Murder of a Hangman

A Redmond and Haze Mystery

Book 13

By Irina Shapiro

Copyright

Cover created by MiblArt.

Table of Contents

Prologue

Giles Britteridge drew a cleansing breath, enjoying the crisp freshness of the March morning. This was his favorite time of year, and the most pleasant part of his day. He enjoyed his morning walk and tried not to think of the business at hand, the myriad problems of running a prison the size of Newgate and the number of inmates and staff under his command. It was taxing and at times maddening, but he took pride in his work and greatly looked forward to his fast-approaching retirement. Another few years and he'd be free of the heap of human detritus he was charged with keeping in line. At least there were no executions or floggings scheduled for today. Even after all these years, watching someone brought so low gave him bouts of indigestion.

Giles approached the entrance he used to access his office and stopped. An innocuous-looking basket sat on the top step, the contents covered with a linen towel. Had someone forgotten it or left it there on purpose? Perhaps some grieving wife had brought a treat for her husband but realized the prison was not yet open for the day. But why would she leave such an offering by the door? Food was dear, and no wife of a common criminal would waste precious resources.

Too curious to simply walk past the basket, Giles bent down and pulled off the towel. A strangled scream tore from his chest, and for a moment he found that he couldn't move or draw breath. He'd seen many a gruesome spectacle in his life, but never had a gruesome spectacle glared back at him. The head was upright in the basket, the eyes open and staring, the hair neatly oiled and brushed. For one mad moment, Giles thought this had to be a sick joke, a theatrical prop left for him to find. He looked around, but no one seemed to be about to enjoy his shock. He reluctantly looked back at the offending object, and only now that he was marginally calmer did he realize that he recognized the face that stared back at him. And then he vomited the breakfast he had so enjoyed only an hour before and banged on the door, desperate to be admitted.

Chapter 1

Tuesday, March 23, 1869

Jason Redmond alighted from the carriage and looked up at the imposing walls of Newgate Prison. The structure was massive, the walls of the prison as high and thick as any castle fortification. Jason understood the need for such establishments, but everything inside him recoiled at the idea of keeping thousands of individuals behind bars and forcing them to live in unsanitary conditions and on starvation rations for years, sometimes decades. It was cruel and ineffective, and in most instances, the punishment was completely disproportionate to the crime they had been charged with. But until the world came up with a better solution for dealing with its criminal element, places like Newgate would continue to exist and take up valuable real estate in some of the world's greatest cities, a stark reminder of what happened when one broke the law and wasn't mentally agile enough to evade the authorities.

Jason's own imprisonment at a Confederate prison camp in Georgia at the end of the American Civil War had been a trial of mental and physical endurance that had left him emotionally shattered and physically broken. There were some things one never forgot or forgave, and there were certain fears that still lived inside one's soul and sprang to the forefront when entering an institution designed to reduce a human being to his or her most basic needs, and more often than not only kept them incarcerated until their appointment with the hangman. Jason had been lucky enough to survive, but most of the people currently housed behind the walls of Newgate would be departing in a pine box to be buried in a pauper's grave with not even a marker to commemorate their existence.

Taking a calming breath, Jason followed Constable Putney to the warden's office at the end of a long stone-walled corridor punctuated by metal doors. The corridor was cold and dim, and Jason felt something constrict inside his chest and wished he could go back outside and ask that the evidence be brought to him so he could examine it in the stark, white-tiled cellar mortuary of Scotland Yard. But he could hardly inform Constable Putney that he was suffering from a case of nerves. Jason drew back his shoulders, stiffened his spine, and followed the constable, walking at a brisk clip until they reached the door. The constable knocked, then pushed it open.

Jason couldn't help but smile in relief when he saw Inspector Daniel Haze, whose pale countenance was illuminated by weak sunlight streaming through the barred window, the rays reflecting off the round lenses of his spectacles. Jason hadn't seen much of Daniel since the abduction of his daughter, Charlotte, and the death of her nursemaid, Rebecca Grainger. Daniel had needed time to grieve a woman he'd cared for deeply and forge a fragile peace with his own feelings of guilt. Rebecca's death had in no way been Daniel's fault, but he routinely resorted to self-flagellation when it came to the tragic decisions of others and blamed himself for his lack of foresight and his inability to prevent the inevitable. Daniel nodded to Jason, but any personal exchange would have to wait until they were alone.

A man of middle years, heavyset and bewhiskered, sat behind the massive desk, his jowls brushing the starched collar of his shirt, his face set in lines of displeasure. He eyed Jason with ill-concealed impatience, since it had taken Jason over an hour to present himself at the crime scene. He'd already left for the hospital when Constable Putney had come in search of him and had had to leave his surgical patients once the constable had tracked him down to answer Daniel's summons.

"Mr. Britteridge, may I present my associate, Lord Redmond," Daniel said as the warden rose laboriously to his feet and gave Jason a stiff bow.

The warden didn't bother to ask what a member of the nobility was doing in his prison or why Jason Redmond was the one to consult on this case instead of some third-rate surgeon who couldn't find gainful employment with one of London's many hospitals and was reduced to butchering corpses to earn his daily bread. He probably knew Jason by reputation, and at the moment, he appeared too shaken by whatever had happened to bother with the social niceties. After a brief greeting of "My lord," the warden launched into a succinct, if somewhat belligerent, explanation instead of allowing Daniel Haze to begin asking questions.

"I arrived at the prison at eight o'clock sharp, as I do every morning. The main entrance had not been unlocked, since the night shift had not left the premises and the day shift had yet to arrive. I discovered a basket, the contents covered with a linen towel. Naturally, I assumed that someone had left an offering of fresh bread or perhaps a ham, given the shape beneath, but when I pulled off the towel, what I saw was a severed head. I immediately sent a message to Superintendent Ransome. We're well acquainted," he added, giving Daniel a hard look meant to remind him that his performance would be harshly judged and discussed with his superior. "I had requested Inspector Yates, but it seems he's been assigned to another case, so Inspector Haze was sent in his stead. Superintendent Ransome assures me that the man is competent and can be trusted to conduct a thorough and well-thought-out investigation."

Daniel looked like he'd just swallowed a wasp but remained silent, allowing Jason to come to his own conclusions and formulate an appropriate response.

"Inspector Haze is not only competent and utterly trustworthy, but he's also a trusted colleague and dear friend, so I would thank you to treat him with the respect he deserves, Mr. Britteridge," Jason said coldly. "Now, if you would answer some basic questions, I will be happy to take the head off your hands."

The warden's fleshy cheeks turned a mottled red, and he inclined his head in acknowledgement of the rebuke. "My apologies, Inspector Haze. I have every confidence in your abilities. It was something of a shock, you see, since I was well acquainted with the victim."

Daniel pushed the spectacles further up his nose and pulled a small notebook and a pencil from his pocket. It would seem

Daniel had been waiting for Jason to begin the interview. Given the obvious lack of evidence, Jason didn't think it'd take long. He settled in one of the hardback guest chairs and waited until Daniel took the other seat. Daniel did not look at him but focused his gaze on the warden.

In retrospect, Jason should have probably allowed Daniel to fight his own battles, but his response to the warden had been a result of his own discomfort at being inside the prison and the memories that crowded his mind despite the pressing issue at hand. A highhanded bureaucrat with no respect for a fellow law enforcement officer had galled him, and Jason had sprung to Daniel's defense without considering Daniel's fragile feelings.

"Inspector Haze, shall we begin?" he asked. Daniel nodded and turned to face the warden. "Mr. Britteridge," Daniel asked. "Do you frequently receive offerings of fresh bread or hams?"

The question clearly took the warden by surprise, and he faltered. "Well, no, but when one sees a covered basket, one immediately associates it with food."

"So this was highly unusual in itself," Daniel summarized.

"Indeed, it was."

"Can you describe the condition of the head when you first saw it?" Jason asked.

"It was just there, sitting in the basket, like a cabbage," the warden reiterated.

"Yes, you have mentioned that, but what I need to know is, was there any blood pooled beneath the severed head? Were the eyes open or closed? Was the head upright, face up, or face down?"

"Ah yes, I see. Of course," the warden muttered, probably a bit embarrassed by his lack of understanding. "The head was positioned upright, the stump of the neck resting on a bit of straw.

There was a smear of blood, but no pooling, as such. The eyes were open, and the hair was neatly brushed."

"Have you searched for the body?" Jason asked.

"Yes. I had my men scour the vicinity, but no body has been discovered as of yet."

"Did they find any traces of blood?"

"They did not."

"And who was this man?" Daniel asked. "You said he was known to you."

"Yes. His name is Philip Hobart. He was one of the hangmen here at Newgate."

"May I see the remains?" Jason asked.

Mr. Britteridge rose from behind his desk, retrieved the basket from a tall wooden cabinet, and handed it to Jason.

"Couldn't bear to look at it," he explained as he resumed his seat behind the desk.

"Thank you," Jason said. Next to him, Daniel silently stared at the contents of the basket.

Jason set aside the plain white towel and studied the head before replacing the towel and setting the basket on the floor at his feet. This wasn't the first severed head he'd seen. After battle, the field was often strewn with limbs, the disconnected stumps resting on earth churned by prolonged cannon fire and soaked with blood. Few had their heads torn clean off, but there had been a few instances, the eyes still staring in horror at the sky they could no longer see. Philip Hobart's head did resemble a theatrical prop since the neck had been cleanly severed, the hair clean and brushed back from a high forehead, and the eyes wide open. The man had been in his forties and possessed of strong, angular features, his bullish expression not softened by death. It was difficult to draw conclusions without the body, but Jason didn't see any signs of struggle or brutal violence. Aside from the fact that the head was no longer attached to the body, it looked remarkably undamaged.

"Can you think of any reason Mr. Hobart's head would be left on your doorstep, Mr. Britteridge?" Daniel inquired.

"Well, I suppose someone wanted to make a point," Britteridge replied.

"What sort of point?" Jason asked.

The warden spread his hands in the universal gesture of having no inkling. "It could have been anything."

"Did Mr. Hobart have any known enemies, or had he received death threats?" Daniel asked.

"Not that I know of, Inspector."

"And did Mr. Hobart work with anyone closely?"

"He had recently taken on an apprentice. Clyde Barkley is his name."

"Is Mr. Barkley currently in the building?" Daniel continued.

"No. There are no executions scheduled for this morning."

"When was the last time you saw the victim and his apprentice?" Jason inquired.

"I saw them both yesterday. Mr. Hobart and Mr. Barkley left separately once their work was done."

"Do you have Mr. Barkley's address? And the address for Mr. Hobart?" Daniel asked, his pencil poised above the nearly clean page of his notebook.

"Of course." Mr. Britteridge opened the top drawer of his desk and withdrew a thick ledger.

From what Jason could see, there was a section for prison employees and one for the inmates, which was considerably thicker. Mr. Britteridge withdrew a clean sheet of paper and copied out the two addresses before handing the page to Daniel.

"Mr. Britteridge, is there anything else you can tell us about Mr. Hobart or his final days?" Daniel inquired.

"Mr. Hobart was a very reticent sort of person. He never lingered after his work was done and did not mix with prison staff. I had invited him to take a drink with me on more than one occasion, but even though he accepted out of politeness, we never progressed beyond the mundane in our conversation. I knew virtually nothing of his life beyond these walls."

"And Mr. Barkley?" Daniel asked.

"Mr. Barkley took his cues from Mr. Hobart and kept his distance, although I do think he's a personable young man and would have benefited from the support seasoned guards could provide to a novice."

"And what will happen to Mr. Barkley now?" Jason asked.

"Well, I suppose he will become a principal executioner in his own right now that his mentor is gone. We have two executions scheduled for next week, and there isn't time to find a replacement on such short notice. Experienced hangmen are in high demand, and our official executioner, Mr. Calcraft, is often called away."

"Is Mr. Barkley ready to take on the role of the principal hangman?"

"I believe he is. I told him so only last week."

"Why?" Daniel asked. "What prompted the conversation?"

"Mr. Barkley had inquired whether he would remain Mr. Hobart's assistant until Mr. Hobart saw fit to retire, and I told him that if he felt he was ready, he could always seek a position as the principal hangman at another facility, perhaps one outside London.

That's when I assured him that I thought he was ready to take on the responsibility and that he should look beyond his duties here at Newgate."

"And did Mr. Barkley wish to seek another position?" Jason asked.

"He didn't say, but he appeared to consider my suggestion. I don't think it had occurred to him until then that he might be ready to strike out on his own."

"And why would you encourage Mr. Barkley to leave? Surely Mr. Hobart would still have been in need of an assistant."

"Mr. Hobart had many years of service left, Lord Redmond. He had no wish to relinquish his position as principal hangman, and he rarely required Mr. Barkley's assistance beyond what was needed in terms of preparation. I think Mr. Barkley was growing frustrated, so I merely pointed out that he had other options available to him. I know it's not the norm to encourage one's members of staff to move on, but Clyde is my son's age, and his father recently passed, so I thought I was doing him a service by speaking to him as a father would."

Daniel made a notation in his notebook, while Jason, satisfied that there was nothing more to say about Clyde Barkley, asked his next question. "Mr. Britteridge, when you say the severed head was meant to be a message, do you mean to the prison authorities or to you personally?"

"I can't conceive of a scenario in which someone would want to send a message to me," Mr. Britteridge said. "Mr. Hobart did not answer to me, since I was not the one to pass sentence on the poor souls he executed. Perhaps the message was meant for the prison governors. Or for our legal institutions, but then it would be more appropriate to leave the head for a High Court judge."

"And what message would someone wish to send to the legal institutions?" Daniel looked baffled by the possibility.

"As I'm sure you're aware, Inspector, public hangings have recently been outlawed. Seems the public has lost their taste for death, at least as a source of wholesome family entertainment," the warden said, his tone so sarcastic, it would be difficult to mistake his meaning. "There are those who believe the death penalty should be abolished altogether. It is a misguided and ill-conceived notion that has absolutely no merit within the guidelines of the law. Fear of death is the only thing that stands between a man or a woman and their criminal impulses. If the death penalty were abolished, the streets would no longer be safe for any of us. Anywhere. Anytime. We would be stripped of all we possess and likely murdered in our beds by those who feel we owe them a better life."

"Is there strong support for the abolition of the death penalty among any factions of Her Majesty's government?" Jason asked.

"Heavens, no. Every educated, rational man understands that to do away with this most basic capital punishment would only wreak havoc on the status quo. And no politician who prides himself on being a realist would sanction such folly, not if they hope to keep their seat and the support and respect of their constituents."

"I don't imagine they would," Jason agreed, also a tad sarcastically, but his true meaning seemed utterly lost on the warden.

"Mr. Britteridge, is there a list of individuals Mr. Hobart has executed?" Daniel asked.

"There is not, but if you think it will assist you in your inquiries, I would be happy to draw one up for you, Inspector Haze. It's easily enough accomplished."

"That would be most helpful," Daniel said. "And perhaps you can annotate it with any pertinent information that comes to mind."

"Such as?" the warden asked.

"Such as whether the family of the condemned might hold a grudge, or if the individual to be executed had continued to proclaim their innocence or admitted to the crime."

"And why would that matter?"

"If the family believed that an innocent man or woman was executed, they might wish to take retribution into their own hands," Daniel replied. "Whereas if the individual had confessed to the crime, the family would understand that justice had been done and accept their loss more readily."

"I'm not privy to the sentiments of the families, Inspector Haze, but I see no reason for them to hold a grudge against Mr. Hobart. He was only doing his job. If they felt their loved one was sentenced unfairly, they would have to take that up with the magistrate or the judge, as they are the instruments of the law. Besides, since the executions are no longer public, the families did not witness the hanging."

"Not those more recently sentenced, but surely there were many executions held before the new legislation," Jason commented.

"Yes, that's true, but do keep in mind, Lord Redmond, that Mr. Hobart sometimes took jobs outside the prison. Contrary to popular belief, we don't hold executions daily, so most executioners will travel for work in order to supplement their income."

"And did Mr. Hobart accept outside commissions often?" Daniel asked.

"I really couldn't say. Since his presence at Newgate wasn't required unless there was a hanging or a flogging on the day's agenda, his time was his own."

"Well, if you happen to remember anything pertinent, do send for me. And please, draw up that list and have it delivered to Scotland Yard as soon as possible," Daniel said as he pushed to his feet.

Jason followed suit, and they were back outside within a few minutes, Constable Putney trailing behind them, the covered basket containing the head of Mr. Hobart carried in his trembling hands.

"Constable, please take my carriage and deliver Mr. Hobart's remains to the mortuary," Jason said.

Constable Putney looked torn between relief at getting rid of the offending object and chagrin at being thus dismissed and missing out on the initial stages of the investigation. He was a clever young man who paid attention and hoped to make his way through the ranks sooner rather than later.

"Of course, sir. You can count on me," he said.

"Joe, you can return home after you leave Constable Putney at Scotland Yard," Jason told his driver.

"I'd be happy to come find you once I'm done, my lord," Joe Marin replied.

Jason suspected that Joe would much rather take part in the investigation by driving Jason and Daniel from place to place than take Katherine Redmond to one of her many charity meetings or wait for her outside a milliner's shop or her preferred modiste. Katherine wasn't one to spend her time chasing fashion, but since moving to London, she had taken a keener interest in looking the part of a lady and often consulted Jason on his opinion of her new acquisitions, which he was more than happy to offer. He liked to see her happy and finally settling into her role as Lady Redmond with confidence.

"Does Lady Redmond not have need of you today?" Jason asked.

"No, sir."

"All right," Jason agreed. "Daniel, where should Joe meet us?"

Daniel consulted his pocket watch, then the addresses Mr. Britteridge had provided. "Let's begin with the widow," he said. "The Hobart residence is not far from here." Daniel showed Joe the address. "Can you collect us at say, eleven?"

"Of course, Inspector. Your lordship," Joe said as he tipped the slouch hat that made him look like a highwayman.

Jason thanked Joe and turned to Daniel, who was ready to set off. "Did you not want to look at the head more closely?" Daniel asked.

"I have seen what I need to for now, and the rest will require more careful analysis. Even without the body, there's much a head can tell us."

"Can it?" Daniel asked, looking dubious.

"It can, which is why I would like to give it my full attention once I get to the mortuary."

"Is it possible to estimate the time of death based on the head alone?"

"I'd say that the victim died less than twelve hours before his head was deposited on the steps of the prison. That's as precise as I'm prepared to be based on a cursory examination."

"So, he would have been murdered sometime after eight o'clock?" Daniel asked.

"Give or take an hour or two, but yes. I would say he was murdered sometime last night rather than this morning."

"That's not much to go on," Daniel said sourly.

"Perhaps Mrs. Hobart can shed some light on her husband's final hours," Jason replied. "At the very least, she can help us narrow the window surrounding the time of death."

"I hope so," Daniel replied. "You heard the warden. He's a long-standing acquaintance of Superintendent Ransome, which means Ransome will be even more combative than usual."

"That he will be. You know how he loves a case that can garner him attention from the press."

"Oh, the press will be all over this one once they get a whiff of the details. Nothing sells newspapers like mindless savagery and a fascinating conundrum."

"I'm not so sure this was a mindless act," Jason replied. "In fact, I would say this looks to have been carefully planned and flawlessly executed."

"Executed being the operative word," Daniel replied.

Chapter 2

Had Jason not known Daniel as well as he did, he might have simply thought Daniel was anxious about the case and worried about disappointing his less-than-supportive superior, but Jason sensed there was something more behind Daniel's concern. Daniel Haze and John Ransome had had their differences in the past, but John Ransome was nothing if not intelligent and ambitious, and Daniel had solved enough high-profile cases to reflect well on the superintendent and earn himself a reputation for being diligent and fair when dealing with suspects. Jason saw no reason Ransome would wish to undermine Daniel, but perhaps Jason wasn't aware of some new development or power shift at Scotland Yard.

Sighing heavily, Daniel allowed his shoulders to relax and his step to slow. "Ransome let it be known that he would be appointing a new chief inspector by the end of the month. I threw my hat into the ring."

Jason suddenly realized that he'd never met the current chief inspector and wondered why that was since he was at Scotland Yard often enough to be acquainted with every detective and constable and know something of their experience and work ethic.

Sensing Jason's unspoken question, Daniel explained, "Chief Inspector Sandin was appointed by Commissioner Hawkins when the position was first created last year. I think the commissioner owed Inspector Sandin a favor and thought a promotion would do the trick. Sandin might have been a good copper in his day, but in recent years he's developed an unfortunate fondness for strong drink. He's become an embarrassment to Commissioner Hawkins and has been asked to quietly retire to avoid any unnecessary unpleasantness."

Daniel shook his head in disgust. "Sandin has not seen the inside of Scotland Yard for nearly as long as I've been in London and has not personally involved himself in any ongoing investigation for nearly as long. Commissioner Hawkins has asked Ransome to choose a competent man, and Ransome is relishing the prospect of watching his inspectors vie for the privilege."

"How many men are in the running?" Jason asked.

"Four, not counting myself. Given their ambition and desire to replace Ransome when he makes commissioner, this is likely to be more of a gladiatorial match than a civilized selection process."

"I see," Jason said. "And you don't think Ransome would consider you for the position?"

"Ransome likes to play favorites," Daniel said. "But it would appear unprofessional to simply name a successor without impartially considering all the candidates. If I don't get a result in this case quickly enough, then I won't stand a chance."

"And does Commissioner Hawkins not have any say in who gets promoted?"

"Have you forgotten that Ransome is the commissioner's son-in-law? The Yard is Ransome's own personal fiefdom. Until he either moves up or retires, his word is law."

"Is this something you really want, Daniel?" Jason asked.

Daniel shrugged. "I don't know. I made my interest in the position known before I had given any real thought to the pros and cons of such an undertaking. To be perfectly frank, I won't be too disappointed if I'm not chosen. I am the youngest detective at the Yard and the most recent hire. It's Ransome's desire to always take me down a peg or two that rankles."

"Then don't let him," Jason said. "You have an admirable record and the qualifications and experience needed for the job. Ransome might like to play favorites, but he also likes to surround himself with men who make him look good. You are such a man, Daniel."

Daniel's smile lit up his gloomy countenance. "Thank you, Jason. I appreciate the vote of confidence."

"You don't need my vote. If this promotion will be awarded on merit, then you have a solid chance of getting the job."

Jason couldn't help but notice the renewed spring in Daniel's step as they turned the corner and stepped into the sunlight, the street beyond out of reach of the shadow of the prison.

"Do you have any preliminary thoughts on the case?" Daniel asked as he consulted the paper with the address once more.

"There are several things we know for certain. Since no body or evidence of the murder was found by the warden's men, we know that Philip Hobart was not murdered either near or inside the prison. He was killed elsewhere, his head left on the steps to make a point. We have yet to discover what that point is, but the head does offer a few clues."

Daniel looked surprised. "What sort of clues? I did not notice anything that might point us in the direction of the killer."

"The edges of the neck were not ragged, so the head was probably severed with one swift blow. This would require a sharp, straight-edged weapon, such as an axe or a machete. Had a knife been used, there would be evidence of hacking and sawing."

Daniel nodded, acknowledging Jason's point. "Anything else?"

"I saw no signs of a struggle, which would suggest that either Philip Hobart never saw the blow coming or had already been incapacitated at the time of the beheading."

"It would be helpful to find the body," Daniel said. "We'd be able to get a clearer picture of the attack."

"It would, but we know the probable cause of death and the fact that the murder most likely had something to do with Philip Hobart's chosen occupation."

"Probable cause of death?" Daniel asked, turning to look at Jason in surprise.

"It is possible that the victim was already dead by the time his head was severed."

"Would you be able to infer that from the appearance of the head?"

"I will check for bruising around the neck and for redness of the whites of the eyes, which would point to strangulation, and see if there's any odor coming from the man's mouth or windpipe, which could be a sign of poisoning. However, if he was shot, run over, stabbed, or murdered in any other way that doesn't involve the head, I would have no way of knowing without examining the rest of the body. What are the chances the body will turn up?" Jason asked.

"Practically nonexistent," Daniel replied morosely. "It could be anywhere by now, since the killer clearly did not want us to find the rest of Hobart quickly or easily or he would have left his remains in some conspicuous place."

"Yes, I agree with you there. The body is probably well hidden for that very reason. It might give too much away."

"I wonder if Mrs. Hobart realizes anything is amiss," Daniel said as he folded the paper and pushed it into his pocket. It seemed they had arrived.

Chapter 3

The Hobarts resided in Budge Row, just down the street from St Antholin Church. At just past ten in the morning, the street, which boasted a number of commercial establishments, was already crowded with shoppers and vehicles that ranged from fine carriages to dray wagons and hansom cabs. The Hobarts did not dwell above a storefront but lived in a three-story redbrick townhome, and Daniel couldn't help but wonder if they occupied the entire building or if the space was divided into several smaller apartments.

Daniel used the brass knocker to announce their presence, and a sullen-looking maidservant of about fifteen opened the door, eyeing them with suspicion.

"The tradesman's entrance is round the back," she said haughtily.

Daniel held up his warrant card. "Inspector Haze of Scotland Yard to see Mrs. Hobart."

She seemed neither surprised nor impressed to find a policeman on the doorstep and shut the door in their faces while she went to inform her mistress that she had visitors. The maidservant returned a few minutes later and held the door open. She did not offer to take their coats and hats, just made a vague gesture toward a door on the left.

"Mrs. Hobart will receive you in the parlor," she said, and walked away, presumably to the kitchen, since the entrance hall smelled of baking bread and soup.

Daniel and Jason removed their hats out of respect for the widow and entered the room the maid had directed them to. The parlor looked well used and, although not overly grand in either size or adornment, boasted several obvious luxuries. There were crisp lace curtains at the windows, a thick carpet that looked hardly worn covered the polished floor, and several ceramic knickknacks and picture frames that had the gleam of real silver were arranged on the mantel. Mrs. Hobart, when she stood to greet them, was not at all what Daniel had expected of a hangman's wife, although, in truth, he couldn't really put into words what he'd thought she would be like.

The woman before them was no older than twenty-two. Her eyes were the color of fine brandy, and her golden-brown hair was parted in the middle and coiled into a knot at her nape. She was very pale, possibly because the unrelieved black she wore looked harsh and unforgiving against her fair skin. Delicate, almost fragile wrists protruded from the lace-trimmed cuffs of her gown, and her slender neck reminded Daniel of a flower stem rising out of loamy earth.

He supposed it was possible that Mrs. Hobart had already been informed of her husband's death, but for some reason, he didn't think she was in mourning for him. She had the dead-eyed stare of someone who'd seen the lowest circle of hell yet still managed to cling to life, her demeanor that of a woman who never expected to feel a spark of hope or even the briefest moment of joy in the years left to her. Sadly, Daniel was all too familiar with that look. He'd encountered it for years in his own wife before unbearable grief had finally taken her from him.

"Mrs. Hobart, I'm Inspector Haze of Scotland Yard, and this is my associate, Dr. Redmond."

Jason always left the introductions to Daniel's discretion when they called on the individuals relevant to an investigation. At times Jason's rank was an asset, and at other times a detriment, since it could only intimidate and embarrass those who didn't move in such exalted circles and felt threatened by the presence of a member of the nobility in their humble home. Mrs. Hobart looked confused but was too polite to ask what they wanted outright. Instead, she invited them to sit, while she sank into an armchair covered with a lace-trimmed antimacassar and folded her pale hands in her lap. She looked from one man to the other, but the vacant look never left her eyes. Daniel thought she was just barely present.

"Mrs. Hobart, I'm deeply sorry to inform you that your husband, Philip Hobart, was found dead this morning. Please accept our deepest condolences on your loss," Daniel said politely.

Mrs. Hobart's eyes opened wider, and a faint blush stained her cheeks, and for a moment, Daniel thought he saw the woman she must have been before tragedy had eviscerated her spirit.

"Dead?" she exclaimed softly. "How?"

"I'm afraid he was beheaded," Daniel said with as much delicacy as he could convey.

Mrs. Hobart's hand flew to her mouth, and her eyes filled with tears. "I don't understand," she muttered. "Whatever do you mean, Inspector? Beheaded by whom?"

"That is what we're tasked with finding out."

"Mrs. Hobart, are you all right?" Jason asked when the woman's eyes turned glassy and her breathing came in short gasps, as if she were about to faint. "Shall I fetch some smelling salts? Or perhaps you'd like a drink?"

Mrs. Hobart shook her head. "Forgive me. It's just the shock," she muttered, but her voice quavered, and she seemed to hover at the edge of consciousness.

Jason walked over to the sideboard and poured a tot of brandy into one of two cut crystal glasses positioned next to the decanter, then pushed it into the widow's trembling hand. "Take a sip, Mrs. Hobart," he instructed. She did. Then another.

"Now take deep breaths," Jason said softly. "And focus on me."

After a few moments, Mrs. Hobart seemed to recover her composure and handed the glass back to Jason, who set it aside. Daniel took out his notebook and pencil, but the look Jason gave him wasn't lost on him. Go gently, it said. Daniel nodded in acknowledgement.

"Mrs. Hobart, may I have your full name?" he asked.

If the widow was taken aback by the question, she didn't show it. "Lucy Jane Hobart."

"Thank you. And who lives here with you?"

"Just Philip," Lucy Hobart said. "And Hattie. She's a maid of all work."

"Is that the young woman we just met?" Daniel asked. Lucy Hobart nodded.

"When was the last time you saw your husband, Mrs. Hobart?"

"Last night."

"And what time was that?" Jason asked softly, his gaze fixed on the widow should she become unwell again.

"We had supper together. We always dine at seven."

"Did your husband retire at his usual time?" Daniel asked.

Lucy Hobart shook her head. "I went up early. Just after eight. I had a dreadful headache, but Philip went out. He said he was going to have a drink at the Queen's Arms. It's just down the road," she explained.

"And did you hear him come in?"

"No," Lucy said, her voice barely audible. "Where was he killed, Inspector?" Her voice trembled, but she seemed determined to remain in control. "Did he suffer terribly before he died?"

"It would have been a quick death, Mrs. Hobart," Jason said. He seemed determined to cosset the widow and spare her unnecessary pain, which was just as well since Daniel could hardly question her if she were unable to answer. He felt terribly sorry for this fragile young woman, but at the moment, she was the only person who could offer him the information he needed, so he had to overcome his pity and press on.

"Where did you find him?" Lucy Hobart asked, her pleading gaze fixed on Daniel. "How long had he lain there?"

"His head was left on the steps of Newgate Prison," Daniel said.

"And his body?" Lucy whispered.

"We have yet to find it. I'm truly sorry, Mrs. Hobart. I know how very distressing this is for you."

"Distressing?" Lucy echoed. "I suppose that's one way of putting it."

"Mrs. Hobart, was your husband worried or upset last night?" Jason asked. "Or possibly even frightened?"

Lucy Hobart peered at Jason. She probably wondered what his role was, since Daniel hadn't explained why he'd brought a doctor along.

"No. Philip was his usual self last night. In fact, he was in fine spirits. Exalted, even," Lucy said slowly, as if trying to recall her husband's demeanor.

"Exalted?" Daniel asked. "By what?"

"He didn't say, but I assumed it had something to do with his work. He never discussed his vocation with me. He didn't like to upset me."

"Mrs. Hobart, how long were you married?" Jason asked.

"Nearly five years," Lucy replied, clearly thrown by the question.

"And do you have any children?" Daniel asked, and caught another warning look from Jason.

The naked pain in the widow's eyes told Daniel everything he needed to know. The Hobarts had recently lost a child. That explained the deep mourning Lucy Hobart was obviously in and the haunted look he'd noticed before he broke the news of Philip Hobart's death.

"I'm very sorry for your loss," Jason said.

Lucy Hobart inclined her head in acknowledgment but didn't reply.

"Does anyone else have a key to this house?" Daniel asked, swiftly moving away from the question of children, since that line of inquiry clearly wasn't relevant to the murder.

"No."

"Could someone have visited your husband last night, after he had returned from the Queen's Arms?"

"I didn't hear anyone," Lucy said. "I wasn't asleep. I don't sleep well these days," she added softly.

"Were you not worried when your husband didn't come to bed?" Jason asked.

Lucy Hobart's shoulders sank even lower. "I lay awake for hours, then took a sleeping draught. When I woke this morning, I assumed that Philip had already left for the prison."

"Did he not normally take breakfast?" Daniel asked.

The young woman shook her head. "Philip never ate before a job. He preferred to wait until luncheon on those days and went to a chophouse in Fleet Street."

"Was there to be a hanging this morning?"

Mr. Britteridge had mentioned that no executions were scheduled for today, but perhaps Philip Hobart had been meant to be someplace else. One of the outside jobs that the warden had spoken of.

"I don't know," Lucy Hobart said. "He never said. I just assumed—"

Daniel looked to Jason to see if he had any other questions, but Jason shook his head. He obviously didn't think Lucy Hobart knew anything that pertained to the murder.

"May we speak to Hattie?" Daniel asked.

"Of course. I'll get her."

She stood and immediately grabbed for the armrest to steady herself. Jason was on his feet in an instant, ready to offer support. He took her gently by the elbow.

"Mrs. Hobart, how much of the sleeping draught did you take?" he asked.

"Only a spoonful. Maybe two."

"Have you eaten today?" Jason persisted.

"I wasn't very hungry."

"You really must eat something. And then you need to lie down. You're in shock."

Lucy Hobart looked at him with gratitude. "Thank you for being so kind. I will do as you say."

"I'm glad to hear it." Jason let go of her elbow.

"I'll send Hattie in to speak to you."

Lucy Hobart left the room, and Jason resumed his seat. "I don't think she knows anything."

Daniel nodded. "She seemed sincere in her grief. And her husband clearly didn't discuss his cases with her."

"It would be highly inappropriate if he did," Jason replied. "No woman, especially one who's recently lost a child, should have to hear such things."

"You've been known to speak of murder with your wife," Daniel pointed out.

Jason grinned. "Katie has a strong stomach, and she'd never forgive me if I treated her as if she were too fragile to hear the truth of my daily reality."

Their conversation was interrupted by the arrival of the maidservant, whose indifferent expression had been replaced by a worried frown.

Chapter 4

Hattie looked from Jason to Daniel and back again, probably trying to figure out who was in charge. She clearly assumed that it was Daniel because she settled her anxious gaze on him. She stood before him with her shoulders slumped and her hands clasped tightly before her, as if she expected to be rebuked or sacked at any minute. There was no doubt that Lucy Hobart had informed her maid of Philip Hobart's death when she spoke to her in the kitchen since nothing else could account for the sudden change in Hattie's demeanor.

Jason knew all too well that the death of an employer was one of the worst things that could befall a woman in service since her position went from being relatively secure to completely uncertain within moments. The Hobarts had a fine house and seemed comfortably off, but Philip Hobart might have been living on credit and the house could be raided by bailiffs, who would remove anything of value as soon as news of the death reached the ears of the hangman's creditors. If that were to happen, Hattie would lose her position, and her home.

"Are you the only servant the Hobarts employ?" Daniel asked.

"Maid of all work, that's me," Hattie replied, a spark of bitterness igniting in her dark eyes.

It was a sizable house, and Hattie would have her hands full with cleaning, cooking, and seeing to all the other myriad tasks that would fill her long workday, from polishing the master's shoes to mending the mistress's unmentionables.

"And where is your room?" Daniel asked, his tone a little kinder now.

"In the attic, Inspector. Sweltering in the summer, freezing in the winter, just as you'd expect. But I don't spend much time up there on account of all I have to do in my waking hours."

"How many hours do you work?" Jason asked.

"Fourteen," Hattie replied without pausing to consider. "From six in the morning until eight in the evening."

"Is that when you retired to your room last night?" Daniel inquired.

Hattie nodded. "Mr. Hobart likes to dine at seven o'clock sharp. I serve supper, then tidy the kitchen, and go up to my room. It's the only time I get to myself," she added wearily.

"Did you see Mr. Hobart at any time after supper last night?" Daniel asked.

"No."

"Did you hear him leave the house?" Jason asked.

"I can't hear the front door from the attic, sir."

"What about Mrs. Hobart? Did you hear her go upstairs?"

"Yes. She went up around eight, same time as me. I was behind her on the stairs, and she wished me a good night before shutting the bedroom door."

"Did anyone ever call on Mr. Hobart in the evenings?" Daniel asked.

"Only Mr. Bram."

"And who's Mr. Bram?" Jason asked.

Hattie's expression softened, and a small smile tugged at her lips. "Mr. Bram is Mr. Hobart's son. He joins the master and mistress for supper once a week."

"But he wasn't here last night?"

"It wasn't his night to dine with them. He usually comes on Wednesday."

"And where does Mr. Bram live?" Daniel asked.

"Blackfriars," Hattie replied. "He's an artist," she added with breathless admiration.

"And he's nice, Mr. Bram?" Jason asked, smiling at the girl.

"Oh, ever so nice," Hattie replied, not bothering to hide her feelings for the master's son. "He's always kind and polite, even to the likes of me. Sometimes he brings me an orange or a penny dreadful to read. He knows I like the stories but can't afford to buy them for myself. I have to be careful with my wages."

"That is kind," Daniel agreed. "And how old is Bram Hobart?"

"Twenty-five, or thereabouts," Hattie said.

"And did Mr. Bram get on with his father and stepmother?" Jason inquired.

"Oh, yes. For the most part."

"Did they sometimes disagree?"

"Mr. Bram thought hanging was medieval," Hattie replied. "I heard him say so when I served at table a few weeks back. He said that repaying murder with murder was bar—" She tripped over the word, but then seemed to remember what Bram had said. "Barbaric," she announced.

"And what did his father say to that?" Daniel asked.

"Mr. Hobart said that the Bible is very clear on crime and punishment. It's a life for a life, an eye for an eye, a tooth for a tooth, and so on," Hattie said. "And Mr. Bram said that if this is the best our justice system can conceive of, then pretty soon everyone will be walking around blind and toothless." She sucked in a deep breath and continued. "Mr. Hobart said Bram was a right fool and should keep his infantile opinions to himself lest he embarrass himself before men of consequence," Hattie rattled off.

"And what did Bram say to that?" Jason asked, curious how the argument had played out.

"Mr. Bram said he has no use for men of consequence unless they require a marble cross bearing their name."

"And did this argument cause a rift between Mr. Bram and his father?" Daniel asked.

Hattie shook her head. "They exchanged barbs from time to time, but they got on most days. All sons provoke their fathers," she commented wisely.

"Do they?" Jason asked, feeling a familiar sadness steal over him when he thought of the relationships between parents and children. He couldn't help recalling some of the arguments he'd had with his own father, convinced they'd never see eye to eye and desperate to prove his point.

"Don't they?" Hattie countered. "My father and brother were always at it hammer and tongs. Never a moment's peace when those two were about."

"Where are they now?" Jason asked. "Do you have family to turn to?"

Hattie shook her head. "My parents are dead, and I haven't seen my brother in years. Got work as a navvy with the railroads. For all I know, he's dead too," she said miserably. She was clearly worried about her future, and Jason hoped Lucy Hobart wouldn't turn Hattie out.

"Is it all right if I go now?" Hattie asked, looking at Daniel. "It's only that I got a kidney pie in the oven."

"Of course," Daniel said. "Thank you for your help, Hattie."

The girl nodded and fled.

"Well, I think we've learned all we can here," Daniel said as he and Jason stepped out into the chilly March morning. He consulted his notes. "The Queen's Arms, I think, since it's near here, and then we can call on Mr. Barkley."

"I'll come with you to the Queen's Arms, but I'm afraid I cannot accompany you to speak to Mr. Barkley," Jason said. "I need to get to the docks. I was going to go after my hospital rounds this morning."

"What business do you have at the docks?" Daniel asked.

"I have to visit the steamship office."

"No word from Mary, then?"

"No."

Daniel nodded his understanding but didn't ask any questions or offer useless platitudes concerning the whereabouts of Mary Donovan. Mary's fate was something of a sore subject these days, especially since Easter was fast approaching and Jason's ward, Micah, would be coming home from school for the holidays and fully expecting to be greeted by his sister and nephew. Jason had yet to discover why Mary had fled Boston, Massachusetts, but at this stage, his primary concern was her safe arrival in London, since the *Arcadia* should have docked nearly two weeks ago. Every day that passed without word compounded Jason's anxiety and forced him to scan the day's headlines for news of the ship. There was nothing in the newspapers, so the only logical next step was to call at the steamship office and ask for news in person.

Chapter 5

The only thing the Queen's Arms had to recommend it was that it was within walking distance of the Hobarts' house. The tavern was dark and dingy, and smelled of spilled ale and old grease. Jason supposed the unforgiving rays of the midmorning sun did few favors for any drinking establishment, but this watering hole seemed seedier than most. He knew little of Philip Hobart, but having seen his house and met his wife, Jason didn't think this seemed like the sort of place the hangman would frequent.

"We're closed," a gruff voice called from the back.

"Police," Daniel called in reply.

A man of about thirty and built like a brick outhouse emerged from a door that must have led to the cellar and eyed them with distaste. Daniel held up his warrant card, and the man mouthed the name as he read it.

"And to wha' do I owes the pleasure, Inspector?" he snarled, baring tobacco-stained teeth.

"What's your name?"

"Smith. Josiah Smith."

"One of your patrons was murdered, Mr. Smith." Daniel had clearly taken an instant dislike to the man, and the feeling seemed mutual, not that policemen were ever welcomed with open arms.

"Oh, yeah? Which one?" Josiah Smith asked. He didn't seem overly concerned, merely curious.

"Philip Hobart," Daniel replied.

The publican smirked. "That's fittin', I 'spose."

Sensing that the man wasn't about to go out of his way to be helpful, Jason stepped forward and laid a half crown on the bar. "For your time," he said smoothly.

The publican eyed the coin, then made it disappear quicker than a skilled pickpocket before offering them a sycophantic grin. "All right, then," he said, his manner now bordering on friendly. "So, what d'ye want to know?"

"Why do you think it was fitting that Philip Hobart should be murdered?" Jason asked.

The publican gave a half-hearted shrug. "On account of 'is occupation. Ye take 'nough lives, I reckon someone'll get a mind to take yers."

"And do you know of anyone who'd want to revenge themselves on Philip Hobart?" Daniel asked.

"It were a general observation, Inspector," the publican said. "I can't name names."

"What can you do?"

"I can tell ye that the 'angman were very much alive when 'e left last night."

"And what time was that?" Jason asked.

"I dunno. Ten, mebbe."

"Was he on his own?"

"'E weren't a sociable fellow. Never seen 'im with anyone."

"How often did he come here?" Daniel inquired.

"'Bout twice a week."

"Publicans are an observant lot. Surely there's something else you've noticed about Mr. Hobart."

The man shook his head stubbornly. “A barman’s like a priest, Inspector. Sanctity of the confessional, and all that.”

“And did Mr. Hobart share anything he needed to confess with you?” Daniel tried again.

“I told ye. ’E weren’t a sociable cove. Sat in the corner and nursed ’is jar in silence. Now, if ye’ve no objection, I’ve got work to be getting on with.”

“Thank you, Mr. Smith.” Jason turned for the door, and Daniel followed.

“That’s the quickest half crown that brigand’s ever earned,” Daniel grumbled.

“It’s a small price to pay for information.”

“What information? He told us nothing.”

“He told us that Philip Hobart left the Queen’s Arms around ten, which narrows the window for the murder by two hours.”

“That’s not much,” Daniel replied sourly.

“No, but it helps. It’s also unlikely that Philip Hobart was involved in an altercation with one of the other patrons, since he mostly kept to himself. Whatever befell him happened after he left the Queen’s Arms.”

“And most likely before he returned home,” Daniel speculated.

“Unless whoever killed him paid him a late-night visit,” Jason said.

“If they did, it would most likely be someone he knew, or he wouldn’t have let them in. I saw no evidence of a break-in.”

"No. And Lucy Hobart would have heard something if there had been an argument," Jason pointed out. "She said she had trouble falling asleep. Surely she would have heard voices."

"The visitor might have arrived after she'd taken her sleeping draught. It's most likely pure laudanum, so she would have been out in minutes."

Jason nodded in assent. "And Hattie would not have heard anything up in the attic, not if she was asleep."

"I hope Mr. Barkley will prove to be more helpful," Daniel said as he pulled on his gloves. "And I trust you will get some answers at the steamship line. Are you available tomorrow?"

"I'm in surgery first thing in the morning, but I should be finished by ten."

"Excellent. Shall I meet you at the hospital?"

"Of course. Can I drop you somewhere?" Jason asked as his brougham turned the corner and came to a stop before the two men.

"No, thank you. I prefer to walk."

Jason tipped his hat, gave Joe the address of the steamship office, and climbed into the carriage. Last he saw, Daniel was walking away, his stride purposeful, his head bowed as if he were deep in thought.

Chapter 6

Jason leaned back against the cushioned seat and closed his eyes. The morning's events were unsettling, and it took a rare case to rattle Jason. Murder was depressingly common, but Philip Hobart's death was truly disturbing in its execution. Whether spontaneous or premeditated, most acts of violence were committed by individuals who wanted nothing more than to distance themselves from the result of their actions. They usually left the body where it fell, self-preservation uppermost in their mind.

Whoever had killed Philip Hobart had gone through the trouble of tidying the head and delivering it to the prison, which would have required not only calm and presence of mind but also nerves of steel. To walk through the streets of London with a severed head in a basket was not the act of an ordered mind but of someone either completely unhinged by hatred or tragically incapable of basic human emotions. And what had they done with the body once it was no longer of use to them? It would have been heavy and unwieldy and would have taken a great deal of effort to dispose of.

Jason didn't have answers to any of the questions that swirled through his mind and decided to set Philip Hobart's death aside until he and Daniel had more information. As the carriage swayed soothingly, Jason's mind turned to the more pressing question of Mary. She had never been Jason's charge, but as Micah Donovan was as dear as a son to him and Mary was Micah's sister, Jason felt the weight of responsibility for the girl. It had taken him over a year to track Mary down after she'd vanished from the Donovan farm in Maryland in 1863. Mary had eventually shown up on Jason's doorstep of her own volition and with a baby in tow, but although Jason had offered Mary a home and unlimited financial support, she had bolted, leaving one-year-old Liam behind.

Eventually, mother and son had been reunited in Boston, where Mary had settled after her chaotic flight from England.

According to Mary's last letter to Micah, she had been married and expecting a baby with her new husband. But that had been months ago, and since then, the situation had altered dramatically. Only Jason didn't know how or why. Alicia Lysander, the medium Jason had consulted during the desperate hunt for Charlotte when the little girl had been abducted, had passed on a message from Micah's deceased mother. Mary was in danger and needed help. Jason was not a true follower of the occult, but Alicia Lysander had proved him wrong on more than one occasion, and he held the woman in grudging respect.

Mr. Hartley, the private investigator Jason had engaged in the past, had informed Jason via telegram that Mary had sailed from New York at the end of February. Why Mary had been in New York, what had prompted her to leave Boston, and presumably her husband, or whether she intended to remain in London had never been addressed, since a follow-up letter from Mr. Hartley hadn't yet materialized. Likewise, Jason had no way of knowing whether Mary had given birth to her child and if the baby had lived.

Armed with the name of the ship, Jason was able to discover that the *Arcadia* was part of the Red Swallowtail Line owned by Grinnell, Minturn & Co. The American steamship line was the only carrier to come into the port of London rather than Liverpool, where most transatlantic voyages either originated or ended.

What troubled Jason more than Mary's unexplained departure from Boston was that Mary had not turned up. A ship from New York to London generally took two to three weeks to arrive. It had been a month since the *Arcadia* had sailed, and it was possible that it had docked days if not weeks ago. If it had, then where was Mary?

Jason had decided to hold off on sending another telegram to Mr. Hartley in the hope that Mary would finally arrive, and all would be explained, but the kernel of worry that had been planted on the night of the seance had taken root and grown exponentially, turning into full-blown fear for Mary and her children. And for

Micah, who, after losing both his parents, wouldn't be able to bear another loss of such magnitude.

The brougham finally drew up before a brick building in Wapping, and Jason alighted and strode toward the door. The office was small and nondescript, with only one elderly clerk seated behind a desk, his spectacles hanging precariously off the end of his nose as he laboriously copied something into a thick leatherbound ledger. There were several filing cabinets lined up against the wall and a map of the world pinned to the expanse of white wall behind the clerk's balding head. The man looked up, pushed his spectacles up his nose, and smiled in welcome.

"Good afternoon, sir. How may I be of assistance?"

"Good afternoon. Is this the ticket office for Grinnell, Minturn & Co.?" Jason asked, wondering if he'd got the wrong place after all.

There was no sign above the door, and nothing except a white and red nautical flag mounted on the wall opposite the map spoke to ownership. Not so much as a sailing schedule or a price list was posted, and the office was so out-of-the-way, Jason didn't think it got much traffic from potential travelers, unless arrangements were made mostly by post and the tickets delivered directly to the customer.

The clerk smiled indulgently. "It is indeed, sir. We have only just recently taken over these premises, so the sign is yet to be mounted above the door. I do hope you didn't have too much trouble finding us." The clerk shot Jason a mildly quizzical look. "Were you interested in booking passage to New York? Home, is it?" the man asked, having obviously noted Jason's American accent.

"Actually, I was looking for information on a vessel bound for London."

"Of course, sir. And what is the name of the ship?"

"*Arcadia*," Jason said.

The man's smile slid off his face, and Jason's stomach muscles clenched with dread. "Was the *Arcadia* not due to arrive by the middle of March?" he asked.

"It was, but it has not made port as of yet. Please, don't worry, sir," the man said in what he probably hoped was a reassuring tone. "We've had reports of storms in the Atlantic. Several vessels coming into Liverpool have also been delayed by a week or more. There's no reason to suspect anything untoward has befallen the *Arcadia*." *At least not yet* seemed to hang unspoken in the air.

"Is there no way to check?" Jason asked, feeling a bit desperate.

Jason realized that what he was asking for was impossible. It was less than three years since the first cable had been laid on the ocean floor by a ship called the *Great Eastern*, telegraphically linking the United States and Britain after decades of failed attempts to revolutionize communication between the continents. The gutta-percha insulated cable that spanned thousands of nautical miles made it possible to send a telegram, but as far as Jason was aware, there was still no apparatus that would enable those on shore to contact a ship at sea. Unless a passing ship came to the rescue of a vessel in distress, there was no way to call for help or send a ship-to-shore message. If the *Arcadia* had encountered inclement weather and been delayed, or if the worst had happened and the ship had sunk in the Atlantic, it might take weeks for the tragedy to be conclusively confirmed.

The clerk peered at Jason over the spectacles that were slowly sliding downward once more and shook his head. Jason was about to take his leave, since there was nothing more the man could tell him, but paused.

"Are you in possession of a manifest for the *Arcadia*?" Jason asked. He wasn't sure if the shipping office would receive a list of passengers ahead of the ship's arrival in port, but it was worth a try.

"Yes, I am," the clerk replied eagerly, probably glad to help in any small way he could. "If you give me the names of the passengers, I can check to make certain they are, indeed, aboard the *Arcadia*."

"Mary and Liam—" Jason wasn't sure which name Mary had given when booking passage so decided to try her maiden name first. "Mary and Liam Donovan." If the man couldn't find them, he'd try Mary's married name, O'Connell.

The man extracted a two-page list from a cardboard folder and ran his finger down a list of names. He stopped halfway down. "Here we are. Mary and Liam Donovan. Steerage."

"Is there anyone else traveling with them?"

"I don't believe so. The lady booked one berth, so I can only assume Liam is a child."

"Yes," Jason replied absentmindedly. "Can you also check for O'Connell?"

"Of course, sir. New domestic servants coming over to take up their posts?" the clerk asked as he ran his finger down the list of passengers.

It annoyed Jason that the man had assumed that anyone with an Irish surname and berthed in steerage would be a servant, but he made no comment. He had greater things to worry about now that he knew Mary and Liam were definitely aboard.

"I'm sorry, sir, but there's no one called O'Connell on the manifest."

"Thank you for checking."

"My pleasure, sir."

Jason took out his card and handed it to the clerk. "Would you be so kind as to send a message to this address if you hear anything, or when the ship finally comes in?"

The clerk looked at the card, and his demeanor instantly changed, his lips stretching into a sycophantic smile. "Of course, your lordship. I will personally inform you the moment any information becomes available."

The way he peered at Jason, Jason could only assume that he expected some sort of recompense for his assistance, so Jason took a crown out of his change purse and slid it across the desk. The man pocketed the coin.

"You're most kind, my lord."

"Thank you, sir," Jason said.

"It's Cleese. Harold Cleese," the clerk added belatedly. "Happy to help, my lord."

"Good day, Mr. Cleese."

"Any luck?" Joe asked when Jason stepped outside and approached the waiting carriage.

"The clerk was able to confirm that Mary and Liam Donovan are on board, but the ship has yet to make port. It's been delayed."

"Best not to assume the worst, then," Joe said stoically. He knew Mary well from her previous visit, and Jason knew from Micah that Joe held Mary in high regard. "That girl's got nine lives," Joe added with an affectionate smile. "Where to now, your lordship?"

"Home, please."

Jason used the time it took to reach Kensington to consider what he'd learned from Mr. Cleese. Mary's husband was not on board, at least not under his own name. And Mary had booked her ticket under Donovan, not O'Connell. The new baby wasn't listed either. There was always the grim possibility that the child had died, but Jason wasn't going to jump to conclusions based on such a minor detail. He did, however, think that Mary had been running away and tried to cover her tracks. Why else would she sail from New York instead of Boston and use her maiden name when she was legally married to Sean O'Connell?

Had the marriage soured already, or was there another, more alarming reason for Mary's flight? Had her husband become abusive or turned out to be a hopeless drunk? Mary had always said that she'd marry a teetotaler, having seen first-hand the effect excessive drinking had on a family, but perhaps Sean O'Connell had managed to fool her. Jason shook his head, dismissing the possibility. Mary would not be so easily fooled. She was a clever girl, if a bit flighty, and Jason was sure that Sean O'Connell must have made a very favorable impression on her if she had decided to throw her lot in with his. Jason wouldn't be nearly as alarmed by Mary's sudden decision to sail to England had the idea that Mary was in danger not been planted at the séance.

But could the danger be the voyage itself? Mr. Cleese hadn't appeared alarmed by the delay, but Jason didn't feel reassured by the man's calm demeanor. Crossing the Atlantic was as dangerous today as it had been a hundred years ago, and even though the accommodations were more luxurious and the food in first class prepared by the best chefs, when it came to weather, nature didn't care how much one had spent on their ticket or whether the bearer was a working man or a member of the peerage. The sea didn't discriminate, and everyone ended up sharing the same watery grave, be they rich or poor, if a ship sank.

Joe dropped Jason off by the front entrance and continued around back to the carriage house. Not ready to share the worrying news, Jason rearranged his face into an expression of bland tranquility and let himself into the house, hoping fervently no one would ask about his day.

Chapter 7

After Jason had left, Daniel bought a pie from a street vendor, consumed it in two bites, then went in search of Clyde Barkley. He didn't find the hangman's assistant at his lodgings in Clerkenwell but was greeted by his mother, who was dressed in widow's weeds. Mrs. Barkley looked sad and frail and appeared to move with some difficulty, but she smiled at Daniel warmly and invited him inside once he explained that he was looking into the sudden death of her son's mentor.

"Oh, that is terrible news, Inspector. I have never met Mr. Hobart myself, but Clyde spoke of him often. He had the greatest respect for the man," Mrs. Barkley said once they were seated in the tiny parlor and Daniel had refused refreshment. He didn't expect he'd be staying long enough for the kettle to boil and didn't care to waste time.

"Did your son and Philip Hobart enjoy a cordial relationship?" Daniel asked.

"Oh, yes. Clyde is a dutiful boy. Always does what he's told. Mr. Hobart would have no reason to be displeased with him."

"And where's Clyde now?"

"He works at his uncle's chemist shop," Mrs. Barkley said. "And a good thing it is too. My brother-in-law needs the help, and Clyde receives a fair wage. My son is careful with his money, Inspector, but the pay he makes from his position as the hangman's assistant does not stretch to meet the expenses of a young man who must now support his widowed mother."

Mrs. Barkley sighed heavily. "I had hoped never to become a burden to Clyde in my dotage, but my husband, God rest his troubled soul, was heavily in debt at the time of his death. He had a fondness for betting on horses, you see," she admitted. "Couldn't stay away from the races. I had to give up the house we'd lived in for nearly thirty years and sell the furnishings to pay off the creditors. Clyde was kind to offer me a home. He's a good boy," she added with an affectionate smile. "He'll make a good husband and a loving father someday."

"And was Clyde at home on Tuesday evening?" Daniel asked.

"Yes, he was. We had supper together, and then I retired at nine. Clyde likes to read for a while before going to bed. He's more of a night owl. Just like his father."

"Might he have gone out after you had retired?"

Mrs. Barkley shook her head. "He rarely goes out in the evening. He doesn't have many friends, and there isn't much for a young man to do on his own, is there?"

Daniel could think of several things a young man could do on his own in a city that boasted establishments catering to every possible taste but didn't mention them to Mrs. Barkley. He had no desire to upset the woman, and it would be easier to ask Clyde himself what he got up to when not in the company of his mother.

"Thank you, Mrs. Barkley," Daniel said. "You've been most helpful."

"Have I? Oh, I'm glad." The older woman looked pleased, and Daniel took his leave.

When Daniel entered the chemist's shop, he spotted only one person behind the counter. The man was no older than twenty, with curling fair hair, wide blue eyes, and a wispy moustache that was probably meant to make him look older but instead put one in mind of a baby bird. He was helping an elderly woman who had rather a long list that included everything from castor oil to tooth powder to Parker's Tonic for improved health. She proclaimed the tonic to be a miracle cure for all her husband's ills and began to list them one by one. Once the woman finally left nearly a quarter of an hour later, the young man turned to Daniel.

"I do apologize for the wait, sir," the young man said. "How may I be of assistance?" His manner was friendly and welcoming, his smile good-natured. And his claret-colored waistcoat was rather fine, the satin embroidered with fanciful birds and colorful feathers.

"Clyde Barkley?" Daniel asked irritably.

The man's brow creased slightly, but his smile didn't falter. "Yes. And you are?" he asked, his unease beginning to creep into his gaze.

Daniel held up his warrant card. "Inspector Haze of Scotland Yard, and I'd like a word. In private," he added when the bell above the door jingled, and another matron of advanced years entered the shop and took up a position behind Daniel.

"Has something happened, Inspector?" Clyde Barkley asked, lowering his voice so as not to alarm the new customer.

"It has indeed, Mr. Barkley. I only need a few minutes," Daniel added when he saw the crease deepen between the man's eyes and his gaze grow anxious.

"Is it my mother?" Clyde Barkley asked, his voice quavering with concern.

"No. Your mother is quite well. I spoke to her not ten minutes ago."

"Oh, thank God." The young man opened a door hidden in the paneling and called out, "Uncle, I need a few minutes. Would you mind manning the counter?"

"Be right there," a disembodied voice called back.

A moment later, a rotund man of about sixty emerged from the back room. He had a shiny pate ringed by curling gray fuzz, bushy muttonchop whiskers, and a moustache that obscured his upper lip. His light blue eyes were magnified by the lenses of his spectacles, and Daniel decided that uncle and nephew resembled nothing so much as a wise old owl and its chick, the undignified images no doubt planted in his mind by a story Charlotte was fond of.

"Uncle Albert, may we use the back room?" Clyde Barkley asked. "Inspector Haze would like a word in private."

"Inspector, eh?" the chemist said, eyeing Daniel with obvious mistrust. "If you imagine we're responsible for someone's death by arsenic or laudanum, you're much mistaken, young man. We keep copious records of all purchases and will alert the police should someone display an unnatural interest in the use of poisonous substances."

"I'm not here to lay accusations at your door, Mr. Barkley," Daniel said. "I simply need to ask your nephew a few questions regarding a case I'm working."

Mr. Barkley nodded and turned to the customer, while Clyde opened a panel in the counter and invited Daniel to follow him into the back room, then shut the door behind them. The room was larger than Daniel had expected, with a long wooden table covered with beakers, jars, and a tablet press that the chemist must have been using since the tabletop just beneath the contraption was covered with loose white powder. There were also shelves filled with various compounds used to mix the remedies the shop sold, as well as dozens of labeled bottles of additional stock.

The young man turned the chair his uncle had been using away from the table, then brought over another chair from the corner. He invited Daniel to sit and took a seat opposite. Clyde Barkley still looked anxious, but he folded his hands in his lap and faced Daniel, his expression clearly proclaiming that he had nothing to hide.

"Mr. Barkley, how long have you been employed as Mr. Hobart's assistant?" Daniel asked. He was gratified to see the surprise on the young man's face. He clearly hadn't expected the question, which was telling.

"Two years now," Clyde said. "Why do you ask, Inspector?"

"When was the last time you saw Mr. Hobart?" Daniel asked, ignoring Clyde's inquiry.

"Last week, Thursday."

"Was there an execution?"

"There was a flogging," Clyde replied. "Why? What's happened?" He was becoming visibly agitated, so Daniel decided to put him out of his misery.

"Mr. Hobart was murdered last night. Beheaded," he added. "His severed head was left at the entrance to Newgate Prison. It was discovered by Mr. Britteridge when he arrived this morning."

Clyde Barkley looked like he was going to be sick. He swallowed hard, then took a deep breath to steady himself. "Beheaded?" he whispered, his eyes huge with shock.

"That's right. He was last seen alive around ten o'clock yesterday evening."

"But I don't understand," Clyde sputtered. "Who would do such a thing? And why?"

"That's what I need to figure out," Daniel replied warily. "It would help to know something about the man. What did you think of Mr. Hobart, Mr. Barkley?" he asked, still watching the young man intently.

Clyde looked nonplussed. "I don't know, really."

"You must have formed an opinion, given that you've known Mr. Hobart for two years."

"He wasn't a talkative man. At first, I tried to engage him in conversation, but then I refrained from making unnecessary small talk. I was there to learn, not to make friends," Clyde

Barkley said matter-of-factly. He didn't seem put out by Philip Hobart's lack of interest in forging a more amicable relationship.

"Tell me, Mr. Barkley, is the position of hangman a desirable one?" Daniel asked.

Daniel thought it would help if he were to understand what had motivated a man to choose such a post for his life's work. Had Philip Hobart felt godlike when he'd executed the condemned? Or had he not felt anything at all, simply going through the motions and making sure the individual was truly dead before leaving to find a spot of lunch?

"Oh, yes," Clyde Barkley replied without hesitation. "It's a most profitable occupation."

"Yet you work in a chemist shop," Daniel pointed out.

"Until I can get work as the principal hangman, I do not receive the same rate of compensation, and since this is my uncle's shop, I can take time off when I need to attend a hanging or a flogging. In the meantime, I am a help to my uncle, and I earn a steady wage."

"And what sort of wage does a hangman earn?" Daniel asked, wondering if the compensation would keep the fashion-conscious Clyde Barkley in whimsical waistcoats.

"The principal hangman receives a guinea-per-week retainer plus another guinea for each hanging. There's also a half-crown flogging fee. If the hangman travels to other prisons to perform an execution, he can charge as much as ten quid per job plus expenses."

I'm clearly in the wrong business, Daniel thought sourly as he contemplated such a windfall. Ten quid would pay his maidservant's wage for two years or go a long way toward renumeration for a new nursemaid for Charlotte, should he finally bring himself to place an advertisement and begin his search.

"And was Mr. Hobart able to command such rates?" Daniel asked, dragging his thoughts from his domestic problems.

"He was, yes. Mr. Hobart trained under William Calcraft himself, who is a very well-known and respected hangman. Mr. Calcraft not only performed the executions, hundreds of them, but also sold pies to the crowds on hanging days, so he made a fortune," Clyde said, clearly impressed with the business-savvy Mr. Calcraft. "Of course, things have changed now that public hangings have been outlawed. One can no longer have a sideline."

"No more pies?" Daniel asked a tad sarcastically, wishing he'd purchased two pies instead of just the one. He was still hungry.

Clyde Barkley appeared aggrieved. "A great hangman did not only do his job but performed for the crowd. It requires great skill to hang someone, Inspector, and an experienced hangman had the potential to attract enormous crowds."

"So most hangmen go into the trade just for the money?" Daniel asked.

"Some do, yes, but some have personal reasons."

"What sort of personal reasons would compel someone to become an executioner?"

Clyde Barkley puffed out his chest with self-importance. "There are those, myself included, who only want to ease others' suffering."

"And how would they ease someone's suffering through hanging?" Daniel asked.

He was genuinely curious. He'd attended a few hangings as part of his professional duties but never took pleasure in the spectacle and did not see how a hangman could view himself as an angel of mercy. He had, however, witnessed a botched execution and could see how some skill was required. Daniel couldn't recall if any of the hangings he'd been to had been carried out by Philip

Hobart, since all his attention had been on the condemned. He did, however, remember William Calcraft, in vivid detail, because the man, already in his sixties at the time, had descended beneath the trapdoor when the victim failed to die quickly enough and wrapped himself around the man's legs, weighing down the condemned until he was finally dead.

The crowd had loved every minute of the spectacle and had held their collective breath as the hangman carried out his duties. Although the condemned man had been convicted of a double murder, Daniel couldn't help but feel pity for the poor bugger whose death had not only been a horror of the worst sort but also a source of entertainment for the jeering crowd, his last moments on earth more awful than any decent, God-fearing person should be willing to countenance. Daniel had never questioned the need for capital punishment, but he didn't believe it should be synonymous with torture or a source of amusement for those who had attended hangings as a matter of course before public executions had finally been outlawed.

Clyde took a deep breath before plunging into an explanation. His eyes were shining, his expression rapt, as if he were describing something miraculous. "You see, Inspector Haze, there are several factors that go into planning a hanging. In the past, William Calcraft, as well as most other hangmen, employed what's known as the short drop. The short drop was only about three feet and was achieved by the removal of an object from beneath the condemned person's feet. It could be a stool, a ladder, or even a cart. Usually, it's a trapdoor that opens when a lever is pulled. This method tends to best serve those who are short and stout, since their weight is enough to strain the rope and they're not tall enough to touch the ground and attempt to support themselves in an effort to stay alive."

Daniel couldn't help but wince at this very detailed description but did not interrupt. Clyde Barkley continued, and Daniel thought he was eager to showcase his knowledge rather than merely educate.

"Most recently, there are those who've been advocating a longer drop, four to six feet instead of the traditional three, in order to ensure a quicker, more humane death."

"And how does an extra foot account for a more humane death?" Daniel asked. Until today, he'd never given much thought to the logistics of hanging.

"The shorter drop is often not enough for the body to jerk hard enough for the neck to break, and as a result, the poor devil might take a long time to die. In years past, this made for entertainment for the crowd, especially if there was strong negative feeling against the condemned, but it's not only prolonged agony for the person being hanged, it's utter torment for their families. There are those who will offer the hangman an *incentive* to make certain their loved one dies quickly," Clyde Barkley added, making Daniel wonder just how generous such an inducement might be.

"Is it legal for an executioner to accept a bribe?" Daniel asked.

"It not illegal, I don't think," Clyde replied.

"And did Mr. Hobart accept such incentives to ensure a particular individual didn't suffer needlessly?"

"He never said so outright, but I have reason to believe that he did, especially of late."

"What changed?" Daniel asked.

"Well, as I'm sure you know, Mr. Calcraft is getting on in years, and there are those who feel it's time for him to retire. And he has been taking fewer jobs since the renewed death threats."

"Death threats?"

"Oh yes," Clyde said animatedly. "This was before my time, you understand. I was just a child, but I have heard about it from some of the older guards at the prison. Mr. Calcraft received his first death threat in 1856, just before the execution of William

Bousfield. It was said that he would be shot on the scaffold. Mr. Calcraft was so afraid, he ran away as soon as he pulled the lever, but Mr. Bousfield failed to die and managed to raise his leg to find purchase on the platform. Mr. Calcraft's assistant tried to push the man's leg off, but Mr. Bousfield would not be deterred and succeeded in elevating himself enough to prevent the noose from strangling him. Mr. Calcraft was forced to return and hang on the man's legs until the culprit was good and dead."

"You mentioned renewed threats," Daniel reminded him.

"Well, there were the Manchester Martyrs. Fenians," Clyde said, lowering his voice confidentially, as if Irish revolutionaries were just outside the door, listening in on their conversation. "That was only a few years ago, but Mr. Calcraft was repeatedly targeted after that unfortunate affair. I heard it said that he refused to execute any more Fenians for fear of meeting with a violent end himself."

Daniel did recall reading about the trial in which three men had stood accused of murdering a police officer. Their hanging had been botched by William Calcraft, and one of the men, Michael O'Brien, had taken nearly an hour to die because the Catholic priest in attendance had refused to allow William Calcraft to yank on his feet, suggesting that would be an act of murder. Daniel didn't quite see how hastening the man's death was any worse than allowing him to suffocate slowly, but the Catholic faith was a mystery to him, and he did not feel sufficiently informed to question the priest's logic.

"So is it your belief that Mr. Hobart accepted bribes from the families of the condemned in order to ensure the victims didn't suffer needlessly?" Daniel asked.

Clyde Barkley shook his head, and spots of angry color bloomed in his cheeks. "That's where you got it all wrong, Inspector. The person being hanged is never the hangman's victim. He's the victim of his own criminal urges. The hangman is only doing his duty, so cannot be held accountable for the condemned person's death."

“You did not answer my question, Mr. Barkley.” Daniel was growing tired of Clyde’s enthusiasm for the profession and the need to pretend that he was simply an instrument of justice rather than the person who caused someone’s death, even though the outcome was determined by an order from the court. “Would Mr. Hobart intentionally allow the person whose family did not offer a bribe to suffer?”

Clyde’s face turned an even deeper shade of red. “He might not be as efficient as he could be.”

“Meaning?”

“For example, if the rope is not affixed properly, the unfortunate person would have to be hanged again. Or if the rope is too long or too short. There are those who say that the individual’s weight and height should be considered, but Mr. Hobart did not subscribe to that belief.”

“And do avoidable mishaps happen often?” Daniel asked.

“From time to time,” Clyde Barkley said vaguely.

Daniel felt sick to his stomach as he contemplated the gruesome details of Clyde Barkley and Philip Hobart’s chosen profession. He thought Clyde’s enthusiasm depraved, but the young man seemed to feel no remorse for his part in the executions.

“Contrary to what you might think, Inspector, the profession of hangman is an honorable one, necessary to the peace and prosperity of a nation. Why, Mr. Calcraft was the one to hang Michael Barrett. Now that was a hanging that drew crowds. Do you remember it? It was nearly a year ago now. One of the last public executions of our time.”

“Yes, I do recall that particular case,” Daniel muttered.

Michael Barrett had also been a Fenian and was convicted of setting off an explosion at Clerkenwell Prison that had killed twelve and wounded over one hundred people. His hanging had been witnessed by thousands, who had cheered loudly as the body dropped. The event had had the atmosphere of a public celebration, with fathers hoisting their children onto their shoulders to get a better view and numerous vendors selling everything from hot pies to oranges to the massive crowd of excited onlookers. Daniel couldn't recall if Michael Barrett had made a speech from the gallows, but it wouldn't have mattered. The sentiment against him had been so strong, no one had cared what he had to say. People couldn't wait to see him die.

Daniel forced his attention back to Clyde Barkley, who was still speaking. "Barrett deserved to suffer for what he had done and pay for the lives he'd taken, and there were plenty who would have happily spared a coin to see him do the hangman's jig. Don't you agree, Inspector Haze?"

"I suppose," Daniel said, not wishing to get into a debate on the justification for intentionally prolonging someone's death. "Tell me, Mr. Barkley, can you think of anyone who might have wanted to hurt Mr. Hobart? Perhaps someone who craved revenge for an execution that was mishandled, or a relative or spouse who blamed him for their loved one's death?"

Clyde's brows knitted in concentration as he considered the question. "There were several families that swore revenge, but it wasn't directly against the hangman, more against the system."

"I'd like their names, please," Daniel said, and flipped his notebook to a clean page.

"The Cassells and the Newberrys come to mind."

"When were their relatives hanged?"

"Within the past few years."

Daniel jotted down the names, then looked back at Clyde Barkley. "With Philip Hobart gone, you will now become the principal hangman," he remarked.

Clyde Barkley's face lit up, as if he hadn't considered the possibility. "Do you really think so, Inspector? Has Mr. Britteridge told you as much?"

"He did mention that he thought you were ready."

"Oh, that would be splendid," Clyde exclaimed. "I really thought I would have to wait years for such an opportunity, but if Mr. Calcraft retires in the near future, which I believe he might, then I suppose I will oversee the majority of the executions at Newgate, and maybe even beyond."

"Mr. Barkley, you do realize that this gives you a motive for murder," Daniel said, watching the young man intently. "You would certainly benefit from the financial windfall such a promotion would bring."

Clyde Barkley looked as if a bucket of cold water had just been upended on his fair head. "Motive for murder?" he echoed. "A windfall?"

"You just told me what a lucrative proposition it is to be employed as the principal hangman. Your financial prospects will have improved overnight now that Philip Hobart is gone."

"I... I hadn't considered that," Clyde stammered.

"Had you not asked Mr. Britteridge how long you might have to wait to carry out a hanging of your own?"

"I did, yes, but that was more of a general question. I never imagined..." Clyde's voice trailed off as he absorbed the implications of Daniel's suggestion. "Inspector, I had no reason to murder Mr. Hobart. I always knew I'd have to put in the time until I was deemed ready, and there was absolutely no guarantee that I would be made principal hangman if he were gone. There are other capable hangmen out there who might have got the job."

"Where were you last night, Mr. Barkley?" Daniel asked.

"I had supper with my mother."

"What time was that?"

"We sat down at seven and were finished before eight. Mother retired at nine. I read for a while, then went to bed at about a quarter past ten. I did not leave the house until just before nine this morning. The landlady can corroborate my account. She has rooms on the ground floor."

"Does your landlady stay up all night keeping vigil?" Daniel asked.

"Well, no, but she locks the front door at nine."

"And you don't have a key?"

Clyde Barkley looked deeply uncomfortable. "I do, but I never use it. I don't often go out in the evenings. I have nowhere to go," he added dejectedly. It was almost as if Clyde and Mrs. Barkley had prepared their statements in advance, but it could also be the truth.

"A young man such as yourself must have friends," Daniel persisted.

Clyde shook his head. "I had one friend from school, Oliver Draper, but Oliver is newly married. I haven't seen him since the wedding."

"And you never take yourself to Drury Lane or partake of the entertainments young men tend to seek out when they're in the mood for female company?"

"Lord, no," Clyde exclaimed. "I have never—" He couldn't bring himself to say the words, but judging by his acute embarrassment and the mottled pink his cheeks had gone, it was safe to say the young man was still an innocent.

Changing tack without warning, Daniel asked, "How long ago did Mr. Hobart's child die?"

Clyde looked taken aback by the question but lifted his shoulders in the universal gesture of ignorance. "I don't know. To be frank, I didn't even know he had a child. As I have mentioned, Mr. Hobart was not a man to discuss his personal affairs, at least not with me."

"Thank you, Mr. Barkley. Do let me know if you remember anything that might be pertinent to the investigation. You can send a note care of Scotland Yard or call in person."

"Oh, I will," Clyde exclaimed, clearly relieved that his ordeal was finally at an end.

"Best of luck to you, Mr. Barkley," Daniel said as he stood to leave.

"Thank you. I do hope you find whoever did this awful thing," Clyde called after him.

Daniel left the chemist's shop and walked down the street, his mind still on the conversation. No matter how hard he tried, he couldn't reconcile youthful, exuberant Clyde Barkley with the sort of man who'd want to hang or flog people for a living. It wasn't the hangman's decision to hang or whip the condemned, but it was his actions that resulted in loss of life, and it took a special kind of person to live with such a responsibility. And Daniel had heard women were applying for the jobs now as well. It didn't bear thinking about.

As he strode toward the hansom stand, Daniel tried to imagine what it would feel like to face the person whose life he was about to take. Would he be able to live with himself, or would he comfort himself with the knowledge that he was performing a necessary public service, one that took courage and skill to execute? It was difficult to know. Many a person questioned the sanity of a man who wanted to join the police service, yet here he was, at the start of yet another murder inquiry. And although he sometimes hated Ransome for saddling him with the more bizarre cases, he also felt an undeniable tingle of excitement at the prospect of investigating each one.

And while Daniel reflected on gruesome occupations, he couldn't help but consider Jason's choice of work. What sort of man would want to cut open a body after death to learn its secrets? Daniel didn't think there was anything cruel or depraved about Jason, but Jason cut into a corpse the way most men sliced into their fillets of beef. Were different people emotionally predisposed toward certain occupations? Daniel supposed it was a lucky person who had the ability to choose. Most people either followed in their parents' footsteps or undertook whatever work they were able to get without an education or an apprenticeship.

Ten quid per hanging was nothing to sneer at, Daniel mused as he crossed the street. If a hangman accepted several jobs a year that paid such a sum, he could be set for life in a few years' time. Daniel certainly didn't earn such a generous wage. Still, there was something to be said for meting out justice rather than simply eradicating the criminal element. But were he and the hangman not simply two sides of the same coin? Daniel apprehended the criminal. The hangman executed the criminal Daniel had delivered to the courts. Perhaps their deaths were more on Daniel than they were on the hangman.

These morbid thoughts did little to help Daniel focus his mind on the case at hand, so he inwardly rebuked himself for going down the path of absurdity as he approached the first cab in a line of hansoms at the corner. He gave the driver Bram Hobart's address and climbed in. The only person responsible for being hanged was the person who had committed the crime, he reassured himself as the cab lurched away from the curb. The policeman, the judge, and the hangman were simply appointed tools of justice that would remain at a safe distance from any person who elected to live a respectable, law-abiding life. Thus mollified, Daniel turned his thoughts back to the case.

Chapter 8

Bram Hobart's studio was located in a disused warehouse in Upper Thames Street. It was so close to the river that the odors of wet mud, dead fish, and filthy mudlarkers, who were out in full force now that the tide had gone out and left all sorts of detritus on the shore, assaulted Daniel's nose and chased away his unsatisfied hunger. There was no sign and no windows to punctuate the walls, the building nothing more than a square brick box.

No one answered when Daniel knocked, but the door was unlocked, so he went in. He was met with stares from a dozen unseeing eyes and involuntarily took a step backward, then became deeply annoyed with himself for becoming rattled. The faces belonged to statues that lined the walls and were cast in shadow. The entire space, which was inadequately illuminated by two narrow skylights, was filled with mournful-looking angels, gargoyles, and blank-faced Romanesque busts. The man responsible for this army of stone effigies was standing on a ladder beneath one of the skylights, chiseling away at an angel's folded wing.

"Mr. Hinkley, your order is packaged and ready to be collected," Bram Hobart said.

He used the chisel to point toward a human-sized parcel wrapped in burlap and resting atop a low wheeled cart in the corner. The statue was cushioned by a thick mattress and had the appearance of a shrouded corpse. "Do be careful with it," Bram added.

Daniel approached the ladder and held up his warrant card but doubted that Bram Hobart could read the small print from his elevated position. "Inspector Haze of Scotland Yard," he announced.

"Oh, dear," the man said with a sardonic smile, and stepped off the ladder to stand before Daniel. "What am I meant to have done, Inspector? That's just a statue." He pointed toward the wrapped parcel. "On my honor."

"Am I addressing Bram Hobart?" Daniel asked, just to be sure he had the right man.

"You are. It's actually Abraham, but I detest the name. Conjures up a Biblical patriarch with a flowing white beard, bared teeth, and a dagger in his grip," he said with distaste. "What sort of man would be willing to sacrifice his only son?" Bram asked conversationally. "Not one I care to be named after. Is that blasphemy?" he asked, one shapely eyebrow lifting theatrically. "If it is, then guilty as charged. Take me away." He held out his wrists to be cuffed and laughed.

The man's flippant attitude irritated Daniel, but then it seemed Bram Hobart had not yet heard the news of his father's death and probably assumed that Daniel's visit was related to some other inquiry. Daniel studied the man for a long moment, giving himself time to form an opinion. First impressions were important in his line of work, and although they often proved incomplete, they were not to be discounted since they offered a unique opportunity to take someone's measure. Despite his irreverence, Daniel thought that Bram Hobart was probably more sensitive than he let on and used his arrogance as a shield against those with the power to hurt him. Surely a man impervious to suffering couldn't produce the delicate features of the angel that rose from the block of marble before Daniel, a being that looked not only ethereal but completely shattered by tragedy.

"Do you like it?" Bram asked, following the direction of Daniel's gaze.

"It's beautiful," Daniel replied truthfully.

Now that he looked at the angel's face more closely, he thought it reminded him of someone, but he'd seen so many graves guarded by angels, he supposed after a time they all began to resemble each other. Daniel focused on Bram Hobart's features instead. He had only seen Philip Hobart's head, but Daniel could discern no likeness between the two men. Unlike Philip, who had dark hair and dark eyes, Bram Hobart had thick auburn hair and deep-set blue eyes that danced with amusement. His generous mouth quirked at the corners and was nothing like his father's thin-lipped leer.

Bram put Daniel in mind of an Irishman or a Scotsman, particularly since he had the physique of an outdoorsman, not someone who spent his time in a poorly lit studio. Bram was clean-shaven and sloppily dressed in an untucked linen shirt and twill trousers that were covered with marble residue. His shoes were scuffed and covered in a thick layer of stone dust. He was tall, lean, and graceful, and seemingly unconcerned by Daniel's unexpected visit.

"Mr. Hobart, I'm sorry to inform you that your father was murdered last night," Daniel said.

Bram stared at Daniel, then reached out and placed his hand on the ladder's rung, as if to steady himself.

"What?" he gasped. "How… How do you know he was murdered?" Bram asked, and swallowed hard, making his Adam's apple convulse in his pale throat. "Where did you find him?" Bram's face had gone the color of his angel, his eyes now radiating pain.

Daniel hesitated, wishing he could cushion the truth, but he wasn't in the business of mincing words, especially when addressing grown men.

"I'm afraid he was beheaded, Mr. Hobart. His head was left in a basket on the steps of Newgate Prison."

Bram's knuckles turned white as he tightened his grip on the rung. "Beheaded?" he echoed. "Who by?"

"That's what I'm trying to discover. I will need to ask you some questions."

"Yes, of course. But first I need a drink. Care to join me, Inspector?"

"I'm on duty," Daniel replied. "But you go ahead."

Bram Hobart walked over to a small cabinet, extracted a dark brown bottle, and tipped the contents into his mouth, drinking until the bottle was empty. He set it aside, wiped his mouth with the back of his hand, and pulled up a chair. Having dropped into it with an air of resignation, he said, "I'm ready."

Daniel wasn't invited to sit, so he remained standing and looked down at the sculptor, who sat with his head bowed, his arms resting on his thighs. Daniel could smell the spirits Bram had consumed but didn't think the drink had impaired his judgment, even though he had to have downed nearly half a bottle. Bram Hobart looked stone sober.

"When was the last time you saw your father?" Daniel asked.

"A few days ago."

"Can you be more specific?"

"Wednesday. We dine together on Wednesdays," Bram said.

"How did he seem when you saw him?" Daniel asked. "Was he frightened or worried about anything?"

Bram shrugged. "My father wasn't a person who discussed his feelings at the dinner table. In fact, he never discussed them at all, at least not with me."

"Why was that?"

"You have to be a certain kind of person to do what he did, don't you think?" Bram asked.

"Yes, I expect you do, but surely, as his son, you knew him better than most."

"I didn't. My mother died when I was seven. My father barely looked at me, much less tried to offer words of comfort or hope for the future. After the funeral, I was sent away to live with my mother's elderly aunt in Dartford. Father came to visit once a year, on Boxing Day. That was the extent of our interaction until I turned seventeen."

"What happened then?"

"Aunt Helen died, so I returned to London. My father allowed me to stay with him for a while, but then evicted me when he married Lucy."

"Why did he evict you?" Daniel asked, genuinely curious.

"He said I was a grown man, and my upkeep was no longer his obligation."

"Did that make you angry?"

"Not at all," Bram replied. "He was right, and although Father wasn't aware of it, I did have something to fall back on. Aunt Helen left everything to me, since I was her only living relative. It wasn't much, but it was enough to secure a ten-year lease on this place and help me to start my business. I am much happier living on my own. My rooms are modest but comfortable, and my landlady is not only a competent cook but a comely widow who doesn't object to a bit of company in the evening," he said with a suggestive smile. "If a man's home is his castle, then I'm king of the heap."

"I see," Daniel said. "And was your father equally happy with his domestic arrangement?"

Bram Hobart shot him a look of pure astonishment. "Have you not heard a word I said? My father did not discuss his marriage with me."

"Yes, I heard what you said, Mr. Hobart, but you did spend time with your father and stepmother. Surely you formed an opinion. Were your father and stepmother well suited?"

Bram Hobart considered this. “Yes, I suppose they were. Lucy is a quiet, unassuming woman. Just the sort of partner my father needed.”

“They had a child,” Daniel prompted.

“Yes. A boy. Samuel. He died a few weeks ago.”

“What was the cause of death?”

“He passed in his sleep.”

“Was a physician called to examine the child?” Daniel asked.

Bram’s expression became pained once again. “Finding a cause wouldn’t have brought Sam back, and it was imperative to bury the child as quickly as possible.”

“Why was that?”

“Because of Lucy’s fragile mental state. She was inconsolable. When she found Sam unresponsive in his cot, she sat with him for hours, rocking and singing to him, as if he were merely asleep. It was heartbreaking. My father had to forcibly take the dead child from her and deliver it to the undertakers or she would have remained that way until she lost what was left of her wits. My father wanted Lucy to remember Sam as he was in life. Cherubic,” Bram added under his breath.

“And how did your father take Samuel’s death?” Daniel asked.

“How do you think?” Bram retorted.

“Was your father more invested in Samuel than he was in you?” Daniel asked, even though the question seemed cruel in view of the child’s sudden death.

“My father’s every thought was for that boy. He doted on him.”

So not as much of a cold fish as Bram intimated, Daniel thought. "Mr. Hobart, can you think of anyone who'd want to see your father dead?"

"You mean aside from the dozens of families whose loved ones he'd sent to their graves?"

"Was there someone particularly vocal in their anger?"

"I wouldn't know. As I said, my father didn't confide in me."

"Did your father have any friends?" Daniel asked with a sigh.

He was growing desperate. He'd interviewed several people closest to Philip Hobart but had learned very little of the dead man. He was still as much of a mystery to Daniel as he had been that morning, when Daniel had been forced to stare at his head.

"My father was fond of Charlie," Bram announced.

"And who's Charlie?"

"Charles Dafoe of the Ferryman Inn in Wood Street. My father always went to the Ferryman on Friday nights."

"Was your father a creature of habit?" Daniel asked.

"Yes, I suppose he was."

"Did you ever join him at the Ferryman?"

"I was never invited," Bram replied bitterly. "That was reserved for people he liked."

"And were there many of those?"

"No, just Charlie. And Lucy."

"Did your father not like you, Mr. Hobart?" Daniel inquired.

"Fathers and sons don't always see eye to eye, Inspector, especially when they fail to form a strong bond early on. My father felt my desire to be a sculptor was not only impractical but self-indulgent. Ironically, we both earned our bread from death. He sent people to their deaths, and I erect stone monuments to mark their graves."

"What would your father have you do instead?" Daniel asked.

He thought Bram Hobart had to be doing well for himself, given the never-ending demand for monuments and gravestones. Of course, as an artist, this sideline probably wasn't his life's passion, only a way to pay the bills. There wasn't much call for classical sculptors these days, not unless they had a reputation that preceded them and were hired for loftier projects.

"He thought the Royal Navy would be a fine choice. Charlie's son joined several years ago."

"Did you ever consider his suggestion?" Daniel asked, more to flesh out the relationship between father and son than because he thought it had any bearing on the murder.

"I get seasick, Inspector. Didn't fancy puking my guts out." Bram leaned back in his chair, his blue gaze fixed on Daniel. "What will you do with my father's head?"

"It was delivered to the mortuary at Scotland Yard. We still hope to find the body."

"And if you don't?"

"If we don't, then the head will be released to you once the surgeon has had a chance to examine it."

"Surely the cause of death is obvious if he was beheaded," Bram said.

"Yes, but the surgeon would like to have a closer look."

Bram nodded his understanding. "Please, inform me once the surgeon is finished with his examination. I don't think Lucy should have to see my father like that. Not after…" His voice trailed off, but Daniel thought he was referring to Samuel's death. "I will see to all the arrangements."

"As you wish, Mr. Hobart," Daniel said, and turned to leave.

By the time he reached the door, Bram Hobart was back on his ladder, chipping away at the angel's wing.

Chapter 9

Daniel stepped outside and consulted his watch. It was just past three, the perfect time to call at the Ferryman Inn, before the after-work crowd began to file in. He would have walked, but Ransome would be expecting a report by five, so his time was limited.

Daniel found a cab and instructed the driver to take him to Wood Street. The traffic was surprisingly heavy, the roads congested with wagons, carriages, and an omnibus that moved at a snail's pace and blocked the road every time someone needed to get off. Daniel's stomach rumbled with hunger when he passed a butcher's shop and spotted a fat ham hanging in the window, surrounded by strings of sausages and a platter of chops. The pie Daniel had eaten hours ago had done little to assuage his hunger, but it was hours yet until supper. He hoped Grace would have something nice for him, and for a split second wished she'd join him at the table so he wouldn't have to eat alone.

Daniel sighed. After he spoke to Charles Dafoe, he'd have to return to Scotland Yard to deliver his report, and only then would he be free to leave for the day. Not that he had anything to go home to, Daniel thought morosely. Rebecca was gone. Charlotte was in Essex, spending a few weeks with her doting grandmother. And Grace retired to her room as soon as she tidied the kitchen after supper, eager for a few hours of rest from the never-ending domestic chores. Daniel spent his evenings reading by the fire, his only escape the fictional world of Charles Dickens' *Our Mutual Friend.* He'd read it before. Sarah had purchased it for him as soon as it was published, and it was still a favorite. A comfort at a time when he felt bereft and alone.

The Ferryman Inn occupied an old Tudor building, the wattle and daub exterior brightened by flowerboxes affixed beneath the mullioned windows. The interior was dim and smelled of hops, and the dark beams in what had once been a white ceiling were so low, Daniel instinctively ducked, even though he knew they were at least a foot above his head. A few patrons sat at the scarred wooden tables, nursing their jars of ale and talking amongst themselves. Most likely regulars who didn't have much to occupy them during the day.

A middle-aged man whose belly strained against the buttons of his stained waistcoat stood behind the bar, lazily wiping tankards that shone with grease from handling by countless fingers. Wooly muttonchops accentuated his heavy jowls, and his hair, which must have been black once upon a time, was a halo of graying waves. Eyes as black as the buttons on his coat followed Daniel as he approached the bar, the man's expression one of deep suspicion.

"Good afternoon," Daniel said. "Do I have the pleasure of speaking to Charles Dafoe?"

Normally, Daniel would simply show his warrant card and get down to business, but Charles Dafoe was his only remaining lead and the person who had, at least according to Bram Hobart, known Philip Hobart tolerably well. Daniel couldn't afford to antagonize him.

"You do, but I haven't seen you here before," the publican replied.

"I'm Inspector Haze of Scotland Yard. I'm investigating the murder of Philip Hobart. I believe you knew him."

The man's mouth went slack with shock. "Philip is dead?"

"He is."

"How?"

"By beheading."

"Sweet Jesus!" Charles Dafoe exclaimed. He looked like he was about to make the sign of the cross but thought better of it and redirected his hand to rest on his heart. "May the good Lord rest his troubled soul," he said, bowing his head piously.

Daniel thought the man might be Catholic, possibly a descendant of French immigrants, given his surname, but didn't care to advertise his faith, especially to a police detective. Charles Dafoe turned around, reached for a bottle of whisky, and poured two glasses. "Here, Inspector. Join me in toasting Philip's memory."

Daniel couldn't help but wonder what it was about the deceased that inspired those who knew him to instantly reach for a bottle of spirits. He didn't really want to drink, especially not on an empty stomach and just before reporting to Ransome, but if he didn't, Charles Dafoe might take offense and refuse to speak to him. Daniel obediently picked up the glass and joined the publican in a toast.

Charles threw back the drink, slammed the glass on the counter, and leaned forward, his sour breath warm on Daniel's face. "You find whoever done this, you hear? Philip didn't deserve to die that way."

"I've spoken to a number of people, Mr. Dafoe, but I know as little of the man now as I did when his head was found on the steps of Newgate this morning."

"Alfie," Charlie hollered. "Mind the bar."

A boy of about thirteen appeared from what had to be the kitchen and positioned himself behind the counter. "You can trust me, Uncle Charlie," he said, his expression tense, his fingers reaching for the rag Charles Dafoe had been using to polish the tankards.

"Good lad," the publican said as he lifted a section of the counter and invited Daniel to follow him into the office at the back.

The room was small and windowless and smelled of dust, stale tobacco, and mouse droppings. Daniel took the guest chair while Charlie settled his considerable bulk behind the cluttered desk.

"Tell me about Philip Hobart," Daniel said, lowering his voice in an effort to invite a confidence. He sensed that Charlie was truly grief-stricken and hoped the man would tell him something worth hearing. "How long had you known him?"

"Since he was a boy," Charlie said. He nodded his shaggy head, his eyes soft with memory. "Philip's father, Roger Hobart, used to drink at the Ferryman, and let me tell you, Inspector, a nastier drunk you had never encountered. Took his fists to his wife and son every time he so much as had a drop in him. Philip was terrified of his father, and with good reason. Roger became so enraged when he learned his wife was with child again, he tried to beat the babe out of her, just like he had all the others. Kicked her in the stomach over and over. She died, the poor lass. Bled to death on the hearth rug. Philip must have been eight then. He sat by his mother's body all night, keeping vigil."

"Was Roger Hobart charged with murder?" Daniel asked, pity for the child Philip Hobart had been swelling in his breast. Why was it that people were capable of such cruelty, especially toward those they were meant to love and protect?

Charles Dafoe scoffed. "'Course not. No one wanted to kick that mad dog, not even the local constable, not when Roger Hobart could turn on him next. The death was attributed to natural causes."

"What happened to Philip?"

"Philip took a beating nearly every night until, one day, his old man drank so much, he couldn't find the strength to raise his fists. Roger stumbled, fell, and struck his head on the corner of the mantel. Died in the exact same spot as his long-suffering wife. Philip had no family, no one to take him in, so he found himself on the street as soon as it was time to pay the rent. The poor lad barely had two farthings to rub together. And it was a cold winter that year," Charles said with a sigh.

"How did he survive?" Daniel asked.

"My father took him in. I always thought he felt guilty for selling Hobart the ale that so enraged him. It was atonement, of sorts."

"So Philip lived here with your family?"

Charles scoffed again. "My old man didn't feel *that* guilty," he said. "He put Philip to work. Didn't pay him, as such, but Philip got two meals a day and a pallet in the cellar in return for an honest day's work. We were of an age, he and I, so after a time, we became like brothers."

"How did Philip Hobart become a hangman?" Daniel asked, grateful for the insight into Philip Hobart's past that Charles Dafoe had provided.

"It was when he turned fourteen that he got a place at Newgate. Worked as a night gaoler. The wage was reasonable, and Philip couldn't sleep in our cellar forever. But he still worked at the Ferryman during the day, for a wage now. Philip saved his earnings and learned what he needed on the job and eventually convinced Mr. Calcraft to take him on as his assistant. I think it was his mother's murder that set him on that path. Philip believed in retribution, and justice."

"And what about his own family?" Daniel asked. Understanding something of the victim was helpful, but none of these revelations seemed pertinent to the crime.

"Philip married young. Personally, I don't think he much cared for Annie. She was a real gabber, that one. Couldn't muzzle her with a gag, but she got with child, and he did right by her."

"Was Philip Hobart that honorable of a man?" Daniel inquired.

Charles Dafoe shrugged. "I reckon he needed something to call his own. A place to lay his head at the end of the day, and Annie gave him that. And, of course, after the way his own mother had been treated, he took responsibility for his spawn."

"Was Annie Bram's mother, or was there another wife before Lucy?"

"She was, but Annie died in childbirth when Bram was just a child. Philip sent him to live with Annie's aunt, Helen. Thought the boy would have a better life with the old spinster."

"So Philip sent Bram away because he loved him?"

Charles smiled knowingly. "I see you've spoken to Bram already. Always did carry on about not being wanted. He's old enough to know better."

"Bram said his father visited him once a year," Daniel pointed out.

"Philip had never seen love or known it for himself, Inspector. Even his own mother hardly noticed him. The poor woman was too frightened of her husband to worry overmuch about her son. And Annie, for all her ceaseless prattling, never said nothing worth hearing. Philip didn't know how to talk to the boy."

"And the current Mrs. Hobart?"

Charles smiled again, this time affectionately. "I think Lucy was the first person Philip ever truly loved. He was besotted with her. And when she gave him a son, his happiness was complete." Charles sighed. "But then the poor little mite passed. It was very sudden. I think it broke them both, Inspector."

"Mr. Dafoe, I'm grateful for the information you have provided, but what I need to understand is who'd seek retribution against Philip Hobart. Was there anyone who'd nursed a grudge against him, or had maybe even threatened him outright? Did Philip fear for his life?"

Charles Dafoe cocked his head to the side as he pondered Daniel's question. "I don't know that he feared for his life, but there was one cove who'd made threats."

“And who was that?” Daniel asked, his notebook at the ready.

“Barnaby Stack, his name was. Came in here one night, claiming Philip had intentionally made his brother suffer ’cause the Stacks couldn’t raise enough tin to pay for a quick death.”

“Would Philip Hobart have done such a thing?”

Charles shook his head. “I don’t believe so.”

“And where would I find Mr. Stack?” Daniel asked.

“That I couldn’t tell you. Haven’t seen the man in ages, and when I did, it’s not as if we exchanged pleasantries.”

“Thank you, Mr. Dafoe.” Daniel pushed to his feet. “I appreciate your assistance.”

“You find the bastard that did this, Inspector Haze. Philip didn’t deserve to die, not like that. Not like some butchered animal.”

Perhaps not, Daniel thought, but traditionally, beheading was considered not only the more dignified but also a more humane way to die, hanging reserved for the lower orders, who didn’t deserve such consideration. What did that say about Philip Hobart’s killer, and Hobart himself? Had the killer given Philip Hobart an honorable death as a sign of respect, or was there another reason he had wished to separate the head from the body and leave it on the prison steps?

Chapter 10

Daniel left the Ferryman and made his way to the underground railway stop. He hated traveling beneath ground and found the experience not only disconcerting but downright hair-raising, but at the time of day when everyone was closing up shop and heading home from work, it really was the fastest way to get to where he needed to be. The journey passed without incident, and Daniel walked the rest of the way to Scotland Yard, taking the time to organize his thoughts about the case. Ransome valued a succinct delivery and a clear plan of action, something Daniel had yet to formulate. He entered the building and headed directly for the superintendent's office.

"Good evening, Inspector Haze," Sergeant Meadows called out. "This was delivered for you." He handed Daniel a sealed envelope that bore the return address of Newgate Prison. It had to be the list of executions Philip Hobart had overseen and, hopefully, the addresses of the condemned persons' families.

"Make any inroads on our headless corpse?" Sergeant Meadows chortled.

Daniel turned on him. "A man is dead, Sergeant. Brutally murdered, his remains desecrated. Find that funny, do you?"

Sergeant Meadows went red in the face but didn't avert his gaze. "My apologies, Inspector. It was crass of me to poke fun."

"Yes, it was. See you don't do it again."

"Yes, sir. I'm sorry, sir."

Daniel didn't bother to reply. He had been too hard on the man, but he wasn't about to apologize. In a job like theirs, humor and irreverence went a long way toward accepting the mindless brutality and senseless death they encountered every day. No matter how hardened a policeman became, there was always someone who could penetrate the shield they had erected around themselves to protect their fragile sanity. It was much easier to accept a death that was the result of a tavern brawl or a premeditated poisoning than a murder in which the perpetrator had reached new levels of depravity and had probably taken great pleasure from the shock value of their evil act.

Whoever had killed Philip Hobart would most likely be devouring the newspapers tomorrow, looking for the story of which they were the star. Was that why they had resorted to butchery, to make the front page? Perhaps. Or perhaps there was some other reason, one Daniel had yet to understand, a reason that had nothing to do with notoriety and everything to do with crime and punishment.

Daniel strode purposefully toward Ransome's office. As usual, the door was open, the superintendent seated behind his desk, his pensive gaze fixed on a photograph mounted on the wall. He started when Daniel materialized in the doorway.

Ransome beckoned him forward. "Come in, Haze. I've been expecting you."

Daniel removed his bowler but didn't bother with the coat. He wouldn't be staying long. He lowered himself into the guest chair and faced his superior as he tried to gauge Ransome's mood. Ransome looked tired and defeated, but Daniel didn't think that had anything to do with the case. And as far as Daniel knew, there were no other high-profile cases open at the moment, just the usual thefts, stabbings, rival gang murders, and hold-ups. He wondered if Ransome was ill but didn't think it appropriate to inquire. Ransome wouldn't appreciate his concern and would most likely bristle at the insinuation that he looked less than robust and not fully in charge of his personal fiefdom.

"How did you make out today?" Ransome asked as he leaned back in his chair and studied Daniel from beneath hooded eyelids.

"There are no obvious suspects as of yet, sir," Daniel replied. "The only person who had something to gain by Hobart's death is his assistant, Clyde Barkley, but there was no guarantee that he would be appointed principal executioner if his mentor died, so he would have been taking a senseless risk if he decided to murder his superior. Likewise, I don't see the point of leaving the head on the steps. If Barkley wanted Philip Hobart dead, he could have murdered him in a less obvious and physically demanding manner."

Ransome nodded. "Still, beheading his predecessor would be one way for Barkley to get the job. I hear it's a lucrative occupation."

"So it is, but Clyde Barkley did not strike me as someone who's either impractical or violent."

Ransome raised an eyebrow at that. "He murders people for a living."

"He does, but not on his own initiative. Clyde Barkley sees what he does as a service to society, and it isn't his decision to take someone's life. This case is vastly different."

"I imagine it's a fine line between killing on the court's order and killing to serve one's own goals. It would be a mistake to discount Clyde Barkley on the strength of a first impression."

"I quite agree, sir, which is why he's at the top of my list."

"Who else is on this list?" Ransome asked. Normally, he would be challenging Daniel, goading him, but today Ransome seemed almost indifferent, like a tiger that was dozing before the hearth like a housecat rather than angrily pacing its cage.

"I think I should speak to the families of the individuals Hobart had executed. Three names in particular cropped up."

"You think it might be revenge?"

"I think that's very possible. The method of the murder leads me to believe that the motive does not lie in Hobart's personal life. He was executed."

“An eye for an eye?” Ransome asked. “Rather Biblical, wouldn’t you agree?”

Daniel nodded, his mind still on his own theory. “Perhaps the killer wanted to underline a connection to Newgate but couldn’t undertake a public hanging without getting caught.”

“So he beheaded his victim and left his head on the step, like a calling card.”

“Precisely.”

“It would help if we knew what he did with the body.”

“It would, but I would wager to guess that the killer disposed of it immediately after the execution, since he or she had no use for it. It could be anywhere.”

“You think this could have been done by a woman?” Ransome asked.

Daniel smiled, despite the gruesome manner of the murder. “Lord Redmond advises me never to discount the possibility, sir. An angry woman is capable of anything.”

“I won’t argue with you there, Haze. Who knows what sort of lunatic we’re dealing with,” Ransome said warily. “How do you intend to proceed?”

“I am in possession of a list of executions Hobart had carried out and will begin speaking to the families first thing tomorrow,” Daniel said.

“You think someone actually blamed Hobart for carrying out a sentence?”

“I think someone might have blamed him for being unnecessarily cruel.”

“Oh?” Ransome asked, one eyebrow lifting again.

"A suggestion was made by Clyde Barkley that Philip Hobart accepted bribes to ensure a quick death. I have visited Hobart's home, and he was very comfortably off."

"You think Hobart regularly supplemented his income?"

"He may have, or it could be a fabricated accusation, made by a man who resented his superior and is happy to see him dead."

Ransome pulled out his watch and consulted the time, then stuffed it back into the pocket of his navy blue waistcoat and pushed wearily to his feet. "I must get home, Haze. My wife's been unwell."

"I'm sorry to hear that, sir. I wish her a speedy recovery."

Ransome nodded. "Thank you. Goodnight, Inspector."

Daniel walked past a contrite Sergeant Meadows and stepped into the purpling twilight of the spring evening. He was more disturbed by Ransome's admission of his wife's illness than by the lack of progress on the investigation. Ransome never revealed details of his personal life, and Daniel surmised that Mrs. Ransome had to be very ill indeed for him to cross the line between the personal and the professional. The poor man had to be distraught. And perhaps he'd shared his anxiety with Daniel because he thought Daniel would understand, having lost his own wife not so long ago.

Daniel lifted the collar of his coat against the evening chill and began to walk. Even though he was tired and hungry, he had no reason to rush. There was no one waiting for him. His gut twisted with grief and guilt when he thought of the beautiful, vivacious Rebecca and recalled how she'd looked in death, as still and white as the marble angel she'd been found beneath. He'd attended the funeral but had not visited Rebecca's grave since and thought that perhaps he should pay his respects. Daniel sighed heavily. Except for Charlotte, nearly everyone he'd ever loved was dead.

Daniel tried valiantly not to give in to self-pity, but life had been a sore trial this past year, and more than once he'd thought that he might drown in grief if he allowed himself to dwell on the magnitude of his loss. He was tired of swimming against the current, tossed on the swells as he tried to keep his head above water. His tired soul needed a rest, a safe port where he could shelter for a while until he felt stronger. There was no one except Jason to share his troubles with, and although he was sympathetic, there wasn't much Jason could do to help Daniel come to terms with his losses. Jason had suffered losses of his own. And now he was worried about Mary and Liam. Jason would be heartbroken if they died, not only for Micah but for himself as well. He was the sort of man that grew attached to people and wanted to step in to keep them safe. But people didn't always welcome a benefactor, and Mary had seen Jason's desire to help her as patronizing rather than well-meant, but the girl had been nursing her own wounds at the time.

The old adage said that time healed all wounds, but Daniel didn't believe that. Not anymore. Some wounds went too deep to ever heal properly. They kept reopening and leaking, draining the body of vitality, and bleeding all joy from the soul. After a time, they grew a layer of scar tissue, just like the scar on Daniel's back, where Jason had removed his kidney after he'd been stabbed, but the pain remained, even if it was a phantom pain that lived only in the mind.

Suddenly, Daniel couldn't bear another moment of loneliness and hurried home. He'd invite Grace to sup with him tonight. They could both use the company.

Chapter 11

Jason arrived at home a few hours before dinner to discover that Katherine had taken Lily for a visit to her friend Adelaide Powell's house, where Lily could play with the Powells' little girl, Dorothy. He rang for Henley to draw him a bath and lowered himself into the steaming water, very pleased with the plumbing he'd had installed in his grandfather's outmoded house. Jason lay back, shut his eyes, and considered the case, both because he really was intrigued and because he had no wish to continue to dwell on Mary's whereabouts.

Everything about the case seemed wrong, from the carefully draped head to the dramatic manner of its discovery. Why would anyone go to such trouble to murder someone unless they were either quite deranged or looking to dress the killing up as a riddle? Jason had yet to decide which possibility he was leaning toward, but he thought that in either case, the murder itself was not the objective. If one simply wanted to end someone's life, there were myriad ways to do that without drawing quite as much attention to themselves. Clearly, the killer didn't have much faith in the police, imagining that the "mutton shunters," as the policemen were sometimes referred to, would not be able to discover any viable clues and fail to solve the case, leaving the killer to walk free.

Jason admired Daniel's dedication to his craft, but this case would require more than dogged police work. To solve this crime, Daniel would have to get into the mind of the killer to understand why he had felt the need to go to such lengths to desecrate the body. And what Jason suddenly realized was that he had been referring to the killer as "he" in his mind. Was he convinced this was the work of a man? A woman could certainly be deranged, and a strong woman might have lopped off the head without much difficulty, especially if the victim was already incapacitated, but something about this murder felt masculine. Jason had no wish to jump to any unfounded conclusions, nor did he have enough information to formulate a plausible theory. He had no solid evidence to go on, just as he had no proof that something awful had befallen Mary and Liam, but every time he thought of them, something inside him clenched like a fist.

Jason wasn't a superstitious person, nor did he imagine that some people were marked for tragedy, but if there was such a thing as bad luck, Mary had been blessed with it double. Why had she left Boston? Jason asked himself again, despite his resolve not to worry. Had Mary planned the journey to England, or had it been a spontaneous decision driven by some unforeseen event? Would she eventually go back? If he didn't hear anything by the end of the week, he'd send a cable to Mr. Hartley. Perhaps news of the vessel had reached New York. Jason needed answers, and soon, if only for Micah's sake. He couldn't bear to break Micah's heart again.

Letting out a heavy sigh, Jason sank deeper into the water, rested his head against the porcelain tub, and tried to clear his mind. He was just beginning to drift when Henley knocked on the door and entered, a fluffy towel draped over his arm.

"Sorry to disturb you, my lord, but it's time to dress for dinner," he announced.

Jason pried open his eyes. "Is my wife back?"

"She is, sir. I saw her ladyship heading up to the nursery."

"I'll be out in a minute," Jason said.

"Very good, sir," Henley said, and placed the folded towel on a marble-topped cabinet near the tub.

Jason reluctantly got out of the tub, dried off, and headed toward his dressing room, where Henley had laid out his clothes for the evening. Jason dressed and went downstairs, where he was halfway through a pre-dinner drink in the drawing room before Katherine breezed in, looking sprightly in a new gown of emerald chiffon.

"You look stunning," Jason said as he came forward to greet her.

Katherine's face lit up. "Do you like it? I wasn't sure the color suits me."

"It's perfect," Jason replied. "Would you like a sherry?"

"Maybe just a small one," Katherine agreed, and took her customary seat.

Jason poured Katherine a drink and settled across from her.

Katherine took a dainty sip, then set the glass down on an occasional table. She gave Jason a quizzical look. "Did you make it to the docks?"

"I did. The *Arcadia* has yet to dock," Jason said. "But storms have been reported in the Atlantic," he rushed to add when he saw her worried expression. "Several other vessels have been delayed but have arrived safely."

Katherine nodded. "Let us pray that's all it is, a delay."

"Until we know different, we shouldn't jump to conclusions," Jason agreed.

Katherine studied him for a moment, and he knew that there was no hiding his thoughts from her. She knew him too well, and if he were honest, he was interested to hear her opinion of the day's events.

"I was called to Newgate Prison today," Jason said. "The hangman's head was left on the steps in a basket."

"Oh, dear," Katherine said, shaking her head in dismay. "What of the body?"

"Could be anywhere."

She sighed. "Every time I think human beings no longer have the power to shock me, I find myself proven wrong."

"As do I. This is an odd case."

"Do you have any leads?"

"Not as of yet." Katherine looked so dispirited that Jason decided to change the subject. "Tell me about your visit to the Powells."

Katherine's relief at not having to discuss the case was almost palpable. "Oh, it was lovely. The girls were just darling. They played very well together, and Adelaide and I had a cozy chat."

"I'm glad you had a good day," Jason said, pleased that at least one of them had.

"My lord. My lady. Dinner is served," Dodson announced in his usual haughty manner as he entered the drawing room.

"I believe Mrs. Dodson has been experimenting again," Katherine said under her breath as they made their way toward the dining room. "Something about calf's tongue was mentioned. Or was it pig's feet and truffles?"

"If they ever find me unexpectedly deceased, just tell them I was dispatched by British cooking," Jason muttered as they entered the dining room and took their seats.

"I will be sure to do that, my dear," Katherine promised, and grinned at him in a way that made him want to skip dinner altogether and call it an early night.

Chapter 12

Wednesday, March 24

Armed with the list of executions Philip Hobart had carried out, Daniel headed to St. George's Hospital to meet Jason. He was eager to share everything he'd learned and hoped that Jason could coax a theory, no matter how far-fetched, from the little information Daniel had been able to extract from the previous day's interviews. Jason joined him outside, and they repaired to the Coffee Brewery, a coffeehouse Jason favored that was frequented by members of staff due to its proximity to the hospital. It was a charming place that boasted stained-glass windows that bathed the patrons in a rainbow of gentle light on sunny days and gave the place a cheery feeling on overcast ones.

Once they placed their order, Jason patiently listened to Daniel's account. Then, once their order had been delivered to the table, the coffee poured and made to their liking, Daniel asked the question that had been on his mind since his conversation with Clyde Barkley.

"Jason, what's your opinion on hanging? Is what Clyde Barkley said true and there's a degree of showmanship involved? I had always assumed that it was straightforward and didn't require much in the way of skill."

Jason's expression became pained. "As with any form of execution, some measure of skill is required, and as with human beings the world over, there are those who will look to either profit from the undertaking or give vent to their malice. Just as a firing squad can kill the condemned instantaneously with a bullet to the heart or the head, they can also riddle the accused with bullets and leave them to die in agony as they bleed to death. Same can be said of hanging. If carried out correctly, hanging can be a humane way to die, but only if the neck is instantly broken, which is where the longer drop comes in. Immediate unconsciousness is followed by rapid brain death, so the victim doesn't suffer, at least not during the hanging itself. There's still the period of emotional anguish as the date of the execution approaches, but that's something else entirely."

"And are hangings often botched?" Daniel asked.

"More often than you might imagine, both due to the incompetence of the hangman and the inadequacy of the apparatus. The condemned person's weight and height really should be taken into account in order to minimize unnecessary suffering, but although there are proponents of improving the method, they are few and mostly ignored."

"Yes, Clyde Barkley did mention something about that."

"Is he a suspect?" Jason asked, clearly wishing to get away from the logistics of breaking a person's neck.

"I will reserve judgment on Clyde Barkley for the time being," Daniel said. "It's quite possible that he had decided to get rid of Hobart in order to expedite his ascent to the position of principal hangman, especially now that there are those who are calling for William Calcraft to retire due to his age and track record. However, even if Barkley was confident of securing the promotion, I see no reason for him to carry out such an elaborate scheme. He could have knifed Philip Hobart between the ribs as he walked home from the Queen's Arms and taken his purse. It would be assumed that Hobart was a victim of a robbery, and no one would ever consider Clyde Barkley as a suspect in the attack. An opportunistic killing rather than a well-thought-out plan would be the most logical way to go."

"Do you still think that the motive lies in Hobart's work?" Jason asked.

"Having spoken to Mrs. Hobart, Abraham Hobart, and Charles Dafoe, it's quite clear that Philip Hobart did not have a wide social circle or seek out entertaining diversions. He was a quiet, reticent man who saw no point in casual friendships and only spent time with those close to him. And those individuals seemed to have held him in high regard."

"What about the son? Seems there was some resentment there."

"There was, but show me a son who doesn't at times feel unloved by his father. Bram Hobart indicated to me that his father doted on young Samuel. Perhaps he felt a bit slighted, having been sent to live at his aunt's house after his mother died. But according to Charles Dafoe, Philip did that to ensure the boy had a better life than he would have had with an unmarried and often distant father. Bram might not have seen it for what it was, but it was an act of kindness."

"Is it ever an act of kindness to send one's child away at a time when they need a parent most?"

"If Philip Hobart did not feel that he could be the father Bram needed, then I suppose it was. Besides, you said yourself, on more than one occasion, that it would have been the prudent thing to do to leave Micah at home rather than take him to war, the way Liam Donovan did."

"That's hardly the same thing," Jason protested.

"Maybe, but just as Mr. Donovan had thought he was doing what was best for his son, so did Philip Hobart."

"All right," Jason conceded. "I take your point."

Daniel nodded, satisfied, and continued. "Philip Hobart had performed fifty-six executions since becoming the principal hangman. He'd also flogged several dozen inmates, but only three of them have died since, of causes unrelated to the flogging. I think it's safe to eliminate them from our inquiry for the time being. Which leaves fifty-six families that might have wanted revenge. Three names, specifically, have been mentioned. Stack, Cassell, and Newberry. I think we need to start by questioning them."

Jason took a sip of his coffee and set the cup down, his expression thoughtful. "If we hope to solve this case, we need to locate the body."

"And what do you expect the body to tell you?" Daniel asked, surprised by Jason's response to the plan he'd outlined.

"It will tell me approximately where Philip Hobart was murdered," Jason replied. "Which, in turn, might narrow down the list of suspects."

"How?"

"It would be easy enough to conceal a severed head, but it's not so easy to hide a headless body. I can't imagine that the killer would move the body very far from the place of execution. It would be extremely heavy and unwieldy, not to mention conspicuous. Likewise, the crime scene would retain some evidence of the killing. As soon as the head was separated from the body, a copious amount of blood would pump from the neck, covering a wide area, unless a bucket or basin was positioned beneath the neck ahead of time."

Jason took another sip of coffee and continued. "As far as we know, Philip Hobart left the Queen's Arms around ten o'clock. His head was discovered ten hours later by the warden. The victim was dead at least a few hours by then, so we're looking at the hours between ten and six. Possibly even earlier, since the individual who delivered the head to Newgate would not want to be seen and would likely have left the basket before sunrise. Unless Philip Hobart was either forcibly taken or went with the killer willingly, the crime scene would have to be somewhere between the Queen's Arms and the Hobarts' home."

"Do you not think that someone would have stumbled on a headless body by now?" Daniel asked.

"Not if it's well concealed."

"They might have thrown the body in the river."

"Yes, they might have," Jason agreed. "But they'd still have to get it to the river, unless Hobart was beheaded on the bank."

Daniel shook his head. "None of this makes any sense."

Jason cocked his head to the side. "Could there be some sort of symbolism to this killing?"

"How do you mean?"

"A political group, perhaps. The last person to be publicly executed was Michael Barrett, the Fenian who was said to have set off the explosion in Clerkenwell. I remember reading about the case shortly after I arrived in England. There was strong doubt about his guilt, and many felt that he had been sacrificed to appease the Tories and uphold the actions of the police. Could this be revenge for Barrett's death?"

"Michael Barrett wasn't executed by Philip Hobart."

"No, but didn't Philip Hobart assist William Calcraft that day?"

"He may have. I can't recall," Daniel admitted.

"It might be a connection worth exploring."

Daniel nodded. He hadn't considered the possibility, but Jason had a valid point. Although Daniel read the papers as a matter of course, he never paid much attention to the Fenian cause. He detested politics and thought that any nation should consider itself lucky to be part of the Great British Empire and accept the progress and enlightenment such a patronage offered. To attempt to throw off British rule through armed conflict was madness that was sure not only to fail but to bring about serious and lasting repercussions.

"The Fenians don't stand a chance, even if they do find underhanded ways to retaliate," Daniel said, and instantly regretted his outburst.

"The Americans didn't stand a chance either when they stood up to the might of Britain. And look at us now," Jason replied with a smug grin.

"It's not the same."

"Isn't it? Why shouldn't the Irish be independent? It's their country, after all."

"Ireland is part of Britain," Daniel protested. "Just like Scotland."

"And don't the Scots want their independence as well?"

"It's a fantasy peddled by reckless idealists who prey on people's discontent and hope to incite armed conflict."

"If there's such strong discontent, then perhaps there's good reason for it," Jason countered.

"As long as there are human beings, there's always discontent," Daniel said.

"And as long as a tiny percentage rules over millions of people, that discontent will always turn violent."

"Let's focus on the one act of violence we're tasked with solving," Daniel said, wishing only to change the subject.

Jason's opinions frequently unsettled him and made him question everything he'd been taught to believe since boyhood. What did it matter what Daniel thought about any of it? It wasn't as if he had the power to bring about change. He was one man, and his only responsibility was to apprehend those who'd broken the law, right here in London. The world was too big a place for him to concern himself with.

"I need to examine the head," Jason said, his thoughts having obviously moved on from armed rebellion back to the matter at hand. "I didn't have enough time yesterday, and the light in Britteridge's office was poor."

Daniel nodded. "Let's go to Scotland Yard, then. You can complete your examination, and I will speak to Ransome about searching the area and consult him regarding a possible political connection."

Jason threw a few coins on the table and pushed back his chair. "Sounds like a plan," he said.

Chapter 13

When they arrived at the Yard, Jason headed directly to the mortuary, where he divested himself of hat and coat and donned the leather apron he used to protect his clothing from the bodily fluids of the cadavers he worked on. Philip Hobart's head was still in the basket, the towel draped over it to keep it from frightening unsuspecting visitors. The basket was atop a cabinet, most likely placed there by the police surgeon, who'd left the room less than tidy after his last postmortem. Jason removed the towel, extracted the head from the basket, and laid it on the table. The window set high in the wall provided enough daylight to examine the remains, but Jason reached for a magnifying glass, nonetheless, determined to see anything the naked eye might have missed.

He studied Hobart's face carefully. He'd never examined a victim of beheading before. On a field of battle, there was no need. The dead were collected and tossed haphazardly into mass graves along with whatever limbs were left strewn on the ground. Jason's only interest had been in those still living. He had read accounts of the mass beheadings in France, though, and knew that if the executioner was skilled and managed to sever the head with one clean stroke, death was instantaneous, but the victim's brain took a few moments to catch up to the rest of the body.

Facial expressions sometimes changed, and the victim's eyes continued to move for several seconds after the head was separated from the body. In years past, when public beheadings had been a spectacle, the crowd had sometimes been treated to the victim's expression of incredulity as the executioner held up the head for everyone to see. There was that last moment of awareness before the eyes dimmed and the mouth went slack as brain activity ceased. As far as government-sanctioned murder went, beheading was probably one of the more humane options, and traditionally reserved for the nobility and all those who had earned an honorable death. Was that the reason Philip Hobart had been beheaded? Was this a badge of honor, a final nod to his skill as an executioner, perhaps from one member of the profession to another? Or was this something else entirely, a final insult to a man who'd profited so handsomely from death?

When Jason was a boy, his father had liked to tell him stories about his native Britain, and Jason had lapped up tales of bravery and treason, asking to hear about rebels who'd had no fear of death, even though they knew what awaited them on the scaffold. William Wallace had been a favorite, possibly because Geoffrey Redmond had not described the Scotsman as a traitor but as a hero of his people, a man who deserved grudging respect.

Perhaps Geoffrey shouldn't have been as graphic in his descriptions of drawing and quartering, but rather than fearful, Jason had been fascinated by how much a human body could take before finally succumbing to death. To be hanged almost until death, emasculated, and then disemboweled was probably the worst possible way a person could die. It was the highest form of torture, reserved for those who were considered reprehensible and undeserving of mercy. After death, they were beheaded, their body divided into four parts to be displayed around the city as a deterrent to anyone who might be tempted to betray their sovereign and their country.

Was it possible that Philip Hobart had been drawn and quartered like some medieval renegade? Given the appearance of the neck and the eyes, Jason didn't think so, since there were no obvious signs of hanging, but until he could examine the rest of the body, he couldn't conclusively rule it out. Had Philip Hobart been a doctor or a solicitor or even a fisherman, Jason might not have considered the possibility, but given what the man had done for a living, Jason couldn't discount a killing that echoed executions of the past.

Pulling up Hobart's eyelids, Jason peered into his eyes but saw nothing that would give him a clue. Likewise, he didn't notice anything he hadn't previously spotted when he'd seen the head at Newgate. The edges of the neck were clean and smooth, the spinal cord most likely having been severed with one well-aimed blow. It must have been so swift, the stroke of the weapon had not even disheveled Philip Hobart's thick, well-oiled hair that remained neatly brushed back from the high forehead. Once Jason clocked that minor detail, he grinned and cursed himself for a fool before getting to work.

Chapter 14

Half an hour later, Jason thoroughly cleaned his hands, collected his things, and headed back to the ground floor to find Daniel. Daniel was in with Superintendent Ransome, so Jason knocked on the doorjamb and was invited to enter.

"Ah, Lord Redmond. Always a pleasure," Ransome said, although he didn't look pleased at all. "A corker of a case," he observed once Jason settled in the guest chair next to Daniel. "Death by beheading," he said, shaking his head in wonder. "What's next? Mounting the heads of our enemies on spikes and leaving them displayed atop the city's gates?"

Jason allowed himself a small smile. "Philip Hobart did not die by beheading," he said, taking both Ransome and Daniel by surprise.

"How do you know that?" Ransome asked.

"While examining the remains, I noticed that the victim's hair was still neatly brushed and oiled. His hair would have been in disarray and splattered with blood when he was beheaded, even if the deed was done with one quick stroke. I examined the skull more carefully and discovered a fracture in the parietal lobe. The blow was rendered with something heavy that might have had a sharp edge. I believe the cause of death was blunt force trauma to the head. That opinion can of course change once the rest of the body is found and I'm able to perform a complete autopsy."

"And this blow to the head did not cause any bleeding?" Ransome asked, looking highly dubious.

"Oh, it did," Jason replied, perhaps a little too smugly. "The blood was washed away and the hair dried, brushed, and oiled to conceal the wound."

"So the body was beheaded afterward?" Daniel asked, looking like a man who was in the process of re-evaluating all he knew.

"The body was beheaded after the blow to the head but before the coverup."

"Which brings me back to my original question," Ransome said. "Was this a revenge killing with ties to something that happened at Newgate? Haze here thinks it might have been carried out by the Fenians, but to date, we've had no reports of any attacks carried out by Irish nationalists against targeted individuals. The Fenians are known for attacking British forts and other military installations, so I think you're barking up the wrong tree there, Haze."

Normally, Superintendent Ransome would have delivered that last part with a lot more relish, enjoying the power to humiliate a subordinate who'd made a glaring error, but today, Ransome's observation was matter-of-fact, his demeanor that of a father educating a child rather than a headmaster taking a pupil to task.

"Yes, sir," Daniel muttered, obviously slighted.

"The case could be related to something that happened at Newgate, but now that we know the victim was actually killed by a blow to the head, this changes my perspective somewhat," Jason said.

"In what way?" Ransome asked.

"The killer would not be likely to transport a headless corpse across town, but if Hobart was already dead but still intact or simply unconscious, the killer might have moved him without attracting as much attention, especially if he had come prepared."

"Prepared with what? An axe?" Daniel asked.

"With a mode of transportation," Jason replied. "If the killer had his own carriage or wagon, he wouldn't have too much difficulty moving the corpse to wherever he needed it to be. Anyone who saw them would assume that Philip Hobart was either unwell or too drunk to move under his own steam. The killer could then take the body to a predetermined location, behead Hobart, clean the head, and deliver it to Newgate before the sun came up. This also rules out the possibility that this was some sort of ritualistic killing designed to resemble known modes of execution."

"That still leaves the question of the rest of the corpse," Ransome pointed out. "If that's how it happened, then the remains could be anywhere in this city."

"Unfortunately, that's true, Superintendent, but I still think it would be prudent to search the area between the Queen's Arms and the Hobarts' residence. Perhaps the killer had no intention of transporting the body and only had need of the head. He could have hit Hobart over the head, dragged him into an alley, beheaded him with whatever weapon he had brought, then left the body where it fell."

"Lord preserve us," Daniel said with feeling.

"Lord preserve us, indeed," Ransome echoed. "The killers in this city are becoming more imaginative by the day. A knife between the ribs or bullet to the head is not good enough for them anymore."

"Don't worry, sir. We still have plenty of those," Daniel reassured him sourly.

Ransome looked thoughtful. "Perhaps we should issue a public appeal. If anyone happens to trip over a headless corpse, they should immediately inform Scotland Yard." He looked at Daniel. "Haze, get on to the newspapers, then take Constables Putney and Collins and search the area as Lord Redmond has suggested. Well, off with you," he snapped when Daniel failed to move quickly enough.

Jason was about to follow Daniel, but Ransome forestalled him. "A word, your lordship." Jason sat back down. "Haze, shut the door on your way out," Ransome called after Daniel.

Ransome looked deeply uncomfortable, and for a moment, Jason thought he might change his mind about whatever it was he wished to talk about, but then Ransome drew in a sharp breath and faced Jason across the expanse of his neatly organized desk.

"I was wondering if I might beg a personal favor of you," Ransome began.

"If there's something I can do to help." Jason didn't want to commit himself until he heard the nature of this favor, but something in Ransome's panicked gaze told Jason that the superintendent wouldn't be asking unless he were truly desperate.

"It's my wife," Ransome said. "She's been unwell."

"Have you consulted a physician?"

Ransome averted his gaze and nodded, and Jason thought the man was fighting back tears. "Laura is with child," he said at last. "We were so happy," he rasped. "So excited. It's been six years since our son was born, and we very much wanted to expand our family."

Jason waited, giving the superintendent time to get to the crux of the matter.

Ransome sighed deeply. "Laura has been experiencing severe pains, and there's been some bleeding. Both are getting worse."

"And the physician?" Jason asked gently.

"Dr. Fleisher came highly recommended. He believes Laura might be suffering from something called toxemia and that the pregnancy can kill her. He wasn't able to offer any solutions that would save both Laura and the child." Ransome's pleading gaze found Jason's eyes. "Please, Jason," he whispered. It was the first time he'd ever called Jason by his Christian name, and it spoke to the depth of his despair. "You are the only one I trust with their lives."

"I would need to see Mrs. Ransome right away," Jason said.

A spark of hope lit Ransome's dark eyes. "Perhaps we can go right now."

"Of course."

"I'm very grateful," Ransome said as he sprang to his feet and reached for his coat and hat on the coatrack.

"Don't thank me yet, Superintendent," Jason said as he followed Ransome out into the corridor and then out of the building. "I have yet to determine what we're dealing with."

Chapter 15

They took Ransome's carriage to his residence in Brompton. The two-story house was modest but well kept, the front garden lovingly tended and dotted with early blooms. Ransome led Jason inside, where they were met by an anxious-looking maidservant.

"Superintendent," she muttered as she took their things and hurried away.

John Ransome's gaze went to the stairs, where a woman of middle years, dressed in a somber gown of plum wool trimmed with black velvet, had appeared. Her hair was gently silvered, and although her face was unlined, she appeared tired and very worried. She came down the stairs to meet them.

"How is Laura?" John Ransome asked.

"The same, I'm afraid," the woman said wearily.

"Lord Redmond, my mother-in-law, Mrs. Hawkins," Ransome said as the woman came closer.

"It's a pleasure to meet you, Mrs. Hawkins," Jason said.

If Mrs. Hawkins was surprised by his presence, she didn't show it. "My lord," she said deferentially and looked to her son-in-law for an explanation.

"Lord Redmond is a renowned surgeon, Mama," Ransome said. "He will help Laura."

Mrs. Hawkins' gaze sharpened, her brows knitting as she took him in. Jason thought he caught a glimmer of mistrust in her eyes. Perhaps it was his American accent that had put her off, or maybe her reaction had more to do with him being a surgeon. English surgeons did not receive the same level of training as medical doctors and were thought no better than butchers, the prejudice going so far as to deny them the title of doctor. The surgeons were referred to as mister, to denote their lowly status. Jason claimed the title of Dr. Redmond because he had attended university and had earned his degree, but Mrs. Hawkins was not aware of that and probably thought he wasn't knowledgeable enough to diagnose her daughter's condition.

"I do hope so," Mrs. Hawkins said stiffly, and headed toward what had to be the parlor.

Ransome led Jason up the stairs, and he caught a glimpse of a frightened-looking boy peering between the balusters from the floor above. Jason smiled up at the child, but the little boy watched him warily, refusing to smile back.

Ransome stopped at a door at the end of the corridor and knocked lightly. "My dear, are you decent? I've brought someone to see you," he called out.

"Come in, John."

The voice sounded weak, but when they entered the room, Laura Ransome managed a smile for her husband and the stranger who had entered her bedroom. She appeared to be in her late twenties, some years younger than her husband. Her chestnut hair was spread out on the lace-edged pillow and her blue eyes were pained, underlined by dark smudges that marred her milk-white skin. Laura's hand flew to her side, and she gasped with pain when she tried to raise herself to a sitting position. She leaned tiredly against the pillows, ready to receive her visitors.

"Laura, this is Lord Redmond. Remember, I told you about him? He's a doctor. From America," Ransome added, as if that would convince his wife of Jason's skill.

"Mrs. Ransome," Jason said, and inclined his head in greeting.

"My lord," Laura said. She sounded a bit breathless. "A pleasure. I've heard so much about you."

"Some good, I hope?" Jason teased.

He was surprised that John Ransome would discuss him with his wife, but then again, Katherine knew all about Ransome, so perhaps it wasn't so strange that his name had been mentioned.

"Oh, of course," Laura said. "John thinks you would make an excellent detective, and he's never wrong."

"Come now, my dear," John Ransome said, and Jason thought he detected a hint of a blush on his lean cheeks. "I'm not infallible."

Laura Ransome smiled at her husband, devotion shining from her eyes. John reached out, took her hand, and brought it to his lips, his gaze one of pure adoration. Jason was surprised to realize that this was a happy marriage, where both partners were equally devoted to each other, and felt ashamed of himself. He'd believed the gossip that had implied that John Ransome had only married the commissioner's daughter to further his own interests and hasten his advancement. That clearly wasn't the case.

"Laura, I asked Lord Redmond to examine you," John Ransome said. "I shared Dr. Fleisher's diagnosis with him."

"What exactly did Dr. Fleisher propose?" Jason asked.

"Nothing," John Ransome said angrily. "He said we should put our faith in God."

Laura's gaze grew anxious, and her slim fingers began to pleat the fabric of the coverlet. She was clearly frightened, and with good reason.

"Mrs. Ransome," Jason said gently, "if you will permit me to examine you, perhaps we can come up with a course of treatment."

Laura's gaze brightened. "Do you think there's something you can do to help us?"

"First, I need to make a diagnosis, and then we can discuss the options."

"What options are there?" John Ransome asked. He looked more hopeful as well, and that made Jason uneasy. He couldn't make any promises until he knew precisely what he was dealing with.

"Let us talk after the examination," he said. "Mrs. Ransome, may I?" Laura nodded. "Superintendent, if you wouldn't mind waiting outside," Jason said.

Ransome looked to his wife before replying. Laura gave him a small nod and a watery smile.

"It's all right, Johnny," she said softly. "Go on."

John Ransome gave a stiff bow and left the room, closing the door softly behind him.

Jason sat down on the side of the bed and gently touched Laura's forehead to check for a temperature, then reached for her wrist. Her pulse was elevated but not alarmingly so. He smiled at the frightened young woman.

"How far along are you, Mrs. Ransome?"

"About three months," Laura said. "I was so happy to learn I was with child. John and I have been longing for another child, but years went by before it finally happened." Laura's eyes filled with tears as she looked at Jason. "Dr. Fleisher says I have some horrid condition that might kill us both. John is terrified. He might seem resilient, but he's really very sensitive."

Jason never thought of John Ransome as emotionally fragile, but many a strong man had been undone by his love for a woman, and his children. And Jason's heart went out to Laura. She was so young and hopeful. She was looking to him to save her and to preserve her family, but there was only so much a physician could do. If Dr. Fleisher was correct, then the only alternative Jason could offer was to terminate the pregnancy in order to safeguard Laura's life. He wasn't at all sure that Laura would be receptive to the suggestion.

"Let's see if Dr. Fleisher is correct in his diagnosis," Jason said softly. "Tell me everything you've been experiencing."

"I've had some bleeding. And pain, right here," she said, and touched a spot just beneath her ribs on the right side. "Also here." Laura touched her lower abdomen, also on the right side. "And my shoulder hurts."

"And have you experienced headaches, nausea, dizziness, or periods of confusion?" Jason asked.

"I have felt nauseated and had rather a severe headache yesterday, but no dizziness or confusion."

"And did Dr. Fleisher take your blood pressure?"

Jason owned a portable Marey sphygmograph, but he didn't have his medical bag with him so wasn't able to measure Laura's blood pressure accurately. He saw no outward signs of elevated blood pressure but would have liked to check regardless, just to be sure.

Laura looked confused. "No. I don't believe he did," Laura said. "But I'm not certain. I've never had my blood pressure taken."

"Did Dr. Fleisher strap anything to your wrist?" Jason asked.

"No."

Jason decided not to focus on Dr. Fleisher's ineptitude and moved on. "Are you able to eat, Mrs. Ransome?"

Laura shook her head. "I was able to take some broth yesterday evening, but I don't have much of an appetite."

"Did Dr. Fleisher perform a physical examination?"

Laura shook her head. "He just asked questions."

"Do I have your permission to examine you?"

Laura looked mortified at the prospect but nodded, too desperate for Jason to help her to give in to embarrassment. Jason pulled away the coverlet to reveal Laura's abdomen. She wasn't showing yet, the white lawn of her nightdress clinging to a still-slim waist. Jason laid his hands on Laura's stomach and moved them slowly, inching from the pelvic area toward the diaphragm. So early in the pregnancy, it was difficult to detect significant changes, but what Laura was describing did not fit the symptoms of toxemia. Jason moved his hand to the spot that pained Laura and pressed carefully. Laura cried out, her eyes widening as he used his fingers to palpate the area.

"I'm sorry for that," Jason said. "I had to be certain."

"Was Dr. Fleisher correct?" Laura asked, naked fear in her eyes.

"I don't believe he was," Jason said. "Let's bring your husband back in, shall we?"

John Ransome looked nearly as terrified as his wife when he reentered the bedroom. "Well?" he asked gruffly.

"Based on Mrs. Ransome's symptoms, I don't believe she's suffering from toxemia. One of the tell-tale signs of that condition is dangerously elevated blood pressure that persists for the duration of the pregnancy. It's accompanied by headaches, dizziness, nausea, and confusion."

"So if it's not this toxemia, what's ailing my wife?"

Jason sighed. He hated to tell this hopeful couple that their baby couldn't be saved, but there was no help for it. "Based on my examination and the symptoms Mrs. Ransome has described, I believe what we're dealing with is an ectopic pregnancy."

"I beg your pardon?" Ransome said.

"It's very rare but highly dangerous. The developing embryo has attached itself to Mrs. Ransome's fallopian tube."

The Ransomes looked perplexed, probably never having heard the term, so Jason tried to explain the situation in terms they would understand. "What that means is that the baby is not growing in the womb but in a narrow tube that will eventually rupture. Such an outcome can lead to death."

"Oh, dear God," Laura exclaimed. She reached out a hand, and her husband clasped it tightly.

"What can be done?" Ransome asked.

"I will need to operate, and soon."

"And the baby?" Laura whispered.

"I'm sorry, Mrs. Ransome, but there's no saving the child. Right now our priority is your well-being."

Laura Ransome colored slightly but met Jason's gaze. "Will you surgically remove my womb?"

"I may have to," Jason replied. "That largely depends on the location of the implanted embryo."

Laura began to cry, but John Ransome faced Jason, his face set in lines of determination. "Please, save my wife."

"Superintendent, I would like you to bring Mrs. Ransome to St. George's Hospital this afternoon." Jason consulted his watch. "I will inform the matron to expect her by five o'clock. I will operate on her tomorrow morning."

"I will not have my wife ogled by medical students," Ransome barked, focusing on the one element he thought he could control.

"It will be a closed theater. Just myself and two surgical nurses."

"May I be present?"

"You may not," Jason replied. "But I will apprise you of your wife's condition as soon as I'm able."

Ransome nodded. "Thank you, Jason."

"I will see you both tomorrow," Jason said, and was about to take his leave when John Ransome caught up to him in the corridor.

"Please, accept the use of my carriage. I will remain here with Laura, so my coachman is entirely at your disposal. If you could just send him back by four, that will give me plenty of time to get Laura to the hospital."

Jason would have liked to refuse, but having ready transportation would save him a considerable amount of time since he now had to return to the hospital to make arrangements for tomorrow's surgery.

"Thank you, Superintendent. I will gladly take you up on your generous offer."

"Think nothing of it."

Jason could see the anxiety in the man's eyes and wished he could reassure him, but it was too soon to make promises. He wouldn't know for certain what he was dealing with until he opened Laura up tomorrow and saw for himself where the embryo was situated and how much of her anatomy would fall victim to his scalpel.

"I will take good care of her, John," Jason said.

"I know you will."

John Ransome clapped Jason on the arm and hurried outside to inform his coachman that he was to take Jason wherever he needed to go.

Chapter 16

After a stop at the hospital, Jason asked Ransome's coachman to take him to the Queen's Arms. Daniel and the two constables were sure to still be in the vicinity, engaged in the search for the headless corpse, and Jason wanted to offer his assistance. Jason asked the coachman to wait until he located Daniel. If Daniel had come and gone, then Jason would ask the man to drop him at home, since he saw no reason to return to Scotland Yard.

"What did Ransome want?" Daniel asked as soon as he caught sight of Jason striding toward him.

"He wished to consult me on a medical matter," Jason replied.

"Is this about his wife?" Daniel asked, lowering his voice. "He'd mentioned that she's been ill. Is it serious?"

"I'm sorry, Daniel, but I'm afraid I must keep the details confidential," Jason said with an apologetic smile.

"Of course. I understand," Daniel said, but he did look a bit put out, having likely expected Jason to tell him what was going on in confidence.

"Have you found anything?" Jason asked, eager to redirect the conversation toward the case.

"Not a thing. We've searched nearly every alley between here and the Hobarts' home, checked the cellar at the tavern in case Philip Hobart never left there alive, and questioned every crossing sweep and shopkeeper between the tavern and the Hobarts' home, but no one seems to have seen anything. Many of them knew Philip Hobart by sight, but they didn't see him on the night he was murdered since he would have passed by long after closing time. No one noticed anything strange the following morning or came across a headless corpse." Daniel's shoulders drooped with disappointment. "I don't think we're going to find anything of use here."

Jason stopped and looked around. "I agree. I don't believe Philip Hobart was beheaded here."

"Really? What changed your mind?"

"I think the killer waited for Hobart to leave the tavern, then hit him over the head once he deemed it safe to proceed. Once Hobart was unconscious, his assailant loaded him into a conveyance of some sort and drove away. If not dead already, Hobart would most likely have died on the way."

"Is it at all possible that he was still alive at the time of the beheading?" Daniel asked.

"It is possible, but given the severity of the skull fracture and the amount of intracranial hemorrhaging such blunt force trauma would cause, I can't imagine he would have survived long. And once the head was severed, the killer prepared the head and disposed of the body."

"But what did he do with it?" Daniel exclaimed.

"If it were me and I had a conveyance at my disposal, I'd throw it in the river," Jason said casually. "By the time the head was discovered in the morning, the body would have been carried away on the current."

"It might have washed up on the tide or been spotted and dragged ashore," Daniel pointed out.

"We'd have heard about it by now, wouldn't you say?"

Daniel nodded. "Well, either the body floated out to sea or was dumped somewhere. I've asked the editor at *The Daily Telegraph* to run an appeal for information. It should run in tomorrow's edition."

Jason shook his head. "That's a good idea, but I don't think we will learn anything. Whoever did this had thought it through and did not want us to find Hobart's remains."

Daniel nodded. "Given the number of dilapidated buildings and abandoned warehouses along the Thames, the body could be anywhere, feeding the rats and decomposing in peace. The killer might have even taken it across the river."

"Anything is possible," Jason agreed. "Once the killer had the head, the body was no longer of any use and could only serve to implicate him or her in the murder."

"Nothing about this case makes sense," Daniel grumbled. "And this," he pointed to Constable Putney, who was cautiously peering into a dank alley and poking a heap of refuse with a stick, "is a waste of time. I propose we start with Barnaby Stack, then question the other two families that were mentioned by name. If the interviews yield no information, we work our way down the list."

"Even if one of the individuals on your list had a hand in the murder, they're not likely to admit to it, are they? Not when there's nothing to connect them to the crime."

"No, but this," Daniel said, holding up the list of Hobart's executions, "is the only lead we have to go on. Until we know more, this is the only logical course of action."

"Where does Stack live?" Jason asked.

"Near Wapping."

"Then I will ask Ransome's coachman to take us there and then send him home. Ransome will need the carriage this afternoon."

Daniel looked intrigued but wisely didn't ask any questions. Instead, he informed the constables that he was leaving and instructed them to return to Scotland Yard under their own steam, a journey that would most likely commence only after a visit to the Queen's Arms for a well-deserved pint.

Chapter 17

Barnaby Stack lived in a ramshackle building that looked like it was one strong gust of wind away from collapsing into a heap of rubble. It was still light outside, but the room he invited them into was dim and smelled of boiled cabbage, cat piss, and damp. The furniture, what there was of it, was threadbare, and the floorboards were scuffed and uneven. The man himself looked much like his abode, old and decrepit. Lanky gray hair hung in curtains around a gaunt face, and the tatty clothes draped the man's skeletal frame as if he'd either availed himself of a larger man's castoffs or had lost a lot of weight. Barnaby Stack looked like a man who spent too much on strong drink and not nearly enough on food.

Invited to sit on a rickety settee, Jason and Daniel opted to stand, while Barnaby folded himself into a worn armchair, rested his bony elbows on filthy antimacassars, and leaned his head back. He looked exhausted.

"Mr. Stack, Philip Hobart was murdered two nights past."

Barnaby Stack stared at Daniel, his mouth opening in what could only be shock. "Was he, indeed?" he asked, clearly relishing the information.

"You were overheard threatening him at the Ferryman Inn," Daniel began.

Stack let out a phlegmy cough and shook his head. "That were years ago, Inspector. I don't have it in me to threaten anyone anymore."

"Nevertheless," Daniel continued. "Why did you threaten him?"

"Because he were a heartless swindler," Stack said. "He took pleasure in the suffering of others."

"You mean your brother?" Jason asked.

Stack nodded. "Rodney were only twenty-five when he were sent down. I didn't have the coin to pay for a quick death, so I had to watch my little brother dance at the end of that rope, his eyes bulging, his tongue hanging out, his trousers soaked with piss, and worse. Hobart did that on purpose, he did," Stack exclaimed, the outburst bringing on another fit of coughing. "People enjoy a spectacle. A prolonged, agonizing death."

"What was your brother's crime?"

"Murder," Stack said. "Killed a man who were harassing his sweetheart. It weren't on purpose, mind. Rodney punched the man, and he went down like a sack of turnips. Never got up. Rodney never meant to kill him. Only warn him off, like."

"I'm sorry," Jason said, ignoring the pointed look Daniel gave him. Murder was murder in his book, intentional or not.

"Rodney were me only family," Barnaby Stack said quietly. "He were the only person who cared if I live or die."

Now that Jason looked at the man more closely, he thought that Barnaby Stack wasn't as old as he'd first thought. Forty, maybe. But there was no light in his eyes, and no hope left in his heart. Even if Barnaby had something left to live for, Jason didn't think he'd last out the year.

"Mr. Stack, when was the last time you saw Philip Hobart?" Daniel asked.

Stack shrugged. "Not since that night at the Ferryman. I were in me cups," he said softly. "And I were missing Rodney something fierce."

"Do you often go to the Ferryman?" Daniel asked.

"Nah. Went there 'cause I heard Hobart went there, regular-like. I wanted to look the man who'd tortured and humiliated me brother in the face."

"What were you hoping to see?" Jason asked. "Remorse?"

Barnaby Stack shook his head. "Not remorse, but compassion maybe. A spark of humanity. Hobart laughed at me and told me to get lost. Said I were a pathetic wastrel and would end up like me brother if I weren't careful."

"And were you careful?" Daniel asked.

"You think I killed him?" Stack seemed amused by the possibility.

"You had a motive."

"So I did. And so did plenty of others. Philip Hobart was a cruel man who made a tidy profit from those as could afford to pay him off." Barnaby Stack smirked. "I wish I'd killed him, Inspector. I really do."

"Where were you on Monday night?" Daniel asked.

"Right here, Inspector. And no, I don't have anyone as can vouch for me. I were on me own, as I am every night. You want to arrest me, be me guest."

Barnaby Stack held out his scrawny wrists, but Daniel made no move to cuff him. Instead, he looked to Jason, who gave a small shake of his head.

"Thank you, Mr. Stack," Daniel said. "Don't leave town."

Stack hacked again, flecks of blood landing on his grubby sleeve. "And where would I go?"

Since the question did not require an answer, the two men headed for the door. They drew in long breaths of fresh air as soon as they were outside, glad to be out of that fetid room and away from Barnaby Stack's misery.

"He couldn't have done it," Jason said. "Not without an accomplice. He's too weak."

"What's wrong with him?"

"I think he's consumptive, but it could also be cancer. I can't be certain without examining him, but he doesn't have long. A few months at most."

"A dying man doesn't have anything left to lose," Daniel remarked.

"No, he doesn't, but I just don't see it, Daniel. If he wanted to murder Hobart, he could have followed him after he left the Queen's Arms and whacked him over the head. Why bother with the rest of it and risk getting caught?"

"For the pleasure of seeing Philip Hobart humiliated."

"Knowing Hobart is dead seemed enough to satisfy him. And even a dying man wants to retain some control over the manner of his death. I don't think Barnaby Stack would like to die at the end of a rope like his brother."

"He could have found someone willing to do the deed," Daniel mused.

"He could have, but he clearly doesn't have the funds to hire someone, and I doubt anyone would be foolish enough to risk their own neck to satisfy a dying man's need for retribution without a sizeable incentive."

Daniel nodded. "I agree with you there. And he did seem genuinely surprised by the news."

"Surprised and pleased. Philip Hobart's death must seem like an unexpected gift, one Barnaby Stack never imagined he'd receive. Perhaps in his mind, Hobart's death was a form of divine retribution."

"There was nothing divine in what happened to that man. Someone wanted revenge, and they took it."

"Well, whoever carried out this murder was a lot stronger and angrier than Barnaby Stack," Jason said. "I don't think this crime was prompted by something that happened years ago. This pain was fresh."

"You know what they say," Daniel remarked. "Revenge is a dish best served cold."

Jason shook his head, finding himself unable to agree. "This dish was still steaming, if the execution is anything to go by."

"Shall we call on the Cassells?"

"I'm afraid I won't be able to join you. I have early morning surgery tomorrow and I need time to prepare."

Daniel looked disappointed but nodded in acknowledgement. "I hope the public appeal throws something up, besides the usual riffraff trying to claim a reward with a pack of lies."

"I didn't realize a reward was offered," Jason replied.

"It wasn't, just for that reason."

"So you're relying entirely on someone's desire to assist the police?"

"I'm relying on the lack of reward to weed out dozens, if not hundreds, of false leads," Daniel replied irritably. "We don't have the manpower for all that rigamarole."

This statement didn't really call for a response, so Daniel smiled tiredly and said, "Have a good night, Jason."

Jason tipped his hat and walked away, his mind already on tomorrow's procedure.

Chapter 18

Daniel consulted the list, then hailed a hansom and made his way to Freida and Leonard Cassell's last known address in Clerkenwell. Their son, David, aged twenty-two, had been executed four years ago. The charge: murder. David Cassell had shot his business partner in the head in a dispute over profits. The list didn't specify what sort of business David Cassell had been engaged in, but Daniel highly doubted it was anything the authorities would consider legitimate.

A young, heavily pregnant woman opened the door and looked at Daniel warily, as if she expected him to try to sell her something or ask for a donation to some charitable society.

"Good afternoon, madam." Daniel held up his warrant card. "Is this the home of Mr. and Mrs. Cassell?"

The woman shook her head. "They've gone."

"Would you happen to know where they went?" Daniel tried again.

"Canada," the woman said. "I reckon they wanted a fresh start after their son was hanged for murder. Mr. Cassell had kin in Quebec. He was a Frenchie," she added confidentially.

"How long ago was that?"

"It'll be three years this July."

"That's very precise," Daniel said.

"That's when Will and I married," the woman said, her face finally relaxing into a small smile. "We moved right in. The Cassells sold us all their furniture and household goods, and a very reasonable price we got too. We couldn't believe our good fortune."

"I daresay it would be too expensive to ship their possessions to Canada."

"You're probably right there, Inspector. Not worth the trouble or the expense. But they did leave some nice pieces, and books. Will likes to read. Says a man should do everything in his power to better himself."

"Did the Cassells have any other children?" Daniel asked, wondering if someone might have remained behind.

"A daughter. Imogen. She was twelve or thirteen at the time. A strange little thing. Fretted something awful about the sea voyage. She was convinced they'd all drown."

"And she definitely went to Canada with her parents?" Daniel asked.

The woman nodded. "My Will saw them off at the railway station. They needed a hand with the luggage, and he offered. He's kind, my Will," she added, and her smile grew wider. "Helpful."

"Thank you," Daniel said.

"Good day to you, Inspector."

Daniel walked away, his thoughts on the Cassells. He could certainly understand the need for a fresh start, and there was nothing unusual in selling their possessions. They might have needed money to pay for the voyage, or maybe they had planned to purchase new things once they reached their destination. Had they intended to use the money to pay someone to kill the man who'd taken their son's life, it would stand to reason that they would have done so before they left, not nearly three years after their departure and four years after David's death.

He supposed it was possible that one or all the Cassells had returned to England with the intention of avenging David's death, but unless Daniel checked passenger manifests for every ship that had come into every port in England for the past year at the very least, he'd have no way to either prove or disprove this theory, and in truth, he didn't think it likely.

Daniel didn't cross the Cassells off his list just yet, but for the time being, he thought it prudent to limit his investigation to the people who were still in London. And that meant the Newberrys.

Chapter 19

Albert and Hester Newberry lived in Kentish Town, their lodgings above a haberdashery shop on Fortress Road. Daniel couldn't help noticing that the sign above the shop looked new, gold lettering against a dark green background surrounded by a whimsical border. The sign pronounced the shop to be called Nestor's Notions. The bow window gleamed, and the display within featured everything from shiny buttons to colorful ribbons and an array of thread in every color of the rainbow. Daniel decided that he would stop in after speaking to the Newberrys and purchase a pretty new ribbon for Charlotte and some black lace for his mother-in-law, to thank her for looking after Charlotte these past few weeks. Harriet had always been partial to lace collars and caps but had been wearing only black lace since Sarah's passing. He'd deliver the gifts when he went to Birch Hill to join Harriet and Charlotte for Easter, assuming this case was closed by then and he could afford to take a few days off.

The woman who opened the door to his knock had to be in her fifties, a stooped, graying wraith who looked at Daniel with incomprehension when he presented his warrant card. She wore a gown of black bombazine, and a black cap covered her thinning fair hair. Her eyelashes and brows had all but faded, leaving her dark eyes to stare at him from a pale, gaunt face.

"Mrs. Newberry?" Daniel asked when the woman failed to say anything or invite him inside.

"Yes," she answered softly.

"I'm Inspector Haze of Scotland Yard. I would like to ask you a few questions, if I may."

"What about?" Mrs. Newberry asked. Her expression had grown anxious, and she peered behind Daniel, as if she thought he might have brought reinforcements.

"May I come in?" Daniel asked. "I assure you, this will only take a few minutes. There's no need to be frightened," he added, seeing the panic so clearly written on her face.

It was clear that Mrs. Newberry did not want him to come in, but good manners prevailed, and she led him into a small parlor that faced the street. It was a serviceable room with comfortable, if well-worn, furniture and faded velvet curtains that blocked out most of the light since they were only partially open. Only one ornament graced the room, a photograph of a young woman prominently displayed on the mantel, the pewter frame gleaming dully against the dark green and silver pattern of the faded wallpaper. The young woman bore a striking resemblance to Mrs. Newberry and had to be Margaret Newberry, the young woman who had been hanged by Philip Hobart not two years ago.

"Do sit down, Inspector," Mrs. Newberry said.

Daniel chose the armchair, while Mrs. Newberry perched on a matching settee. She clasped her trembling hands in her lap, gripping her fingers so tightly that the knuckles turned white. Daniel wondered if she was that nervous or if perhaps she was afflicted with shaking palsy and the trembling had nothing to do with his presence. Mrs. Newberry fixed her gaze on him, silently inviting him to explain his presence.

"Mrs. Newberry, Philip Hobart was murdered on Monday night."

Mrs. Newberry's expression did not change, and Daniel wondered if she even knew who he was referring to, but then her mouth quirked at the corners and she grinned joyously, the smile lighting up her eyes and giving Daniel a glimpse of the beautiful young woman she must have been in her youth.

"Thank you, Inspector. I'm very pleased to hear it," Mrs. Newberry said. "I do hope he suffered."

"I think he probably did," Daniel replied, although he really wasn't sure if Hobart had been awake or even alive for the final act.

Mrs. Newberry seemed to relax. "Would you like some tea, Inspector?" she asked, her eyes still glowing triumphantly. "The kettle's just boiled."

"Thank you. That's very kind."

His hostess left him to his own devices and returned a few minutes later with a laden tray. She poured him a cup of weak tea, added a splash of milk and two cubes of sugar per his request, and handed him the cup before serving him a miserly slice of raisin cake. The cake was stale and didn't have enough sugar or raisins, but Daniel was starving and would have wolfed it down had Mrs. Newberry not been watching him so intently.

He suspected that the cake was meant to last for a week at the very least, and the sugar cubes he'd taken would not be easily replaced. The room was clean and tidy, but Mrs. Newberry's gown was frayed at the cuffs and hem, and the lace trim on her collar had been carefully mended. If she had ever owned anything of value, she'd long since sold it. Mrs. Newberry lived in genteel poverty and probably watched every farthing for fear of ending her days in a workhouse, alone and with nothing to look forward to but a pauper's grave.

Mrs. Newberry broke off a dainty piece of cake and popped it into her mouth. The shaking in her hands seemed to have subsided. "Tell me how he died, Inspector," she said, her gaze bright and interested. "In detail."

"Mr. Hobart was hit over the head and then beheaded," Daniel said.

He was somewhat unnerved by the woman's obvious delight, but then again, if she had blamed Philip Hobart for her daughter's death, then her reaction made perfect sense, even if her pleasure in a man's death was wholly unchristian.

Mrs. Newberry only served to underline Daniel's observation when she nodded and exclaimed, "May he roast in the fires of hell for eternity."

Trying to hide his shock, Daniel schooled his features into an expression of bland neutrality and said, “Mrs. Newberry, tell me about Philip Hobart.”

Mrs. Newberry shook her head. “I won’t speak of that man. But I will tell you about my daughter.” Her gaze went to the photo on the mantelpiece, and she sighed, the joy of only a few moments ago no longer in evidence. “My Margaret was a good girl. A kind and loving young woman who’d never hurt a fly.”

Mrs. Newberry looked at Daniel, probably thinking that he was going to point out that Margaret Newberry had been hanged for murder, but Daniel remained silent, hoping Mrs. Newberry would continue to talk.

“Margaret had big dreams. She wanted to run our shop one day. Be her own mistress.” Mrs. Newberry smiled wistfully. “She was clever too, and good with figures. Albert always said she had the business sense of a man. Margaret used to laugh and tell him that women were just as clever as men, but they had to downplay their intelligence in order not to damage the fragile male pride. That was why she never wanted to marry. She said she’d live her life doing as she pleased. I used to chide her and tell her that a woman was happiest as a wife and a mother, but Margaret scoffed at that.”

“What happened, Mrs. Newberry?” Daniel asked gently. He could see the pain in the older woman’s eyes and knew the idyll she recalled hadn’t lasted long.

“My husband died. Albert climbed the ladder to fetch a box of embossed buttons for a customer, reached out to pull the box off the shelf, like he had so many times in the past, and his heart gave out. He cried out and clutched at his chest, and by the time he fell to the floor, he was gone. Margaret was there. She saw it happen. She was heartbroken to lose her father, but that wasn’t the end of our trouble.”

Mrs. Newberry pulled a handkerchief from her sleeve and dabbed at her eyes. “It turned out that Albert had borrowed money from the bank some years before. He never said. Didn't want to worry us, I expect. He was paying off the debt monthly, but when his creditors heard that he'd died, they called in the loan. They wouldn't extend a line of credit to a woman, not when she didn't have a man willing to guarantee the loan. Margaret and I were forced to sell the shop to Mr. Nestor. He offered us a fair price and permitted us to keep these rooms, but after we paid off the principal sum and the interest, there wasn't much left."

Mrs. Newberry sighed. "Margaret had to find employment, and although she'd helped Albert in the shop for years, no one around here would give her a job. After a time, she had no choice but to look further afield. She eventually found a position with Harding, Howell, and Co., in Pall Mall. At the haberdashery counter." Mrs. Newberry smiled sadly. "Margaret was so excited to work in such a prestigious establishment. London's first department store, she had called it. For the first time in months, Margaret was happy, and excited. She thought that maybe she could work her way up to a higher and better paying position. She would have too. I'm certain of it."

"What went wrong?" Daniel asked.

"The floor supervisor, Mr. Whitley, had something of a reputation among the girls, but of course, Margaret wasn't aware of that when she accepted the position. He left her alone for the first few weeks, allowed her to settle in, and then the harassment began. He'd call her into his office under some trumped-up excuse and try to make free with her. Margaret said that some of the girls simply went along with it because they couldn't afford to lose their positions, but my Margaret wasn't that sort of girl. She resisted."

"How did Mr. Whitley take that?"

"He redoubled his efforts, and when Margaret continued to refuse, he became more aggressive. He threatened her," Mrs. Newberry said, her voice shaking with anger. "Said that if she didn't do as he asked, he'd accuse her of theft, and she'd spend years in prison. After that, Margaret handed in her notice. On her last day, Mr. Whitley called her into his office to collect her wages. When Margaret went in, he locked the door and assaulted her."

Mrs. Newberry was crying softly now, and Daniel could only imagine how painful it had to be for her to recount the details of her daughter's downfall.

"He pushed her up against the desk and tried to…" Mrs. Newberry's voice trailed off. "Well, you know," she said at last. "In her desperation, Margaret grabbed a marble ashtray and hit him over the head. She only wanted to stun him so that she could get away, but the man died of a brain bleed two days later. Margaret was charged with murder."

"I'm sorry," Daniel said, and meant it. The circumstances of the assault should have been taken into account, but the judge who had presided over the case had clearly only focused on the outcome and not the events that had led up to the murder.

"Mrs. Newberry, it is my understanding that you made threats against Philip Hobart," Daniel said.

Mrs. Newberry shook her head. "I did not make threats, Inspector. After Margaret was arrested and sent to Newgate to await trial, I began a letter-writing campaign in the hope of getting Margaret a fair trial. I also wrote a letter to the newspapers, but it was never published. And I wrote to all the young ladies that had worked under Mr. Whitley. Three of them came forward and testified on Margaret's behalf. They had been accosted and threatened by Mr. Whitley as well."

But they weren't the ones to crack his skull, Daniel thought. *And lucky for them too.*

"Who was the judge that sentenced Margaret to death?" Daniel asked.

"Judge Grant. I knew it was all over as soon as I heard he'd be presiding. Everyone referred to him as Hanging Grant, and with good reason. His judgments were always harsh, and more often than not unfair, more so to women. He wasn't interested in justice. That man was drunk on his own power."

Daniel nodded in agreement. He'd met Oliver Grant quite recently and had been the one to collar him for the murder of his sister. It was only now that Daniel recalled that it had been Philip Hobart who'd hanged Hanging Grant.

"The three men responsible for what happened to Margaret are all dead," Daniel observed.

"Yes, they are, and although it's cold comfort, Inspector Haze, since their deaths will not bring my Margaret back, it helps me to sleep at night knowing that perhaps there is some divine justice after all."

"Did you harbor resentment toward Philip Hobart?"

"He hanged my only child. And she didn't die easily, Inspector. The drop did not break her neck, so it took her some time to die. I know a few minutes is nothing to most people, but when you're suffocating, every second is an eternity. Margaret died in the sort of agony no human being should ever have to endure."

"And do you believe Philip Hobart intentionally prolonged her death?" Daniel asked.

"I don't know if it was intentional, but I know it was awful. I stood right there, at the front, where Margaret could see me, but after a time, she couldn't see anything. The blood vessels in her eyes burst from the pressure, and the crowd cheered. They said she looked like a demon."

"How did you ever survive that?" Daniel asked gently, feeling sorry for this heartbroken woman despite his vow to remain dispassionate and objective.

"I wish I hadn't. I prayed to the good Lord to take me," Mrs. Newberry said. "What did I have to live for? My husband was gone. My daughter had been disgraced and tortured until she was mercifully dead. All I wanted was to lie in the cool earth next to the two people I loved most in the world, but it seems the world is not done with me just yet. My child has been dead for two years, but I continue to live on. Bereft. Alone. Useless. And destitute."

"I'm sorry, Mrs. Newberry," Daniel said again.

"What are you sorry for, Inspector?" Mrs. Newberry asked warily. "Sorry that Margaret was accosted by a man who took advantage of his position? Sorry that her life was cut short when all she'd tried to do was defend herself? Or sorry that a well-respected judge cared nothing for fairness and sentenced her to death?"

Daniel nodded. He wasn't about to defend the system that so frequently meted out harsh punishment in cases where a lesser penalty would do. Margaret Newberry had killed a man, but she had acted in self-defense, and Mr. Whitley would still be alive and well if he had not abused his power over a defenseless young woman. A prison sentence would have served just as well, but Margaret had stood no chance once she came before Oliver Grant.

Daniel set down his teacup and stood. "Thank you for speaking to me, Mrs. Newberry. I really am sorry to have caused you further pain."

"You didn't, Inspector. Knowing Philip Hobart died violently doesn't diminish my grief, but it does restore my faith in the Almighty."

Daniel didn't think the Almighty had anything to do with Philip Hobart's gruesome fate but decided to keep that opinion to himself. He thanked Mrs. Newberry for the tea and cake and took his leave. The weather had turned while he was inside, and fat drops of rain landed on the brim of his bowler and slid beneath the stiff collar of his shirt and down his neck, making him shiver. Rivulets of rainwater ran down the striped awning of Nestor's Notions, and puddles quickly formed to reflect a leaden sky and the hulking redbrick buildings that lined the street. An old nag pulling a delivery wagon loaded with casks plodded past him, the driver and the horse staring fixedly ahead and looking as wretched as Daniel felt.

Never before had he questioned the British legal system, believing it to be a shining example of all that was impartial and just, a beacon of fair-mindedness that should be a lesson to the rest of the world, but seeing the husks left behind by that very system made Daniel feel hollow inside, the chasm that had opened in his chest filling with doubt and pity. Guilty or not, did anyone really deserve such an agonizing, dehumanizing end? And was every murder equal in its intent? Surely there were degrees, as in the case of Margaret Newberry. Had a young woman who had simply been defending herself from the unwanted advances of a lascivious man deserved the same fate as a thug who'd knifed someone in a dark alley, his only intention to help himself to his victim's purse?

Daniel shook his head as if that simple action might dispel his troubled thoughts. Jason, with his unshakable sense of fair play and liberal views, was rubbing off on him and forcing him to question everything he had believed his whole life. Perhaps it wasn't a detrimental thing to examine one's beliefs from time to time, but it did make for uncomfortable introspection that often resulted in personal growth one had never sought in the first place.

No longer in the mood to shop for gifts, Daniel pulled down his hat, raised his collar, hunched his shoulders against the lashing rain, and hurried toward the corner, hoping he'd find a passing hansom before he was soaked through.

Chapter 20

After dinner, Jason excused himself and headed to his study. He shut the door, lit the lamps, and opened the window, enjoying the sound of the driving rain. It washed the air clean of coal smoke and reminded him of spring nights in New York, when he had been a medical student and often stayed out late into the night with his friends instead of studying for exams. Spring rain also brought other, less pleasant reminders of sleeping out in the open at Andersonville Prison and shivering all night in what was left of his tattered uniform until the hot Georgia sun made the wool steam and burned his exposed skin, but Jason chose not to dwell on those.

Jason pulled out the anatomy manual he'd recently ordered from Edinburgh. The publication had the most up-to-date representations of the female reproductive system, and he pored over the images, his finger tracing the delicate outlines of the diagram as he visualized every step of the operation and the time it might take to complete it. Not for the first time, he wished he had a reliable partner, someone he could ask to take the surgery tomorrow. It wasn't that he doubted his skill, but it was never good practice to mix the personal and the professional, and although Jason wouldn't call John Ransome a friend, he did hold the man in high regard and worked with him often enough to worry about fracturing the relationship.

Which was also precisely why he couldn't turn the case over to another surgeon, not when he understood what was at stake. Jason treated his fellow surgeons with respect and deferred to their opinions when the situation called for it, but he also knew that with the exception of a few sympathetic souls, they treated their patients like slabs of meat and didn't much care what became of them once they were wheeled away from the operating theater. If Laura Ransome died or spent the rest of her days mourning the children she never had, whoever had operated on her wouldn't give her a passing thought. Jason wouldn't entrust her to another surgeon any more than he would allow some hack to operate on Katherine, or any other woman he cared for.

What happened tomorrow could alter Jason's relationship with John Ransome forever and have an impact on Daniel's prospects at Scotland Yard. John Ransome was a fair man at his core, but he was also someone who didn't forgive or forget, and a favorable outcome was never guaranteed. At times, the patients deemed hopeless managed to survive, while those whose chances were excellent never rallied. In Jason's experience, recovery had much to do with the individual's desire to get better, and if Laura Ransome had lost all hope of ever bearing another child, she just might give in to melancholy and undermine her own chances.

Jason could only imagine the turmoil John Ransome must be in tonight, awaiting the outcome of the procedure and knowing that the course of his family's life would change irrevocably come tomorrow. Jason held the future of the Ransomes in his hands, and he found the responsibility unbearably heavy. He smiled absentmindedly when Katherine knocked and entered the room.

"Can I get you anything before I retire?" she asked.

"Thank you, my dear, but I'm nearly done in here."

Katherine walked over to the table and glanced at the open volume. "You are worried," she said.

"I am. Perhaps it would have been prudent to ask another surgeon to step in."

"Jason, you take too much upon yourself," Katherine rebuked him gently.

"How do you mean?"

Katherine looked away, and Jason knew that she didn't want to say anything that might sound like outright criticism, especially the night before a surgery, when he couldn't afford to dwell on pointless distractions.

He laid his hand over hers. "Tell me, Katie."

"Jason, I know that the things you've seen and done have robbed you of your faith in God," Katherine began softly. "And I can hardly fault you for your anger and disillusionment, but skilled as you are and determined as you feel to help others, ultimately, their fate is not up to you."

"Are we still speaking about Laura Ransome?" Jason asked.

"Laura, and Mary," Katherine replied.

"You mean Mary is not mine to worry about."

"Of course you can worry, and it does you credit that you care so deeply, but Mary is a grown woman, Jason. A wife and a mother. You must allow her to make her own mistakes without forever urging her to accept your help. If she wants it, she'll let you know."

If she's even still alive, Jason thought morbidly. "Thank you, Katie. I know you're right." He smiled at his wife. "And I will stop playing God now, both personally and professionally."

"I didn't mean—" Katherine began, but Jason shook his head.

"I know what you meant, and I value your honesty. Sometimes a man needs the wisdom of a woman to help him see more clearly." He lifted Katherine's hand to his lips and planted a gentle kiss on her cool fingers.

"Let's go to bed," Katherine said.

She went to shut the window, while Jason closed the manual, set it back on the shelf, and turned off the lamp. Katherine silently slid her hand into his as they walked up the steps toward their bedroom, and although Jason was still apprehensive about the surgery tomorrow, he felt marginally lighter for having been relieved of the responsibility for life and death. Whether it was

God, fate, or simply a person’s own resolve to forge their own destiny, the outcome didn’t lie solely in his hands, and for that he was grateful.

Chapter 21

Thursday, March 25

Jason arrived at the hospital before the morning editions of *The London Illustrated News* and *The Daily Telegraph* hit the still-dark streets. He was relieved not to have to hear the newsboys yelling themselves hoarse as they hawked the day's leading story in an effort to appeal to those who relished tales of violence. The morning was foggy and wet, a gusty chill wind whipping at Jason's coat and hat. He stopped by the doctors' lounge, hung up his damp things, and pulled on a clean smock over his shirt and waistcoat. Many surgeons sauntered into the operating theater covered in the blood of the patients who'd come before, but Jason always took his soiled smocks home and had Fanny soak and wash them until the linen was once again pristine. The surgical patients were frightened enough without having to stare at reminders of someone else's suffering as they breathed in the ether that would offer them a respite from pain.

Jason found Laura Ransome awake, her face a pale oval in the dim corner where her bed was situated. Most patients on the ward were still asleep, but the nurses were already gliding between the rows of beds, taking out bedpans, checking vital signs, and issuing stern reprimands. Laura looked terrified, her eyes huge as she searched Jason's expression for any hint of the surgery's possible outcome.

"The theater is ready for you, Dr. Redmond," Nurse Lowe said as she approached the bed. "Shall I prepare the patient for surgery?"

"Please, give us a moment, Nurse," Jason said. He turned back to Laura. "How are you feeling this morning?"

"I'm frightened," she answered.

"It's only natural that you should feel uneasy," Jason replied in an effort to soothe her.

"It's not the surgery I'm afraid of," Laura said. "I'm terrified of disappointing my husband." Her eyes filled with tears. "John longs for another child."

"No child could ever make up for the loss of a beloved wife," Jason said.

"Did John tell you that?"

"He didn't need to. It was all there in his eyes. Now, let's get you ready, and I will see you in the operating theater."

"Is there a chance I might die?" Laura asked, her voice catching on the last word.

"Absolutely not," Jason lied with a confidence born of years of reassuring frightened patients.

Laura seemed to relax and offered him a watery smile. "See you on the other side, Dr. Redmond."

"You can count on it." Jason laid a hand over Laura's and squeezed gently, then turned on his heel and walked away.

For the next hour, Jason's entire focus was on Laura Ransome. The box of sawdust beneath the operating table was crimson with congealed blood, and the woman on the table before him was whiter than the sheet that covered her from pelvis to toes. An ether mask covered a good portion of her face, and her abdomen lay splayed before Jason, the organs glistening in the light of the lamps. Nurse Lowe suctioned the blood as Jason bent over Laura's body, wielding his scalpel with the precision of an artist applying the final strokes to the masterpiece of his heart.

"Let's close her up," Jason said once he straightened and set the bloodied scalpel aside.

Nurse Bramson, a recent hire who had steady hands and nerves of steel, handed him a threaded needle, and Jason sutured the incision, using small, even stitches to avoid leaving a thick, ropy scar. Laura was a young woman and would feel self-conscious if left with such a souvenir. As soon as he finished and the wound was neatly bandaged, Nurse Bramson removed the ether mask, and a porter was summoned to take Laura to a private room Jason had reserved for her immediate recovery.

The two nurses remained to tidy the theater, while Jason thoroughly washed his hands with carbolic and cleaned his instruments before returning to the doctors' lounge. He removed his smock and cap and stowed them in a cotton sack Fanny had provided for that purpose, returned the instruments to his medical bag, ran a hand through his disheveled hair, and headed down the corridor to check on Laura. She would be coming around and beginning to feel pain from the procedure.

Laura was tucked up in the narrow cot, Nurse Lowe stationed by her side. Jason and the nurse engaged in a wordless exchange in which Nurse Lowe assured him that all seemed well, and the patient was comfortable and her vital signs steady. Laura's eyelids fluttered as she regained consciousness, and her hand immediately went to her stomach, then fell away when she felt the thick gauze bandage.

"Laura, how do you feel?" Jason asked as he bent over her. She was still deathly pale, but her breathing was even, and her gaze was becoming less cloudy as she tried to focus on him. "Are you in pain?"

Jason would prefer to hold off on the morphine, but if Laura was suffering, then he'd give her a small dose to take the edge off the pain.

"I feel tired," Laura muttered.

"Then try to sleep. I will tell your husband you're out of surgery."

"Johnny." The name was a barely audible exhalation, but Jason heard the longing and wished he could allow John Ransome to come and sit by his wife's side, but that would be a violation of the hospital's policy. No visitors were allowed in the recovery room.

"John will be able to visit you tomorrow," Jason promised. "I'll be back shortly," he said to Nurse Lowe. "Come get me if Mrs. Ransome develops a fever."

Nurse Lowe nodded in understanding and returned her attention to the patient.

Leaving the ward, Jason retrieved his coat and hat and went in search of Superintendent Ransome. He found him outside, pacing nervously, his head bowed, and his hands clasped behind his back as he walked past the benches reserved for convalescing patients. Ransome came to an abrupt stop and faced Jason, his expression so tortured, Jason's heart went out to the man.

"The surgery went well, and Laura is resting comfortably," Jason said, and watched John Ransome's tension give way to relief.

Jason didn't bother to explain that he'd removed the embryo but hadn't been able to save the fallopian tube that had already begun to rupture. Another few days and the situation would have turned dire, possibly fatal. He saw the question in the other man's eyes and smiled encouragingly.

"Barring any unforeseen complications, Laura should recover fully after a few weeks on bed rest. Although I would strongly recommend a period of marital abstinence for at least a month, she should be able to conceive again and carry to term in the future."

"And this ectopic…" Ransome's voice trailed off since it was clear he wasn't quite certain how to phrase the question.

"Happens very rarely and is not likely to occur again. Lightning doesn't strike twice in one place," Jason said, and hoped that was true.

Ransome's face broke into a smile of gratitude. "I don't know how to thank you, Jason. I was terrified of losing Laura. I would have been content as long as I knew she was safe, but Laura—" He made a gesture meant to imply that all women were a bit irrational, and Laura would probably never forgive herself for what she had perceived to be her failure as a wife.

"I understand," Jason said. "And I will personally oversee Laura's recovery."

"Thank you," John Ransome said with feeling.

He looked uncertain, so Jason clapped him on the arm. "Go home, John. There's nothing you can do at present, and I will send for you should there be any unforeseen change. I will inform the front desk that you may visit with Laura tomorrow, so they will let you upstairs."

"How long will Laura remain in hospital?" Ransome asked, jutting his chin toward the building.

"A week at the very least," Jason said. "I will not discharge her until I'm confident she's no longer in danger of infection."

Ransome nodded again. "May as well go to work."

Jason watched Ransome leave, then returned to the hospital. He would remain on hand for a few hours to make sure Laura Ransome did not develop a fever. He returned to the doctors' lounge, poured himself a cup of tea from a freshly made pot and sweetened it liberally to keep a bout of hypoglycemia at bay, then settled into one of the comfortable club chairs before unfolding the newspaper someone had left behind. The headline in *The Daily Telegraph* screamed:

SCOTLAND YARD STUMPED

SUPERINTENDENT RANSOME CALLS ON PUBLIC

TO LOCATE HEADLESS CORPSE

The article went on to give the particulars of the murder, playing up the gruesome details for the benefit of their horror-craving readers. Jason folded the paper and tossed it aside, disgusted with the public's appetite for murder. He didn't bother to look at *The Illustrated London News*, knowing there would be a crudely executed sketch of the severed head on the front page, the victim glaring from the basket in a way that not only accused the killer but the police. The editors seemed to expect Scotland Yard to apprehend the culprit without delay in what could only be described as a feat of hitherto unheard-of deductive prowess. These sorts of editorials made Jason angry since they whipped up public discontent and called for results that bordered on the miraculous.

Jason hoped that Laura Ransome's condition would give Daniel a few days' reprieve from Ransome's ire, since it seemed the investigation had ground to a halt. As far as he knew, Daniel didn't have any new leads and they had yet to understand the motive for the murder. There was a knock on the door, and then one of the porters poked his head in.

"Dr. Redmond, Detective Haze to see you. He's downstairs."

"Thank you, Mr. Grimes." Jason pushed to his feet, already hurrying toward the door.

Daniel was aware that Jason was in surgery this morning, so if he had seen fit to come to the hospital, there must have been an important development in the case. Jason hoped for Daniel's sake it was a breakthrough.

Chapter 22

Daniel was in the vestibule, standing with his back to the staircase, his gaze fixed on the still-bare trees just beyond the window. There was no mistaking the tension in his neck and shoulders or the hard set of his jaw when he turned around, as if sensing Jason's imminent approach. Jason nodded to a former patient who'd come in to have his bandages changed, skirted a couple of laborers who'd brought in a friend who was bleeding profusely from a tear in his leg, and approached Daniel from the side once he finally managed to cross the unexpectedly crowded foyer.

"Daniel, what happened?" Jason asked, not bothering with the social niceties.

"The body has been found."

"Already?" Jason exclaimed, amazed that the appeal to the public had yielded results so quickly.

Daniel shook his head. "The body was discovered before the first copies hit the pavement this morning."

"Really? Where?"

"In the cellar of the Ferryman," Daniel said. "It was stuffed into a barrel. I would very much like your help in assessing the remains before we move them. I have a hansom waiting outside."

Jason inhaled deeply. He hated to leave Laura Ransome unattended, but unless she suffered an unexpected hemorrhage, she'd be safe under the watchful eye of Nurse Lowe for a short while.

"I'm afraid I can only spare you an hour," Jason replied.

Daniel nodded curtly. "That should suffice."

"Give me a moment."

Jason returned upstairs, issued detailed instructions pertaining to Laura's care, and informed Nurse Lowe where he'd be in case of an emergency. Then Jason grabbed his things and hurried back to the foyer, where Daniel was pacing impatiently.

"Were you able to learn anything of interest yesterday?" Jason asked once they were settled in the hansom and on their way to the Ferryman.

Daniel filled him in on his interview with Mrs. Newberry. "Margaret Newberry was hanged several years ago, and her mother is barely scraping by, from what I could see. Perhaps she has been scrimping all this time, her need for justice the only thing keeping her from succumbing to her grief," Daniel mused. "She most definitely could not have done it herself. She's not tall enough to have hit Philip Hobart on the head, and she's certainly not strong enough to have loaded his body onto a conveyance without help."

"She could have had an accomplice," Jason speculated, "but I really don't see the point of beheading the man and delivering his head to Newgate. If the bereaved wished to make Philip Hobart suffer in the way their loved one had, then it would make more sense to hang him."

"And they could have strung him up from any tree or lamppost in London and watched him die," Daniel replied.

"Precisely. I really think that the beheading was the whole point, and we have yet to understand the connection between the method of murder and the motive."

"What if there is no connection and whoever did this simply has a twisted sense of humor and a very sharp axe?"

"In my experience, there's always a reason, even if it's one most rational people can't possibly understand. Let's take a look at the body and see what it tells us about how Philip Hobart died," Jason suggested. "Perhaps we'll be able to fit in some of the missing pieces."

“Well, I think we’ve just been handed a Charles Dafoe-sized piece of the puzzle,” Daniel said, smiling for the first time that morning.

“Was he the one who found the body?”

“He was, but that doesn’t mean he didn’t already know it was there. Reporting it to Scotland Yard might be a clever ruse to throw us off the scent.”

Jason nodded. “Possibly. Or perhaps he was genuinely shocked to find his friend’s remains and wants to see justice done.”

“Let’s see what the scene tells us,” Daniel replied.

The traffic was surprisingly light, and they arrived at the inn in good time. The Ferryman was closed to customers, but Jason and Daniel were admitted by the publican’s wife. Mrs. Dafoe was a woman of middle years, whose mourning attire was relieved only by the soiled white apron tied around her waist and the unnatural pallor of her skin. She had the look of someone who rarely went outdoors and spent most of her time in the dim confines of the tavern.

Mrs. Dafoe didn’t bother to hide her displeasure at the disruption in business and made up for her husband, who had been rendered speechless by the morning’s discovery, with a torrent of angry words. She turned on Daniel, her hands on her bony hips and her bosom heaving with outrage.

“You get that thing out of here right now, Inspector,” she demanded. “And I had better not see the Ferryman mentioned in the papers, you hear? We struggle to keep our heads above water as is, what with the price of coal and the fancy new public house that opened across the road. If word gets out that a headless body turned up in our cellar, we’ll be done for. Sure, they’ll come to gawk and gossip, but once the curiosity wears off, where will that leave us, I ask you? Nowhere, is where,” she said with furious finality. “No one will want to drink at a tavern where the ale might’ve been used to pickle a dead cove.”

"I'm sorry for your trouble, Mrs. Dafoe," Daniel said patiently. "We will remove the remains as quickly as possible."

"Oh, aye, but can you remove the tittle tattle that will follow us for the rest of our days?" she huffed, her eyes blazing with indignation.

Daniel didn't reply. To put an end to the speculation once word got out would be about as easy as stopping the tide from coming in and going out. Already there were several people loitering outside the tavern, craning their necks to see who'd be loaded into the police wagon that waited outside. Mrs. Dafoe muttered something unintelligible and bustled off to the kitchen, but not before she bolted the door to keep the nosier of her patrons from barging in.

Charles Dafoe sat huddled at a corner table, his hands clasped before him. He had been staring morosely into space but looked at Daniel expectantly when he approached. Charles might have meant to offer a smile of greeting, but what came out was a grimace so grotesque, it reminded Jason of the Guy Fawkes effigy he'd seen last November, the staring face licked by flames as the crowd jeered and huddled around the bonfire.

"Mr. Dafoe, this is my associate, Dr. Redmond. He will examine the remains before we remove the barrel from the premises," Daniel said.

Charles Dafoe nodded. "It's down in the cellar," he said. Now that he was no longer trying to smile, his expression was one of incomprehension. "I don't understand. How did it get there? Why would someone…?" His voice trailed off as his thoughts turned inward once again. "Philip was my friend," he muttered. "My only real friend. I would never do anything to hurt him." Charles Dafoe peered at Jason. "Will you make him whole again, Dr. Redmond?" he asked, his eyes brimming with tears. "Even in times past, they used to reattach the head after it had been lopped off by the executioner so that the condemned could have a proper burial."

Jason nodded. “You have my word, Mr. Dafoe. I will make Philip Hobart whole again.”

“Thank you,” Charles Dafoe said quietly. “It would mean a great deal to Philip. And to Lucy and Bram,” he added. “It’s important to say a proper goodbye when someone dies.”

“Mr. Dafoe, could I ask you a few questions before I examine the body?” Jason inquired.

Charles Dafoe nodded. “Of course. Anything I can do to help.”

Jason pulled out a chair and sat across from the publican, so as not to tower over him as they talked. Daniel sat down as well.

“How many ways are there into the cellar?” Jason asked.

“Just two. One from the back alley and one from inside.”

“And how many people have keys to the back door?”

“Just myself and my wife,” Charles Dafoe replied. “And both keys are accounted for.” He held up a key ring that held half a dozen brass keys. “Nothing’s missing.”

“You did mention that Philip Hobart had a key to the cellar,” Daniel chimed in.

Charles Dafoe looked incredulous. “That was nigh on twenty-five years ago, Inspector.”

“Was the lock changed since Philip Hobart used the cellar?” Jason asked.

Dafoe shook his leonine head. “No. There was never any need.”

“So it is possible that Philip Hobart’s key was used to gain access.”

“I suppose so.”

"Mr. Dafoe, when was the last time you were down in the cellar before you found the barrel this morning?" Daniel asked.

"Last night. I went down to fetch a cask of ale."

"And was the barrel there last night?"

"I was only down there for a few moments, but I don't think so." Charles stared into the distance as he tried to recall. "No, it wasn't there," he said with more conviction. "I'm sure of it."

"So, someone entered by way of the back alley last night and deposited the barrel with Philip Hobart's remains in your cellar," Jason speculated. "Would you not have heard them? I presume your private rooms are above the tavern."

Charles Dafoe shook his head slowly. "Last orders are at eleven. By the time the stragglers are out the door and we've tidied the taproom, it's past midnight. And then we're up at six the following morning. We're so worn out by the end of the day, Dr. Redmond, we wouldn't hear cannon fire in the next street."

"And which way does your bedroom face?" Jason asked.

"It faces the street. The back bedrooms are empty just now. Our son, Jack, is in the Navy," Charles Dafoe added sadly. "And our daughter passed three months ago. Died in childbirth, the child with her." Charles fixed his gaze on his folded hands. "Her husband, Evan, is at sea with our Jack, so Marie stayed with us. Evan's yet to be told, the poor lad. He'll be gutted."

"I'm very sorry for your loss," Jason said. "May your daughter and grandchild rest in peace."

Charles Dafoe nodded and muttered, "And now this. This will ruin us if it gets out."

"Hardly, Mr. Dafoe," Daniel said. "People enjoy a bit of notoriety with their pint. If I know anything of human nature, the news will bring the punters in."

Charles Dafoe's mouth lifted at the corner, and he scoffed. "If you say so, Inspector. I think Philip would have found that perversely amusing."

"Did Mr. Hobart normally find things amusing?" Jason asked, clearly surprising both Charles Dafoe and Daniel with the question.

"No, not particularly," Charles said. "But he could appreciate irony. The more bitter, the better."

Daniel pushed back his chair and stood. "Thank you, Mr. Dafoe. We'll go down to the cellar now."

He waited a moment, probably to see if Charles Dafoe would wish to accompany them, but the publican turned away, fixing his gaze on the mullioned window and the street beyond. He'd seen his friend's body once. He clearly had no wish to see it again.

"Why did you ask that, about finding things amusing?" Daniel asked as he and Jason walked toward the door to the cellar.

Jason shrugged. "I suppose I'm still trying to form a picture of the man."

"Well, from what I've heard so far, he was hardly a barrel of laughs."

Daniel looked mildly contrite at what he'd just said, but Jason did catch a glimmer of amusement in his dark eyes. He'd been in the job long enough to resort to gallows humor, which, although callous, was also the first step toward becoming a more effective policeman. Perhaps Daniel was ready for that promotion after all, Jason mused as he followed Daniel down the worn stone steps.

The odor in the cellar was a combination of fermenting hops, musty wood, and the earthy scent of root vegetables that were stored in shallow crates set against the wall. There were also several baskets filled with oyster shells, the white residue from the broken shells sprinkling the floor beneath. Their steps echoed on the flagstones as they approached the barrel Constable Collins was guarding. Although the barrel was closed, the constable kept well back, his expression one of ill-concealed horror and his skin waxy in the light of the oil lamp that hung from a hook affixed to a beam in the low ceiling. Constable Collins stepped aside, his relief at no longer being alone with the body evident.

"You may wait outside if you wish, Constable," Daniel said, and the young man bolted.

The barrel was near the steps that led to the alley door, so whoever had delivered it wouldn't have had to go far. It was surprisingly compact for a receptacle that was said to contain the body of a grown man. Jason removed the lid and peered inside. He'd expected the remains to be submerged, but the barrel was empty except for the headless corpse. Jason supposed the barrel would be too heavy for one man to lift if it held liters of liquid on top of the dead weight of the body. Still, even without liquid, it would take a strong man to maneuver it down the steps without making any noise, unless he had an accomplice.

The body was in a sitting position with the legs bent and the arms pressed to the sides, the hands resting on the knees. The severed neck must have chafed against the lid because there was some organic matter on the underside of the wood, but otherwise, the edges were fairly smooth. The shirt collar was stained with dried blood, but the rest of the clothes, which were of good-quality broadcloth, were relatively clean, the corpse still wearing shoes. A thick gold watchchain, just visible between the torso and the thighs, and a wedding ring glinted in the light of the oil lamp.

"Do you still mean to autopsy him?" Daniel asked.

"I do, after I make certain the head fits the body."

"Do you think there are two headless corpses out there?" Daniel exclaimed.

"I fervently hope not. But I do need to ascertain the cause of death."

"But surely we already know the cause of death."

"Appearances can be deceptive," Jason replied.

Daniel sighed and nodded, no doubt recalling some of their earlier cases and the revelations that had come to light as a result of a postmortem.

"You can transport the remains to the mortuary now," Jason told Daniel. "Do not lift out the body or dispose of the barrel."

"Whyever not?" Daniel asked.

"It's too dark in here for me to examine the remains in situ, and I would like to take a closer look at the barrel once the body has been removed."

"As you say."

"Now, I really must return to the hospital," Jason said.

"Jason, I saw John Ransome leaving just as I arrived at the hospital."

"He was waiting for word of his wife."

Daniel looked torn between asking for a more detailed explanation and respecting his superior's right to privacy. "Will she recover?" he asked instead.

"She will," was all that Jason was willing to tell his friend.

"I will question the Dafoes' neighbors and see if anyone heard anything last night," Daniel said once Constable Collins and Constable Putney had lifted the barrel into the waiting wagon and were ready to set off.

"Let's meet at Scotland Yard around three. I should be able to get away by then," Jason replied.

If Laura Ransome was stable, Jason would be able to safely leave her in the capable hands of the staff until morning.

Chapter 23

Daniel spent the next two hours questioning anyone whose windows faced the Ferryman Inn, both front and back. Assuming that the barrel had not been at the Ferryman all along, it would have been delivered sometime between midnight and six in the morning, while the Dafoes were asleep. Given its weight and dimensions, it would have to have been brought by cart. It would be difficult to carry a dead weight in a container with no handles, even if the killer had help. Likewise, to roll the barrel would make too much noise and draw unwanted attention to those involved.

Daniel wondered if he could rule out Charles Dafoe as a suspect for the moment and take him at his word. For one, Charles Dafoe did not have a motive, as far as Daniel knew. And for another, if he had been the one to kill Philip Hobart, it made no sense to alert Scotland Yard when he could have quietly disposed of the body without putting himself in the frame for murder. No one would ever question a tavern owner loading a barrel into a cart and driving off. It would be like suspecting a gravedigger because he carried a shovel, or a butcher because he routinely used a cleaver. Charles Dafoe had seemed sincere in his grief, but Daniel reminded himself that he had met many a convincing liar, and to cross Charles Dafoe off the list of suspects entirely would be premature.

As expected, none of the neighbors had heard anything out of the ordinary or seen anything to arouse their suspicion, mostly because everyone had been sound asleep. One woman, a weary young mother whose baby was teething and had kept her up half the night, said that she might have heard the sound of wheels that stopped near the mouth of the alley sometime after midnight, but she hadn't looked out the window, nor did she find it strange that a conveyance might come down the street late at night. It happened all the time, and it might have been a hansom or the nightsoil man's wagon. There were plenty of people abroad at night, especially those whose work couldn't be done during the daylight hours, like the poor sods who shoveled shit out of London's cesspits and took it away before the city stirred to life.

Having finished with his questioning, Daniel wolfed down a bowl of oyster stew at the Ferryman and washed it down with a half-pint of bitter before making his way back to Scotland Yard. Sergeant Meadows was behind the counter, seemingly engrossed in that week's penny dreadful.

"Anything?" Daniel asked, referring to the appeal.

"No, sir. Nothing yet. Not even the usual reprobates who'll tell you anything you wish to hear for a few shillings. Surprising, that," Sergeant Meadows said. "It's as if the culprit has committed the perfect crime."

"There's no such thing as a perfect crime," Daniel retorted, although he was beginning to suspect that he was dealing with someone very clever indeed.

Daniel had half expected to see Ransome's office empty when he passed it, but the superintendent was at his desk, his expression inscrutable as he applied himself to his correspondence. Daniel had just divested himself of his coat and hat when Constable Putney informed him that Lord Redmond had arrived and requested that Daniel join him in the mortuary. Daniel nearly groaned but managed to contain his irritation. He hated the mortuary and hoped Jason did not expect him to witness the postmortem.

When Daniel joined him, Jason was already in his shirtsleeves, the leather apron tied around his waist. He'd lit the lamps despite the daylight streaming through the window and was standing next to the barrel, his gaze fixed on the headless torso, his head cocked to the side, as if he were visualizing the body being stuffed into the barrel.

"Shall I help you lift him out?" Daniel asked, wishing he didn't have to touch the deceased.

"Please," Jason replied, and grabbed the torso beneath the arms.

Daniel slid his hands beneath the folded knees, and together they hefted the body out of the barrel and laid it on its side on the slab. Ignoring the corpse for the moment, Jason returned to the barrel and bent over it, his head dipping to examine the bottom half.

"Anything interesting?" Daniel asked.

"Not yet," Jason's voice echoed from within. He straightened, grabbed a magnifying glass from a nearby cabinet, and returned to his examination.

"Dammit," Jason exclaimed irritably as his head came up. "Absolutely nothing to go on." Jason rarely gave in to frustration, and although surprised, Daniel could understand just how he felt.

"Can't say I'm surprised. Sergeant Meadows seems to think this was a perfect crime."

Jason glared at Daniel and shook his head. "No such thing."

"That's what I said. I do hope the condition of the body might tell us something."

"Let's lay him flat," Jason suggested.

Daniel tried to keep his gaze focused on the victim's shoes as he helped Jason to straighten the limbs. The worst of the rigor mortis had passed, but the flesh felt cold and unyielding to the touch, even through the fabric of the trousers. The head, when Jason laid it in its proper place, appeared to fit perfectly atop the neck, although the sagging jowls and neck had the wrinkled appearance of a much older man. Daniel averted his gaze, but he could still see the corpse's grisly smile from the corner of his eye and thought he could detect the dark irises peering at him from beneath half-closed lids.

"Why's he grinning like that?" Daniel asked, certain that Hobart's mouth had been closed when they had first seen the head in the warden's office. And the eyes had been fully open.

Jason didn't bother to look up as he studied the point of the joining. "After a day or two, the skin of the nose and mouth begins to draw back, producing the effect of a grin. The flesh loses elasticity and begins to wrinkle, and the eyeballs begin to dry out. All perfectly normal."

"To you maybe," Daniel muttered.

"You can wait upstairs," Jason said, "but I think it would help if you were to remain. I'm not going to cut him open today. I simply wish to examine the body."

Daniel nodded. He'd give his eyeteeth to wait in his office, preferably while he sipped a cup of strong tea and enjoyed a biscuit or two, but if Jason wasn't going to perform a postmortem, Daniel had no excuse. Instead, he steeled himself for what was to come and waited patiently for Jason to examine every inch of clothing before removing the items one by one until the body on the slab was naked, the pallid skin reminding Daniel of a giant white grub.

"Thoughts?" Daniel asked, unable to bear the suspense any longer.

"I am certain that the head and the body belong to the same individual. I do think that Hobart was already dead at the time of the beheading, but it's impossible to tell based on the amount of blood on the clothing. Had he been alive when the head was lopped off, blood would have spurted from his neck, but if he was laid flat, the blood would not have flowed down his body or splattered his feet. I also think that had he still been conscious, there would be some sign of a struggle, but there's nothing obvious. His hands are not bruised or scratched, and the nails are not broken. There doesn't appear to be any organic matter beneath the fingernails, so he did not grab at his assailant or try to fight for his life."

"So it was the blow to the head that killed him?" Daniel asked.

"That's the most logical assumption," Jason said. "My theory is that Hobart was hit on the head from behind while walking home from the Queen's Arms. I see no evidence of multiple blows, so it's likely that that first blow either rendered him unconscious or killed him outright. His body was transported to the place where he was beheaded. If not dead already, Philip Hobart either died on the way or was still unconscious at the time of the beheading."

"And the second crime scene?"

"A private place, where the killer was certain he or she would not be interrupted."

"Like a cellar of a tavern with an empty barrel to hand?" Daniel asked.

"Quite possibly."

"And would there have been a great deal of blood?"

"If Philip Hobart was still alive at the time of the beheading, then there would be a significant amount of blood. There would be less blood if the victim was already dead, but a postmortem hemorrhage will still occur when the blood vessels rupture. However, if the killer laid the body flat and placed a basin or a bucket beneath the neck, the amount of blood at the crime scene would be minimal."

"So, what does the body tell you about the person who committed this murder?" Daniel asked.

Jason considered the question, his gaze skimming the corpse in a way that suggested he was attempting to visualize the assault.

"I think there are two distinct possibilities. The first is that the whole thing was carefully planned. The killer knew exactly where Philip Hobart would be and lay in wait for him. In that scenario, the murder is premeditated, and the perpetrator came armed with a weapon and a ready mode of transportation."

"And the second?" Daniel asked.

"Something happened to cause the killer to follow Philip Hobart from the tavern and hit him on the head in a fit of anger. The shape of the wound suggests a weapon that had sharp corners, like a brick or a sharp-edged rock. An object he could have found just lying around. Perhaps the killer had arrived in a carriage or a wagon, or perhaps he or she hid the body and returned for it."

"So *possibly* a crime of passion?" Daniel mused.

"Not in the normal sense."

"Go on."

"Even if the initial blow to the head was unplanned, the rest was carefully and calmly executed. Having taken the body away, the killer severed the head, washed away the blood, brushed and oiled the hair, making sure to cover the wound, and delivered Philip Hobart's head to Newgate Prison. These were not the actions of a panicked individual."

"Yes, I agree. Is that what leads you to believe that the killer had access to a private, isolated space?"

"Based on the presentation of petechiae and purpura," Jason pointed to groupings of tiny red spots that dotted the pallid flesh, "and judging by the areas of lividity, the body was left on its stomach for hours after death, so the killer was not under any immediate pressure to dispose of the corpse. There's also no obvious reddening along the point of decapitation."

"Which means?"

"This suggests that the head was not severed immediately after death."

"So the killer could have taken the body anywhere and no one would be the wiser," Daniel deduced.

"Precisely."

"In which case, we're right back where we started."

"I wouldn't say that," Jason replied. "We have a working theory and can rule out robbery as the motive since the victim was still in possession of his watch and wedding ring. Both items are solid gold and would fetch a tidy sum at any pawnbroker's."

"But you didn't find his purse. He would have had money on him if he was on his way home from a tavern."

"The purse might have been in his coat pocket," Jason replied. "Or he could have simply taken a few coins to pay for his drinks and had nothing left by the time he departed the Queen's Arms."

"That's true," Daniel conceded. "Do you suppose the coat was removed before the beheading?" Philip Hobart would have been wearing a coat and hat, but neither had been found with the body.

"Maybe to expose the neck," Jason replied.

"Even if the killer sold the coat and hat to a rag shop, we'll never find them. There are hundreds of such places in London, and if the collar is not splattered with blood, there'll be no way to identify the coat."

"Profit was clearly not the motive, so why bother? How much would they fetch?"

"A few bob at best."

"The ring alone is worth considerably more," Jason pointed out.

Daniel lifted the gold ring out of the box Jason used to keep the decedent's belongings and weighed it in his palm. It felt solid and heavy, and the gold could easily be melted and reshaped into anything the jeweler had a mind to create. Whoever had so carelessly left the watch and ring on the body clearly wasn't in need of funds. Daniel pocketed the watch and wedding ring to return to the widow and fixed his gaze on the grinning head.

"And you're certain the body wasn't stuffed into the barrel immediately after the beheading?" Daniel asked. "Perhaps the barrel was left on its side, which would account for this pattern of lividity."

"The killer would have to get the corpse into the barrel either before rigor had set in or once the limbs became slightly more flexible. Had the body gone in right away, the pattern would appear different, even if the barrel was left on its side. Why do you ask?"

"Charles Dafoe has access to barrels and a private cellar to which only two people that we know of have a key. He also owns a horse and wagon. What better way to deflect suspicion than to alert the police to the presence of a barrel containing the body?"

Jason cocked his head to the side as he considered Dafoe's culpability. "That floor was surprisingly clean for a cellar, so it may have been recently washed," he speculated. "But what reason would Charles Dafoe have to kill his oldest friend? And why would he not just chuck the barrel into the river? Why bother alerting the police at all?"

"Perhaps he thought he could outsmart the police by getting ahead of the investigation," Daniel suggested.

"Or perhaps he's being framed by someone who knew of the connection between the two men."

Daniel sighed. "Old friendships are often fraught with jealousies and resentments. Perhaps they fell out."

"Philip Hobart still visited the Ferryman regularly," Jason pointed out. "That hardly speaks to a rift."

“We know that Philip Hobart went to the Queen’s Arms after supper, but there’s nothing to suggest that he didn’t go on to the Ferryman afterward. Charles Dafoe said last orders are at eleven, so the Ferryman would still have been open. If an argument broke out between the two men and Charles Dafoe hit Philip Hobart over the head in a fit of anger, all he’d have to do is drag the body down to the cellar, decapitate the corpse, make the head presentable, and deliver it to Newgate. No one would go looking for Philip Hobart’s remains in the Ferryman’s cellar, so Dafoe might have left the body down there until he was ready to deal with it.”

“The argument would have to have erupted after closing time, or any number of patrons would have witnessed the murder. And don’t forget that Philip Hobart was hit from behind,” Jason reminded him. “Perhaps he was in the act of walking away, or maybe there was no argument and Charles Dafoe meant to kill him all along and simply took advantage of the opportunity he’d been presented with.” He nodded, as if silently confirming something to himself. “It fits, Daniel, but only if Charles Dafoe had a motive for murder.”

“A devoted friend or a cold-blooded killer?” Daniel mused.

“That all depends on whether he had something to gain by Philip Hobart’s death,” Jason said as he covered the corpse with a sheet and untied the apron.

“If Philip Hobart talked to his wife, she might know. And possibly his son. I can’t imagine that Mrs. Dafoe would give anything away, and we have no way of knowing who was at the Ferryman that night. The Dafoes will hardly give up that information if they have something to hide.”

“Perhaps your appeal might still yield some clues.”

“I hope so,” Daniel replied, but he didn’t hold out much hope for a credible witness. “No one has come forward yet. In the meantime, I think I had better reinterview Lucy and Bram Hobart.”

Jason nodded in agreement. “Yes, I think that’s the logical next step.”

“When will you perform the postmortem?” Daniel asked as they left the mortuary and headed toward the stairs.

“Tomorrow afternoon. Shall we update Superintendent Ransome?” Jason asked as they reached the ground floor landing.

“Yes. I suppose we ought to.”

But Ransome had already left for the day. The light in his office was off, the door firmly shut.

“I’ll see you tomorrow,” Jason said wearily once they stepped outside.

It was damp and overcast, and gauzy tendrils of mist drifted off the river and shrouded the world in swathes of thickening fog, putting Daniel in mind of ghostly fingers that reached for one’s throat from beyond the grave. He shook his head to dispel such morbid thoughts.

“Goodnight, Jason. My regards to Katherine,” he said.

“Goodnight, Daniel.”

Jason tipped his head and walked away, his silhouette swallowed by the encroaching fog in mere moments.

Chapter 24

Friday, March 26

Having risen early, Daniel decided he would start the morning by speaking to the Hobarts. He had no other leads at the moment, and Jason would be otherwise engaged until at least noon. Daniel breakfasted on soft-boiled eggs, buttered toast, kippers, and several cups of strong tea, and set off. It wasn't the done thing to call on someone early in the morning, but this wasn't a social call, and Lucy Hobart did not strike Daniel as someone who would loll in bed until late into the morning.

The soupy fog of the night before had dissipated, but a fine mist hung in the air, the sky the color of dirty linen. The pavement glistened with morning dew, and the sleek body of a passing carriage was beaded with moisture, the burly coachman huddled into his coat, his neck drawn in like that of a turtle, and the brim of his hat pulled so low it almost completely obscured his features.

Even if Lucy Hobart was an early riser, it was still too early to turn up at her door, so Daniel decided to walk to Budge Row. There weren't too many people about, and those that were seemed to be moving slower than usual, their expressions closed as they went about the daily task of opening up their shops and setting out their wares. Daniel squared his shoulders against the damp wind, stuffed his hands in his pockets in a most ungentlemanly manner, and allowed his thoughts to roam. He quickly exhausted analysis of the case and moved on to the ever-shifting internal politics of Scotland Yard.

Would the outcome of this case have any bearing on Ransome's choice of chief inspector, or had Ransome already made up his mind? If he were honest with himself, Daniel didn't think he was qualified for the job, but he didn't think Ransome would choose a man on merit alone. He liked to play favorites and often pitted the men against each other in an effort to foster a more competitive environment. He wanted quick, decisive action and satisfactory results so that his name could appear in the papers and reassure the public that he had nothing but their safety and welfare in mind. One truly had to admire the man and his understanding of human nature.

As Daniel approached Budge Row, he resolved to graciously accept whatever Ransome decided and give the newly minted chief inspector all the support and respect the man deserved. Daniel's time would come. He was certain of it, but in the meantime, he had to solve this case to Ransome's satisfaction. And no one knew more about a man than his wife, even if she pretended not to.

Hattie looked harassed when she opened the door to Daniel's knock. There was a smudge of soot on her pinafore and a dusting of flour on her cheek, but the girl quickly rearranged her expression into something resembling decorum and invited Daniel to wait for her mistress in the parlor. Lucy Hobart looked even more fragile than before when she entered the room, her pallor exacerbated by the milky light from the window and the black of her mourning gown making her look like an underfed crow.

"Do you have news for me, Inspector?" Lucy asked once they settled across from each other.

Daniel decided not to tell Lucy Hobart that her husband's body had been discovered at the Ferryman or to hand over Philip Hobart's effects just yet, since he wasn't ready to answer her questions about the state and location of the body. The news might influence her answers, and there was no need for this grieving widow to picture her husband's remains stuffed into an ale cask.

"Not yet, but I do have a few more questions, Mrs. Hobart."

Lucy inclined her head, giving him leave to proceed.

"What did you make of the Dafoes?" Daniel asked, watching Lucy for any change in expression, no matter how miniscule. There was none.

"I have never met them, Inspector," she said.

"But Charles Dafoe was your husband's oldest and closest friend."

"Philip only kept up with Charles Dafoe out of a sense of duty. He stopped in once a week to have a drink but did not seek his society outside the Ferryman."

"But he did tell you about Charles," Daniel probed.

"My husband was grateful to the Dafoes for helping him in his hour of need, but as you might imagine, he didn't want to be reminded of those difficult days."

"Did Philip and Charles have any disagreements of late?"

Lucy Hobart shook her fair head. "Not that I'm aware of. Why do you ask?"

"Long-lasting friendships have their ups and downs, do they not?"

"I wouldn't know, Inspector Haze. I've never had any."

"Did your husband have any other friends from the old days, or maybe someone he'd grown close with as a result of his work?"

"Philip wasn't someone who sought social connections."

"It must have been lonely for you," Daniel tried again.

"Not at all. We preferred our own company."

If Daniel had hoped to learn anything from Lucy Hobart's reactions to his inquiries, he quickly realized that he had overestimated her involvement in her husband's inner life. In fact, he wasn't sure she had one of her own. Lucy reminded Daniel of a china doll, her beautiful face devoid of expression, her gaze fixed on something beyond the window. He didn't think she was intentionally hiding anything from him. She simply had nothing to convey.

"I would like to bury my husband, Inspector. Have you located his remains?" Lucy asked.

"We have," Daniel admitted. There was no longer a reason to withhold the information. "You can have an undertaker collect the body from Scotland Yard on Monday."

Lucy nodded. She seemed relieved, but it surprised Daniel that she didn't ask where the body had been found. Perhaps she didn't care to know. It was too gruesome, and once the image was planted in her mind, she'd never be able to erase it. Daniel took out the wedding ring and the watch and set them on the table before Lucy Hobart. She stared at them but didn't reach out to touch them.

And then the stony demeanor cracked for just a moment, Lucy's expression turning desolate. "I don't know what I'll do without Philip. I've never been on my own."

"I'm sure your stepson will look after you," Daniel supplied.

Lucy sighed shakily. "Bram will discharge his duty, but he's a young man who will have his own family someday." She angrily wiped away a tear that slid delicately down her cheek. "Widowhood wouldn't loom so large if I still had my lovely boy."

"I trust your husband left you well provided for?"

"Yes, I suppose he did," Lucy replied softly.

"Are you familiar with the terms of the will, Mrs. Hobart?"

"Philip left equal shares to Bram and Samuel, with a modest allowance for me."

"So now Bram gets the lot," Daniel said, watching the woman for any sign of resentment.

Lucy shot Daniel a reproachful look. "Bram adored his brother, and I would thank you not to imply that he will be happy to benefit from Samuel's death."

"Forgive me," Daniel said. "I didn't mean to upset you."

"If you have any further questions about the financial arrangements, I suggest you speak to Bram. I'm afraid I don't know any more than I have already told you."

Lucy folded her hands in her lap and fixed her gaze on the window again. It was obvious she wished Daniel to leave her in peace, so he bid her a good morning and took his leave.

Chapter 25

Daniel found Bram Hobart in the same spot as before. He was standing on the ladder, chisel in hand. A thin wire headband held back his hair, preventing it from falling into his face as he worked. His trousers were covered with fine chippings, and the sleeve of his shirt was torn where he must have snagged it on a sharp bit of marble. Reddish stubble covered his lean cheeks, and dark semicircles smudged the skin beneath the eyes. The man looked tired and bereft, but his hand was steady and his arm true when he drove the chisel into the stone. A few more inches of the sculpture he had been working on the last time they'd met had emerged from the marble, and Daniel could now see the hilt of a sword clasped in the hands of the mournful angel.

"Warrior angel?" Daniel asked as he took a moment to admire Bram's work. Archangel Gabriel came to mind, and Daniel couldn't help but acknowledge Bram Hobart's skill as a sculptor.

Bram nodded. "It was commissioned by the Lyles to honor their family's military tradition," he said as he stepped off the ladder. "Colonel Lyle's son was recently killed by the Maori in New Zealand. A sad business. The boy was barely eighteen."

"Yes," Daniel agreed, although he knew very little of the New Zealand wars against the native tribes.

"How can I help you, Inspector Haze?" Bram asked when Daniel failed to state his business.

"I have a few more questions to put to you, Mr. Hobart."

"Fire away. You don't mind if we talk while I make tea, do you? I'm parched."

Bram Hobart led Daniel into a small room at the back where a squat cast-iron stove sat in the corner, a kettle belching steam positioned on top. There was a low cabinet from which Bram extracted a bottle of milk, and tins of tea and biscuits. Two mugs, bowls, and plates stood on a shelf, and there was a ceramic cup that held utensils for two. A desk positioned beneath a skylight was littered with sketches and stacks of bills and correspondence.

"Tea?" Bram asked.

"No, thank you."

Bram made a mug of tea, extracted three Garibaldi biscuits from the tin, then turned to face Daniel, an expression of bland patience on his handsome face.

"We found your father's remains, Mr. Hobart," Daniel said.

Bram sighed. "That's good news, indeed. Poor Lucy has been beside herself."

"I told Mrs. Hobart the body can be collected on Monday."

"I will make the arrangements," Bram said. He took a bite of his biscuit and chased it with a gulp of tea, his expectant gaze on Daniel.

"You didn't ask me where the body was found."

"I'm not sure I care to know. I would prefer to remember my father as he was, not as some sort of Frankenstein monster, stitched together by the undertaker to minimize the horror that befell him."

Daniel nodded and continued. "Did your father and Charles Dafoe ever fall out over the course of their long friendship?"

Bram shook his head. "Not that I know of. Why do you ask?"

"Because your father's remains were discovered at the Ferryman."

Bram set down his mug with a shaking hand and swallowed hard, his Adam's apple bobbing as he forced the biscuit he'd been chewing down his throat. "What are you saying?" he rasped, once he was capable of speech again.

"I'm saying that Charles Dafoe is a suspect, Mr. Hobart."

"No," Bram replied, shaking his head vehemently. "No, I refuse to believe it. Charles and my father were childhood friends. Charles would never do anything to hurt him."

"So, you can think of absolutely no reason Charles Dafoe might hit your father over the head?"

"Absolutely none," Bram replied, but the conviction had gone out of his voice, and his gaze was thoughtful, as if something had come to him but he wasn't quite sure he should bring it up.

"What is it, Mr. Hobart?" Daniel asked. "Have you thought of something?"

Bram sighed and nodded miserably. "The Ferryman is housed in an old Tudor building. I believe the foundation dates back to the Romans."

"So?"

"The inn needed urgent structural repairs. This was about three years back."

Daniel waited patiently, letting Bram share what he needed to say in his own time.

"Charles couldn't afford the work, so he asked my father for a loan. Father was happy to help. He owed the Dafoes a debt of gratitude." Bram gave Daniel a searching look. "Do you know about that? Did Charles tell you what happened to my grandmother?"

"He did," Daniel assured him.

"So you understand. Father couldn't refuse even if he had wanted to, which he didn't. But it was a tidy sum."

"Was the loan ever repaid?"

Bram shook his head. "Not in its entirety. I believe Charles managed to pay off about ten percent. Maybe twenty."

"Exactly how much money did your father loan the Dafoes?"

"I believe it was four hundred pounds."

Daniel let out a low whistle. Four hundred quid was a large sum, and few people would have that sort of money lying around..

"Did your father ever ask for the money back?" Daniel asked.

"He didn't want to embarrass Charles, but he was beginning to despair of ever seeing that money again."

"I see," Daniel said. "Was the loan agreement in writing?"

"No. My father trusted Charles Dafoe implicitly. He didn't ask for a document, nor did he charge him interest."

"That's very generous."

"Yes," Bram agreed. "My father hasn't given me a farthing since I came of age, but when it came to Charles, no sacrifice was too big." He sounded bitter, and Daniel could understand his resentment.

"You stand to inherit it all now," he pointed out.

Bram gave a one-shouldered shrug. "Only because there's no one else."

"And I believe you will receive Samuel's portion as well."

Bram looked unbearably sad. "It's only right that Samuel's portion should go to Lucy. I want to see her financially independent."

"That's very thoughtful of you, Mr. Hobart."

"Selfish more like. I don't want to be responsible for my father's widow for the rest of my days."

"Mrs. Hobart is still a young woman. She might wish to remarry."

"And I hope she does," Bram said. "She deserves to be happy and have a family of her own."

"Do you have plans to marry, Mr. Hobart?" Daniel asked. The fact that there was two of everything on the shelf wasn't lost on Daniel. Bram Hobart was prepared for company, most likely of the female variety.

Bram appeared surprised by the question but answered readily enough. "I'm not courting anyone, if that's what you're asking, Inspector. Marriage is not a priority just now. At the moment, I can't think past burying my father."

"Will you erect a monument in his honor?"

Bram gave a mirthless chuckle. "Yes, the Grim Reaper."

Daniel had never heard of this Grim Reaper, but the insinuation was self-explanatory. "Thank you for your candor, Mr. Hobart," he said. "I'll see myself out."

Chapter 26

Having been handed a new lead, Daniel had no choice but to return to the Ferryman. Money was always a motive, and four hundred pounds was definitely a sum worth killing for. Daniel found Charles Dafoe behind the bar, his earlier despondence forgotten in the face of running a business. The publican looked surprised to see Daniel again so soon but reluctantly waved over his nephew and directed Daniel to the corner table Charles had occupied earlier.

"Have you discovered something new, Inspector Haze?" Dafoe asked once they were seated.

"You might say that. You never mentioned that Philip Hobart had made you a loan of four hundred pounds."

"I didn't mention it because it's not relevant," Dafoe replied evenly.

"It's for me to decide what's relevant and what isn't, Mr. Dafoe."

"All right," Charles Dafoe conceded. "What do you wish to know?"

"What were the terms of your agreement?"

"There were no terms. I needed a loan and asked Philip to help me. He obliged."

"Abraham Hobart said you failed to repay the loan. Is that true?"

"I had some setbacks, that's true enough, but I was always going to pay that money back. I had managed to pay back nearly fifty quid. Philip knew I was good for the rest."

"Mr. Dafoe, your friend's remains were discovered in your cellar, to which, by your own admission, only two people have a key."

"Philip had a key," Charles Dafoe reminded him stubbornly. "Someone might have taken it off him at any time, like that scheming weasel of an assistant. Philip didn't trust that boy. Said he was too ambitious for his own good."

Daniel filed away that bit of information on Clyde Barkley for the moment and returned to the whereabouts of the key, which was the more pressing concern.

"Did Philip Hobart really hold on to a key he'd been given twenty-five years before?" Daniel pressed. "When was the last time he'd used it?"

"Philip hadn't used the key since he felt able to stand on his own two feet, but to him, that key represented something. So to answer your question—yes, he did hold on to it."

"And what did the key represent?"

"Acceptance. Kindness. Support. That's why he never gave it back. It was a symbol of what the Ferryman and the family within meant to him."

"And you took advantage of that symbol. You accepted a loan you never meant to repay," Daniel said.

Charles Dafoe shook his massive head. "Philip never once brought up the money. I gave him a small sum whenever I was able."

"I only have your word for that."

"Is there no one in your life that you trust, Inspector Haze?" Charles Dafoe asked. "Someone whose word is as good as a signed document?"

"There is," Daniel replied, and knew that he would trust Jason not only with any amount of money but with Charlotte's well-being and safety.

"That's how Philip trusted me."

"But did you trust him?"

"How do you mean?" Dafoe asked.

"Did you trust him not to land you in debtor's prison? He could have brought a charge against you."

Charles Dafoe laughed at that. "Philip would never have done that. And even if he did, there was no evidence to support his claim. We never set anything in writing." His eyes narrowed as he nailed Daniel with his shrewd gaze. "And what evidence do you have that would stand up in a court of law, Inspector Haze? You found a barrel containing Philip's remains in the cellar, which I alerted you to. Why would I do that if I had been the one to kill him?"

"You could have done that to divert suspicion while also clearing yourself of the debt," Daniel said.

Charles shook his head mulishly. "Bram knows about the debt. Just because Philip is dead doesn't mean I no longer have to repay the money. Unless you think I was planning to murder Bram next. Wise up, Inspector Haze. Clearly someone is trying to set me up."

"And who would want to set you up, Mr. Dafoe?"

"Someone who doesn't want you to discover a connection between them and Philip, that's who," Charles Dafoe snapped.

"Are you referring to Clyde Barkley?" Daniel asked. Charles had already as good as accused the young man of treachery. He was surprised when Charles clammed up, his expression one of mute resignation.

"Mr. Dafoe?" Daniel prompted.

"I'm referring to Michael Pearson," Charles said with a sigh.

"And who is Michael Pearson?" That was the first time Daniel had heard the name, and he wondered why Charles Dafoe was mentioning Pearson only now, on their third meeting.

"Annie Hobart died in childbirth," Charles Dafoe said. "But the child didn't die with her."

"The child lived?" Daniel asked, astounded by this bit of news.

"He did. But Philip didn't want him. Annie wasn't happy with Philip and was often seen in the company of James Pearson in the months leading up to her death. Philip believed the child was Pearson's."

"And was he?"

"You only have to take one look at the boy to know he's Philip's. He's the spit of him."

"But he goes by the other man's name?"

"James asked his mother to take the child in. She believed Michael might be her grandson and raised him as such. Michael owes his life to Hester and James Pearson."

"Why did you not mention this earlier?" Daniel asked, inwardly cursing the man for his reticence.

"Because I didn't think of it," Charles Dafoe exclaimed. "But Michael was here not an hour ago. He'd heard about Philip's death and reckoned he has a claim to his estate since his mother was married to Philip at the time of her death and he's legally Philip's son."

"Does Bram know about Michael?"

"I don't imagine he does. Philip never mentioned the boy. I doubt he even knew what became of him."

"And you think Michael Pearson would have the motive and the cunning to carry out this scheme?"

"He's a clever lad, Michael. And he harbored a burning hatred for his father."

"But what would drive Michael to murder his father now?" Daniel asked.

"Grief," Charles Dafoe replied. "James Pearson passed recently. He was the only father Michael had ever known."

"Did James Pearson ever marry or have other children?"

"No. I don't think James ever got over Annie. Perhaps that's what bound him to Michael, a love for a woman who was missing from both their lives."

"Why would Michael Pearson leave his natural father's remains in your cellar?" Daniel asked. "And how would he get in?"

"I reckon Michael knows all about the unpaid loan. His grandmother did since the old witch knows everything that goes on in these parts. He probably thought I'd dispose of the barrel in order to protect myself from the prying gaze of Scotland Yard, therefore making myself complicit and clearing the way for him to claim his inheritance. As to how he got in, Michael is skilled with a lockpick. He could have opened the alleyway door easily enough."

"Why didn't you dispose of the body? No one would have anything on you if you did."

"Because I have nothing to hide, Inspector, and because Philip deserves justice."

"Where do I find Michael Pearson?" Daniel asked resignedly.

"At the White Dove," Charles Dafoe replied. "It's been in the Pearson family for generations."

"With James Pearson dead, is Michael not the rightful owner?" Daniel asked. "Surely that makes for a sizeable inheritance."

"The tavern went to James's younger brother, Deacon. And Deacon has two boys of his own. Michael will never own the White Dove, and Deacon feels no loyalty toward Michael. He thinks the boy has lived off his family's charity long enough."

Daniel sighed, amazed at how this investigation kept twisting and turning and forming a circle instead of moving in a straight line toward a satisfying resolution.

"Don't leave town, Mr. Dafoe," Daniel said as he stood to leave.

"And where would I go? This is all I have in the world."

But would you kill to protect it? Daniel wondered as he left the inn once again.

Chapter 27

The White Dove was just down the road, so Daniel decided to call on Michael Pearson to see what he could learn. He wished Jason could accompany him, but Jason was at the hospital that morning and wouldn't become available until later, and Daniel had no time to waste in case Michael Pearson decided to make himself scarce.

Of course, Charles Dafoe could be sending Daniel on a wild goose chase in an effort to deflect suspicion from himself. When all the speculation and misdirection was pared away, the evidence still pointed to Dafoe, since the only tangible proof of involvement had been found in his cellar. Daniel hoped Dafoe wouldn't do a runner, but as the publican had so succinctly pointed out, he had nowhere to go, not without turning his back on his remaining family and his business.

Watery sunshine had replaced the sullen clouds of early morning, and the streets were now crowded with pedestrians, vendors, and crossing sweeps, who jealously guarded their respective corners and darted out into the junction every time an elegant carriage drew near in the hope of making a few shillings. Daniel resolutely ignored the cries of the newsboys, who taunted him with the latest headlines from London's most popular dailies. Bungling Bobbies, the Headless Hangman, and the Necromancer of Newgate—which really was a bit far-fetched—being just a few of the more colorful headlines. Daniel supposed he should be grateful that the headlines didn't mention him by name. Hopeless Haze or Clueless Clodhopper, as he had been called once already, would not be helpful for his career trajectory, especially when Ransome was considering Chief Inspector Sandin's replacement.

Like the Ferryman, the White Dove occupied a historic building, but whereas the Ferryman reminded Daniel of a gently aging Tudor beauty that still felt the need to put on airs, the White Dove was more like a drunken doxy who could barely stand upright after a night of servicing endless clients. The whole building seemed to sag on one side, the top of the ground-floor window frame just slightly askew on the left side, as if the building were about to wink at passersby. No wonder Charles Dafoe had been compelled to sink a small fortune into restoring his tavern. He hadn't had much choice if he hoped the place wouldn't tumble down about his ears.

The White Dove was nearly empty, even though it was almost noon. Only a few tables were occupied, mostly by scruffy workmen who looked as if they'd grown old there. A woman of about sixty stood behind the bar, her black high-necked gown making her look like a specter in the unbroken gloom of the taproom. She peered at Daniel but didn't remark on his presence or offer to serve him, having no doubt pegged him as someone who wasn't there to drink.

"Are you Mrs. Pearson?" Daniel inquired.

"Who's asking?"

Daniel held up his warrant card, and Mrs. Pearson let out what sounded very much like a hiss of displeasure. "What do you want with us?"

"I'd like to speak to Michael."

"Why?"

Daniel didn't bother to reply. He owed her no explanations. "Where can I find him?"

"He's down in the cellar. I'll get him," she snapped when Daniel turned toward the open door that led downstairs and exhaled the unmistakable musty breath of a subterranean chamber. He would have liked to examine the premises but thought he'd speak to Michael Pearson first.

Daniel studied the young man once he came through the door and positioned himself before the bar. Michael Pearson was about seventeen. He wasn't very tall, but his wiry build spoke to agility and strength. And his loosely balled hands certainly looked capable of swinging an axe. He shared Philip Hobart's dark coloring, and Daniel could see something of a resemblance between father and son, but it wasn't as pronounced as Charles Dafoe had led him to believe. Michael and Bram looked nothing alike, though, so perhaps Bram Hobart had taken after Annie.

Michael stared at Daniel sullenly, his jaw working as he tried to control his annoyance. "What d'ye want?" he asked at last. Michael tried to sound indifferent, but Daniel could see the anxiety in his eyes and the way he'd looked to his grandmother for guidance. Mrs. Pearson gave him a reassuring nod but made no move to come closer, retaining her stance behind the bar.

"I want to talk to you about your father," Daniel said.

"Me father is dead."

"Your natural father."

"I hear he's dead too."

"And how do you feel about that, Michael?" Daniel asked.

Michael shrugged. "I s'pose I feel a bit sad," he said, his mouth quirking in a way that didn't support his answer.

"Why is that?"

"Because now I'll never get a chance to kill him meself."

"Was that something you dreamed of doing?" Daniel asked.

Michael sighed, and his shoulders drooped as if a heavy mantle had suddenly been draped over them, probably the weight of nearly two decades of rejection. "Philip Hobart threw me away. Even once I got older, he refused to acknowledge me. I were his son," Michael exclaimed, and Daniel saw the naked hurt in the boy's eyes. "His flesh and blood, his responsibility. He never cared if I lived or died, so why should I care that he's dead?"

"Did you kill him?" Daniel asked straight out.

"No."

"Why should I believe you?"

"Because I had nothing to gain from his death," Michael replied. "Not like I were going to get anything."

"You are legally his son," Daniel pointed out. "You could approach your brother."

"I have," Michael spat out. "I went to see Bram when I turned fourteen."

"And what did he tell you?"

"He said that if I ever needed help, he'd be there, but there weren't much he could do for me if I were looking for a handout. He were struggling himself and didn't earn enough to support a brother he'd known nothing 'bout till that day."

"Did he believe you?" Daniel asked, wondering if Bram had known about Michael all along or if Michael's sudden appearance had forced him to reconsider everything he had believed about his childhood and his father.

Michael nodded. "He did. He even said that I look like our father."

"Did he say anything else?" Daniel asked, curious about Bram's reaction to finding out that the baby he'd thought had died was very much alive.

Michael scoffed. "What could he say? I think he were shocked, but for all that he were gracious. Offered me tea and biscuits and asked after me childhood."

"And did you ask him anything?"

"I asked 'bout our mother. I wanted to know what she'd been like. Bram showed me a photograph." Michael smiled in a way that made something clench in Daniel's heart. "She were beautiful," Michael said softly. "I think she would've loved me."

"And have you seen Bram since?"

"He stops in from time to time, to see how I'm getting on. And I've been to his studio a few times. He's gifted," Michael added, clearly in awe of his older brother.

"He is," Daniel replied. "And now that Samuel is dead, Bram will inherit the lot."

"So I hear," Michael said, his bitterness obvious.

"Think Bram will share the bounty?"

"How should I know? Not like we talked about it."

"Will you be angry if he doesn't?" Daniel asked. He could see Michael considering the question, as if the thought had never occurred to him until that moment.

"Nah," he said at last. "But it'd be good of him if he did."

"I hear you have no claim to the White Dove," Daniel said.

"No, but James put something by for me. I'm leaving, Inspector Haze," Michael said. This time he made no effort to hide his smile.

"Where are you bound?"

"New York. There's no longer anything to keep me here."

"Where were you on Monday night, Michael?" Daniel asked.

If Michael was surprised by the question, he didn't show it. "I were with Sass. She can vouch for me."

"Who's Sass?"

"Saskia Bekker. She's the barmaid. I left with her after we closed and spent the night in her loving arms," Michael added with a saucy grin.

"Does Saskia know you're leaving?"

"She's coming with me. Sass and I are going to be married in New York."

"Saskia starts at noon, Inspector," Mrs. Pearson, who'd obviously been following the conversation closely, cut in. "If you care to wait a few minutes, she'll answer your questions."

The triumphant look in Mrs. Pearson's eyes told Daniel that Saskia would confirm Michael's alibi, whether it was true or not. Michael certainly had good cause to hate Philip Hobart, and perhaps, now that he was leaving for America, he thought he'd be able to get away with this brutal act of revenge. The beheading didn't really square with Daniel's impression of the boy, but he couldn't formulate an opinion based on instinct alone, not when Michael was the product of years of rejection and neglect. Such a wound could fester and lead to unspeakable brutality, even in one so young.

Daniel pulled out his pocket watch and checked the time. He didn't want to miss Saskia's arrival or give Mrs. Pearson an opportunity to warn the girl, but he thought he had enough time to examine the cellar for any incriminating evidence.

"I'd like to look down in the cellar while I wait," Daniel said.

Mrs. Pearson shrugged. "Suit yourself, Inspector. Michael, take him down."

Michael turned and wordlessly disappeared through the door he'd come through a few minutes before. Daniel followed. The cellar was dark and dank, the musty space reeking of spilled ale and rotting vegetables. The ceiling was so low, Daniel had to bow his head in order to avoid hitting it on the crossbeams. Michael lit an oil lamp and held it aloft, casting a pool of light onto the cramped space. It was filled with casks, crates, and pieces of broken furniture that would probably never get fixed. Daniel reached out and took the lantern from Michael, then shone the light into every corner and crevice.

The search yielded nothing but mouse droppings on Daniel's shoes and cobwebs in his hair. If blood had been spilled in the cellar, it would have been obvious since the floor was so grimy, it clearly hadn't been washed in years, maybe decades. Daniel's shoes stuck to the steps leading up to the taproom and then made sucking sounds as the sticky soles tried to bind themselves to the scarred flagstone floor. He ran a hand through his hair, feeling as if the strands were fused together with spiderwebs, and then brushed the thick dust from the lapels and shoulders of his coat.

Mrs. Pearson smirked at Daniel's disgust but offered no apology for the state of her cellar. Instead, she gestured toward an empty table near the wall, indicating that he shouldn't wait by the bar where he was discommoding her police-wary customers. Daniel took a seat facing the door and hoped that Saskia wouldn't use the rear entrance that led to the alley behind the tavern.

Saskia Bekker finally arrived a few minutes later, and via the front door. She was no older than sixteen, a fair-haired, blue-eyed beauty dressed in a low-cut blue gown that showed off her buxom figure to great effect. She headed directly toward Daniel's table when he beckoned to her, assuming he wished to place an order. A constellation of freckles spread across the bridge of her pert nose, and her gaze grew worried when she peered at Daniel's warrant card. She mouthed the name, as if she didn't often read and found it difficult to make out the words. Daniel gestured toward a chair, and she perched on the edge, looking like she might flee at any moment.

"Saskia, I need to ask you a few questions about the night Philip Hobart was murdered," Daniel said. "You know who he was, do you not?"

Saskia nodded, but her gaze flew toward Michael, who stood by the bar.

"It's all right, Sass. Just tell him the truth," Michael called out.

Saskia nodded again and clasped her hands before her, as if she were about to pray.

"Where were you from Monday night into Tuesday morning?"

"I was here until eleven, then Michael walked me home."

"Do you live alone?"

Saskia shook her head. "I live with my father, but he was dead to the world by the time we got in."

"And your father allows you to have a man in your bed?" Daniel asked.

Saskia's cheeks flamed with either anger or shame. Daniel couldn't tell. "If Michael is in my bed, then my father can't touch me," she retorted. "Michael looks out for me."

"And was Michael with you the whole night, or is he just using you as an alibi?" Daniel was intentionally goading the girl to see if she would let something slip.

Saskia's eyes blazed with blue fire. "He has no need to lie. He was with me the whole time. Michael loves me. We're going to New York together, and we're going to be married."

Daniel couldn't help but feel sorry for the girl. Most immigrants thought that the streets in America were paved with gold, and they would make their fortune and live happily ever after. Unless James Pearson had left Michael a tidy enough sum to start a successful venture, Michael and Saskia would no doubt wind up working in some tavern, just like they did here.

Daniel studied Saskia for a long moment. She seemed sincere, but he wasn't convinced. "I can arrest you for interfering with an investigation if I find out you lied to me."

"I'm not lying," Saskia snapped. "Michael didn't kill Philip Hobart."

"And how can you be so sure of that?"

Saskia looked unbearably sad as she looked at Daniel, world-weariness in her young face. "Because he still hoped that his father would acknowledge him, even after all this time. He didn't want anything from him, Inspector Haze. Michael just wanted to know him."

"And did he ever approach Philip Hobart that you know of?"

Saskia shook her head. "He wanted to, but he couldn't bring himself to do it, not again." She sighed heavily. "He was a cold fish, that one. I told Michael he was better off without him. He had a father who loved him."

"But now that father is gone," Daniel reminded her.

Saskia nodded sadly. "James Pearson was a good man, and the world is a sadder place without him in it. He offered us a ticket to freedom, and we're going to make the most of the opportunity. Michael would never do anything to prevent us from leaving. Anything," she reiterated.

"When are you due to sail?"

"In a fortnight, and we're going to be on that ship," Saskia said, her eyes blazing with determination. "There's nothing for us here, Inspector. Not a thing."

"Thank you, Saskia," Daniel said.

He stood, gave Michael a curt nod, and left the White Dove. He had two weeks to arrest Michael should he find proof of his guilt, but there was nothing to suggest that Michael had murdered Philip Hobart. Aside from his well-earned resentment, there was no evidence to tie Michael Pearson to the crime.

As Daniel strode toward the nearest hansom stand, he wondered why Bram Hobart had never mentioned his brother. Was it because he genuinely cared for Michael and wanted to protect him from suspicion, or because he didn't believe Michael had anything to do with Philp Hobart's death? Either way, Daniel felt sympathy for the boy and for the poor girl who was too afraid to sleep alone when her father was in the house. What sort of world was this where a man interfered with his daughter and no one except a teenaged boy cared enough to stop it?

Chapter 28

Jason arrived at Scotland Yard just before noon. He'd stopped by the hospital to check on Laura Ransome and was immensely pleased with her progress. Her pallor had been replaced by a healthier hue, and her gaze was no longer dull or glazed with pain. No signs of postoperative infection or fever were present, and the incision was healing cleanly. Jason had spent a few minutes with Laura, reassured her that she would be going home soon, then checked on several other patients and consulted on two surgical cases with Mr. Harris before heading to the Coffee Brewery. He never ate before a postmortem, but he could use an infusion of strong coffee before he began.

John Ransome wasn't in his office, so Jason went directly to the mortuary. The smell that greeted him when he pushed open the door had yet to reach eyewatering proportions, but it was best not to put off the postmortem any longer since gasses were starting to build up within the abdominal cavity, and soon bodily fluids would begin to leak as decomposition progressed.

Jason hung up his coat and hat, put on his apron and linen cap, and prepared the instruments he would require. He then threaded a needle while his hands were still dry and laid it aside to be used after he completed the autopsy. He would close up the body, then reattach the head. He was in no doubt that a competent mortician could do the same, but he wanted to spare Lucy Hobart any unnecessary pain, and a clumsy seam would only serve to remind her of her husband's ugly and violent end.

Jason was just about to make the Y incision when there was a knock on the door, and Superintendent Ransome entered the room. He glanced at the headless corpse but didn't show any emotion. Unlike Daniel, John Ransome was impervious to putrefying cadavers.

"Can I have a word, your lordship?" he asked.

"Of course," Jason replied, and set down the scalpel.

"In my office, if you don't mind."

Jason removed the cap and apron and hung them on the coatrack, then followed Ransome upstairs. Ransome shut the door to his office and settled behind his desk. He seemed to be studying Jason as if seeing him for the first time.

"Is something wrong, Superintendent?" Jason asked.

Ransome shook his head, but his thoughtful gaze never left Jason's face. "I stopped by the hospital this morning. Laura told me you had just left."

"Mrs. Ransome is recovering as expected," Jason said carefully, wondering why Ransome appeared so pensive.

"Yes, I am aware. My gratitude is boundless."

Ransome went quiet, and Jason waited for him to speak. He was certain the superintendent had not asked him to step into his office and shut the door just to talk about his wife. They could have done that in the mortuary.

"Jason," Ransome began, using Jason's Christian name again.

Jason wasn't sure how he felt about that, not because he preferred to stand on ceremony but because it kept a certain level of formality in place when it came to their stations. John Ransome was not a friend, nor was he really a colleague.

"You are a gifted surgeon, and I know that numerous patients benefit from your dedication and experience, but I can't help thinking that your gifts are wasted."

"How do you mean, Superintendent?"

Ransome sighed. "You have a keen mind and an inborn instinct that's so necessary in successful policing. There are many good detectives on the police service, but none are truly remarkable."

Jason began to raise his hand in protest, but Ransome cut across him. "Please, hear me out." Jason sighed inwardly but remained in his seat.

"As you know, I'm looking to fill the position of chief inspector, and I would like to offer the post to you."

"I'm honored, Superintendent, but I cannot possibly accept."

"I knew that would be your answer, but please, think about it before you make up your mind. You can make a real difference, Jason."

"I'm making a difference already," Jason replied.

"I will never forget what you did for my own family, but you can be an instrument of justice, of change," Ransome implored.

"I appreciate your confidence in my skills, but I have no interest in a formal position at Scotland Yard."

"But you do enjoy the challenge," Ransome said. "I see it, Jason. You thrive on solving puzzles and manage to extract every bit of pertinent information from the most minor of clues when many detectives fumble even when presented with the obvious."

"John—"

"Twenty-four hours," Ransome said. "Give me that. If tomorrow at this time you still feel the same, then I will respect your decision and not trouble you with this again. But this is a unique opportunity that will not come around again, at least not anytime soon. Talk to your wife."

That was an unexpected thing for John Ransome to say, and Jason realized that Laura and John's relationship had to be closer than he had first assumed. Perhaps Ransome saved all his gruffness for the men under his command but deferred to his wife's opinion when at home.

"All right," Jason said. "Twenty-four hours."

"That's all I ask." Ransome smiled. "Give me a chance to win you over."

"I have a postmortem to perform," Jason said, and stood.

"Of course. Pardon the interruption."

Jason was still deep in thought by the time he returned to the mortuary and picked up his scalpel once again.

Chapter 29

Daniel had just arrived at Scotland Yard when Sergeant Meadows hailed him. "Good afternoon, Inspector Haze."

"Good afternoon, Sergeant," Daniel replied. "Have we had any response to the appeal?"

Had a promising lead presented itself, Sergeant Meadows would have informed Daniel immediately, but Daniel still harbored hope that in a city of millions, someone might have seen or heard something useful.

"Only five people came forward. Four of them completely unreliable. Made up tall tales in the hope of claiming a reward."

"But no reward was offered."

"To someone who's hungry, even a mug of hot tea and a biscuit can be a reward," Sergeant Meadows said.

"You said five people came in," Daniel said. Sergeant Meadows handed him a piece of paper. "What's this, then?"

"A Mrs. Hobson came in late yesterday evening. I thought you'd want to speak to her."

"What did she say?"

"She said she saw something odd on Tuesday morning but wouldn't reveal the particulars. Said she'd only speak to the detective," Sergeant Meadows said. "But given where she lives, I thought she might have a valid lead."

Daniel glanced at the address and sighed. Mrs. Hobson lived near Newgate. Daniel pulled out his watch and checked the time. It was past noon, and not only was he starving, he had hoped to speak to Jason. Deciding to call on Mrs. Hobson the next time he was in the area, Daniel decided to wait for the results of the autopsy. In truth, he didn't expect that the woman would have anything of value to tell him, but it would be negligent not to speak to her when she had made the time to travel to Scotland Yard.

Daniel had just made a mug of tea and settled at his desk when his office partner, Detective Yates, came in and dropped into his chair. He looked tired and irritable and reached for Daniel's as yet untouched mug, draining the contents in three long swallows.

"What's wrong, Yates?" Daniel asked. He was thoroughly irritated by the loss of his tea but also curious. Detective Yates was a stolid, experienced copper, not someone to give in to emotion or allow the cases he was working to affect his mood.

"What's right is the better question, Haze. Some days I feel like I'm battling Hydra. I cut off one head, and ten more emerge in its place."

"Care to elaborate?" Daniel asked, deeply surprised that Yates would have heard of the mythical beast, much less worked it into the conversation.

"London is a cesspool, my friend," Yates said. He sounded defeated. "Violent gangs are carving up the East End, Chinamen control the opium trade, and the Frogs are flooding the streets with cheap pornography. Half the women in this city are whores, and the other half live in a world where nothing bad ever happens and their most pressing concern is obtaining an appointment with the most fashionable modiste," Yates spat with disgust, "while their husbands step over dead children left in the gutters to get to the highest-rated brothels and sample the newest merchandise before someone beats them to the punch."

"Nothing new there," Daniel replied morosely, wondering where this tirade was leading.

"Oh, but there is something new," Yates said. He leaned forward and lowered his voice confidentially. "I heard it said that the new chief inspector will not be promoted from within."

"Ransome is bringing in his own man?"

"You can say that. Rumor has it he's offered the job to Redmond."

"Jason Redmond?" Daniel choked out.

"The very one."

"That's absurd."

"Is it? Constable Collins overheard Ransome in his office this morning, talking to your friend about this very thing," Yates said angrily. "Begging, almost."

Daniel thought he was going to be ill. How could Ransome bypass all the detectives who'd worked so hard to clean up London's streets and offer the position to Jason? Jason was without doubt capable and highly intelligent, but he had never expressed a desire to join the service. Jason was a surgeon, a doctor. He made a difference in his own way, and he liked it that way. He'd said so often enough. But perhaps Jason's priorities had changed.

"What did Lord Redmond say?" Daniel asked quietly.

"Turned him down flat, but Ransome wouldn't be deterred. Asked him to think it over for twenty-four hours."

"Did Lord Redmond agree?"

Yates nodded. "And you know what that means."

"What does it mean?"

"Means he's not quite decided, doesn't it? Perhaps with the right incentive…" Yates let the sentence trail off, but Daniel knew what he meant.

Everyone had their price, and maybe John Ransome had figured out Jason's. Daniel exploded out of his chair, grabbed his coat and hat, and strode from the building, ignoring several constables who tried to speak to him about the case. He'd go see Mrs. Hobson. Even if he learned nothing of value, he'd at least have sufficient time to cool off.

Chapter 30

Mrs. Hobson, when Daniel finally tracked her down, was selling eel pies in Newgate Street, her tray nearly empty after the midday rush. Daniel bought the remaining two pies and watched as the woman wearily removed the strap from around her neck and set the tray against the wall. She was no older than thirty, but her swollen ankles and work-roughened hands spoke of hardship and need.

"You came by Scotland Yard, Mrs. Hobson," Daniel said as he took a bite of the first pie, grateful to get something to eat at last.

"I did. I was in the area," Mrs. Hobson explained. "To collect the eels."

Daniel continued to eat his pie, giving the woman a chance to tell her story. She sighed and stepped from foot to foot, as if too tired to stand for a moment longer.

"I was out early on Tuesday morning. I sell bloaters on Mondays and Tuesdays, sheep's trotters on Wednesdays and Saturdays, and eel pies on Thursdays and Fridays," Mrs. Hobson explained.

Daniel nodded. He never purchased bloaters or sheep's trotters from street vendors, both because he didn't care for smoked herring or boiled sheep's cannon and because these dubious delicacies were too difficult to eat while working. But he did enjoy the eel pies, and this one was particularly delicious.

"You're very enterprising, Mrs. Hobson," Daniel said once he'd swallowed the remainder of the pie, impressed with the woman's drive.

Mrs. Hobson shrugged. "I do what I can to feed my children, Inspector. Since my husband died, I've had no one to share my burden."

Daniel nodded sympathetically. "What did you see, Mrs. Hobson?"

"I was walking past the prison, toward Old Bailey Street," the woman began.

"What time was this?"

"Just past four in the morning."

"Where were you going?" Daniel asked.

"I was heading toward Blackfriars Bridge. That's where I buy the herrings, at a stall near the river," Mrs. Hobson explained. "Best price per dozen, but you have to come real early, before they sell out. If I come first, I buy three dozen, so it's worth the early start. And that's when I saw her."

"Who did you see?"

"A woman. I didn't see her face. It was still dark, and she wore a veiled mourning bonnet and a black coat. She was the only other person about, so I couldn't help but notice her."

"Is that all?" Daniel asked. He'd finished both pies and took out his handkerchief to wipe his greasy hands.

"She had a basket slung over her arm, and she seemed frightened when she saw me."

"Did you notice anything else about her? Was she old or young? Stout or slender?"

"Difficult to guess her age," Mrs. Hobson mused. "She could have been anywhere from twenty to sixty, but she was most definitely in mourning. She wasn't very tall, maybe about my height, and not stout, but the way she was walking made me think she might be in pain."

"What made you think that?"

"She walked slow, careful-like."

"Did you see what was in the basket?" Daniel asked.

Mrs. Hobson shook her head. "It was shaped like a cabbage, but it was covered with a towel. I didn't see your appeal for information right away, Inspector Haze. It was only when I unwrapped the herrings from the newspaper that I saw the headline, and that thing in the basket came to mind. I'd think nothing of it if I saw that woman during the day. I'd think she was out shopping. Even those in deep mourning have to eat, but what would a respectable woman—and I reckon she was respectable, judging by the quality of her bonnet and coat—be doing near Newgate at that time of the morning?"

"That is a very good question, Mrs. Hobson," Daniel agreed. "A very good question, indeed."

"Was it helpful, what I told you?" Mrs. Hobson asked.

"It was. And it was kind of you to take the time to report this to Scotland Yard."

Mrs. Hobson's gaze softened, and she suddenly appeared a little less tired. "My husband was murdered, Inspector Haze. Robbed, beaten, and left to die in the gutter for the two bob those heartless ruffians took off him. They never caught whoever done it, so I wanted to keep some poor woman from suffering the torment I've had to live with these past five years, knowing my husband's killers have gone free."

"I'm sorry for your loss, Mrs. Hobson."

She nodded. "Well, I'd best be going now. I've got herrings to smoke and trotters to boil."

Mrs. Hobson did not expect a reward, but Daniel couldn't bear to walk away without thanking her in some small way. He took two sixpence coins out of his pocket and held them out to her. For one brief moment, Daniel thought she might refuse, but she gave a curt nod and pocketed the change. By her own admission, Mrs. Hobson had children to feed. She couldn't afford to be too proud.

"Best of luck to you," Daniel said, and walked away, feeling unbearably sorry for this sad, downtrodden woman who'd been robbed of her man.

Chapter 31

Daniel was out when Jason finished the postmortem, as was Ransome, who had yet to return from a meeting with the commissioner. Rather than wait around, Jason took himself off to a small but elegant restaurant in Queen Victoria Street. There, he enjoyed a well-deserved luncheon of poached salmon with cream dill sauce, roasted potatoes, and buttered peas, and permitted himself two glasses of red wine. The food served to forestall a bout of hypoglycemia—which, judging by the slight dimming of Jason's vision and the tremor in his hands, wasn't too far away—and the wine to take the edge off his anxiety.

The offer from Ransome had been as unexpected as it was flattering. Jason would be lying to himself if he refused to acknowledge that some small part of him wondered what it would be like to take on the position of chief inspector. Medicine was his first love, and he still derived great satisfaction from surgery, but his frustration with the hospital administration and the lack of regard for the patients' well-being exasperated him. Jason often found himself feeling more disheartened than rewarded after days spent at the hospital, particularly when a patient who'd had a fair chance of survival died because of shock or post-operative infection.

Jason pushed away his empty plate. He could always start his own practice, but he would still need access to an operating theater, competent nurses, and a ward where his patients could recover. He could hardly open his own hospital. Or could he? Setting up an operating theater would be a one-time investment, and there were plenty of trained nurses, both those who'd served in Crimea and graduates of Florence Nightingale's school of nursing at St. Thomas's Hospital. Jason preferred to work with experienced nurses, like Nurse Lowe, who was unflappable, but it would be nice to give the younger women a chance.

And he'd had a note from Flora Tarrant, whom he'd met during the investigation into the death of Roger Stillman. Flora wanted to relocate to London and had asked that Jason keep her in mind should he ever find himself in need of an assistant. Jason had liked Flora and thought she was just the sort of young woman who'd relish her independence. And Katherine would wholeheartedly approve of her since she was well acquainted with Flora's parents.

All in all, the scheme wasn't as far-fetched as Jason had first imagined. His grandfather had left him well provided for, and if he sold his parents' house in Washington Square, he would certainly have the freedom to do as he pleased for decades to come. But if he opened a private hospital, he'd have to forego involving himself in criminal investigations since he would no longer be just a surgeon but an administrator as well as an employer. He'd need to hire at least two other surgeons to assist him, nurses, porters, cleaners, and even a cook to cater to the patients in his care.

Shaking his head at the scope of such an undertaking, Jason realized that this was the first time he'd seriously considered selling the house in New York. That in itself was something he needed to think about in greater depth and discuss with Katie. Letting go of his childhood home meant that he might never return to the States, and he wasn't sure he was ready to make that decision, at least not today.

Jason left payment on the table and stepped outside. A private hospital was a nice dream, but he wasn't ready to assume such a commitment. He enjoyed the freedom to choose his cases and his ability to assist Scotland Yard. And most of all, he valued his friendship with Daniel. Whether he accepted the position of chief inspector or devoted himself entirely to medicine, his relationship with Daniel would change, and he simply wasn't ready to forsake a partnership that meant so much to him.

Still, this was too important a decision to make on the spur of the moment and by himself. He owed Katie the respect of discussing the offer with her and thought it was only fair to give her an opportunity to voice her feelings. Setting the subject aside for the time being, Jason returned to Scotland Yard, ready to share his findings with Daniel and Superintendent Ransome.

Chapter 32

"Mrs. Hobart would like to bury her husband," Ransome announced as soon as Jason entered his office and assumed his usual seat. Daniel was already there, his neck and shoulders rigid with tension, his foot tapping rhythmically against the parquet floor. Jason tried to catch his eye, but Daniel looked away, his jaw clenching with what could only be anger.

"Are we ready to release the body?" Ransome pressed.

"We are," Jason replied.

"I expect you have discovered nothing that alters your opinion on the cause of death, Lord Redmond?"

"The cause of death was blunt force trauma to the head, which led to an epidural hematoma. That's bleeding between the brain's protective lining and the skull," he added. "It is my conclusion that Philip Hobart was already deceased at the time of the beheading."

"Well, that's that, then." Ransome adopted the look of a man who had more important things to be getting on with, but Jason forestalled him.

"There's more, Superintendent."

"Oh?" Ransome asked, one eyebrow lifting in surprise.

"Philip Hobart had several historic fractures, which I believe were the result of beatings he'd endured in childhood and adolescence. He also had an enlarged liver but no yellowing of the skin or the whites of the eyes that happens when the individual is afflicted with liver disease."

"So, what caused the enlargement, and why is it important?" Daniel asked, his foot now still.

"It's important because I believe Philip Hobart had a type of cancer known as seminoma, which can be caused by cryptorchidism."

"And what might that be?" Ransome asked, looking at Jason with ill-disguised wariness.

"It's a medical term for undescended testes. In the case of Philip Hobart, the left testis was intra-abdominal, most likely a birth defect that did not affect his ability to engage in sexual congress but would have made him considerably less fertile. Combined with a testicular tumor that's as large as an egg and appears malignant, even to the naked eye, I'd say Philip Hobart was extremely unlikely to have fathered a child in the recent past."

"Are you saying the child that died wasn't his?" Ransome asked, the points of his moustache lifting comically as he considered this new and interesting possibility.

"I can't say with one hundred percent certainty that Philip Hobart was infertile, but it is very probable that someone else had fathered Samuel Hobart."

"What about his other son?" Ransome asked.

"Sons," Daniel corrected him. "Philip Hobart had another son from his marriage to Annie Hobart. Michael Pearson. Philip Hobart rejected the child at birth, believing him to be the son of his wife's lover, James Pearson. The Pearson family took Michael in, but having just met the boy, I'd say it's very likely that he's Philip Hobart's natural son."

"And Bram?" Jason asked. He had yet to meet Bram Hobart, so he couldn't venture a guess.

"Bram Hobart bears no obvious resemblance to his father, but he could take after his mother," Daniel replied. "And there was no photograph of Samuel at the Hobarts' residence, so it's impossible to comment on his paternity."

"If Mrs. Hobart had a lover, then the killing might have nothing to do with her husband's occupation," Ransome mused. "Leaving the head at Newgate could be a clever act of misdirection."

"I did discover something else when I autopsied the head, which might be significant," Jason interjected. "Fine white powder was trapped in the victim's nostrils and on his upper gums."

"Cocaine?" Ransome asked.

Jason shook his head. "The killer washed away the blood from the head wound and applied pomade in an attempt to cover up the injury before delivering the head to Newgate, but they didn't do as thorough a job on the face. It is my belief that when severed from the body, the head fell onto a surface that was covered with dust. I think that's an important clue."

"Dust? How on earth does that help us?" Ransome demanded irritably. "Is nothing about this case straightforward? The commissioner expects an imminent arrest, Haze," he snapped, directing his comment to a bewildered-looking Daniel. "This case is making the judiciary jittery, especially when the newspapers are publishing gruesome illustrations meant to increase their circulation at the expense of the victim. And there are those who are saying that Hobart deserved it."

Ransome glared at Daniel, since he didn't dare include Jason in his tirade. "Where will we be if the criminal element are led to believe that this murder was the result of Hobart's profession and declare open season on our public officials? Who will be next? The judges? The jailers? The police?" Ransome cried, his voice becoming shrill in his agitation.

"If you would allow me to finish, Superintendent," Jason said softly.

Ransome went quiet and had the decency to look shamed by his outburst. "Forgive me. I seem to have allowed the commissioner's concerns to rattle me. I have every confidence in my men." His gaze appeared to include Daniel in that statement, but Daniel shrank beneath his scrutiny, almost as if he'd imagined that Ransome was addressing Jason alone.

"The dust is gritty to the touch," Jason said, and waited for a reaction.

Ransome was none the wiser, but Daniel's reaction was immediate. "The worktable at the chemist's shop where Clyde Barkley works was covered with white dust. Might the dust be from crushed tablets?"

"Possibly," Jason replied. "I discovered a sprinkling of the same residue at the bottom of the barrel. I believe it came from the victim's trousers where the fabric had come in contact with the floor. Without tasting the powder, I can't be certain what it's from."

"Tasting it?" Ransome asked, his mouth turning down at the corners in disgust.

"It could be anything," Jason replied. "Tasting it could rule out a number of possibilities, but I'm not prepared to risk it."

"There was white dust on the floor at the Ferryman's cellar," Daniel said, his expression thoughtful. "It was near the baskets of oyster shells."

"I was thinking that as well," Jason said. "Given that the victim's body was discovered at the Ferryman and there was dust from crushed oyster shells at the scene, that's one more piece of physical evidence that connects Charles Dafoe to Philip Hobart's murder. However, it would be extremely helpful to know if Philip Hobart was aware of his illness."

"Why would that matter?" Ransome asked.

"Given the size of the tumor and its obvious malignancy, I should think that Philip Hobart was experiencing symptoms of the disease. If he was aware of the diagnosis, he would have most likely shared the news with those closest to him, such as his wife and son, and Charles Dafoe, who'd been his confidant since childhood," Jason speculated. "And if the killer knew that Hobart was ill, they could simply bide their time. The cancer would have killed him within a year."

"So what you're suggesting is that the killer was not someone close to the victim," Ransome said. "But Philip Hobart might not have told his loved ones of the cancer, even if he had known."

"I think those who knew him best would realize that he was ill," Jason said. "Even if they didn't know the extent of the malady."

"How would they know?" Daniel asked.

"Based on the appearance of several lymph nodes, I believe the cancer had metastasized. Spread," Jason added when both Ransome and Daniel looked nonplussed. "Philip Hobart would have lost weight and been experiencing loss of appetite, fatigue, and probably pain in his lower abdomen. Anyone who knew him well, like his wife and son, would notice the changes."

"Clyde Barkley didn't even know Philip Hobart had a small son or that Samuel had died," Daniel said. "He would not know of his superior's illness, even if Hobart himself was aware of his condition. Barkley had much to gain, and his uncle's workroom is covered in gritty white powder. Likewise, his mother is in mourning and seemed to have difficulty moving about."

"And how is that relevant?" Ransome asked.

"A street vendor I just interviewed saw a woman in mourning attire at about four in the morning on Tuesday. The woman carried a basket, its contents cabbage-shaped and covered with a towel, and just happened to be walking down Newgate Street, past the prison," Daniel explained. "Mrs. Hobson said the woman appeared to be in pain."

"A woman," Ransome drawled. "So this wasn't a one-man job."

"Doesn't appear that way, sir."

"What are your thoughts?" Ransome asked, addressing both Jason and Daniel. Jason let Daniel take the question since he was still considering what he'd just learned.

"Bram Hobart has inherited his father's estate, and his studio is covered in white marble dust," Daniel said. "However, if he knew of his father's illness, there was no need for him to hasten his death and risk his own life, particularly when he appears to be doing well for himself. He seems to have many lucrative commissions and was genuinely devastated by news of the murder."

Daniel considered the next suspect. "Charles Dafoe owed Philip Hobart a great deal of money, which he was in no position to repay. His wife is in deep mourning for their daughter and grandchild, and the baskets of oyster shells in the cellar could account for the white powder."

"Why do they have oyster shells?" Ransome asked.

"Crushed oyster shells are frequently used in both horticulture and construction," Jason said. "And the Dafoes have recently undertaken repairs to the building."

"And then there's Michael Pearson," Daniel mused. "He has an alibi for the night of the murder, but the alibi was provided by the girl he intends to marry, so there's no way to know if it's legitimate or simply an act of loyalty. His grandmother is in deep mourning for her son, who died recently, or the woman the vendor saw could have been the girl herself, Saskia Bekker, dressed to disguise her features. According to Charles Dafoe, Michael Pearson is handy with a lockpick, and he and Saskia are due to sail to America in a fortnight. Perhaps he thought he'd be long gone by the time the police connected him to Philip Hobart."

"All the suspects seem to be pointing fingers at each other," Ransome said. "But who had the most to gain from Philip Hobart's death, and what does the evidence tell us?"

"There's no arguing with a body in a barrel, sir," Daniel said.

"But would Charles Dafoe be foolish enough to leave the evidence sitting in his own cellar and then report it?"

"More to the point, would he be brazen enough to leave the evidence in his cellar and then report it?" Jason said.

Ransome fixed his dark gaze on Jason. "What's your take on this, Lord Redmond?"

"We have four men who stood to gain from Hobart's death and could have had a female accomplice. Clive Barkley had motive, means, and opportunity, but he had no way to ensure his succession to the post of principal hangman, nor would he have had access to the Ferryman's cellar unless he knew that Philip Hobart still carried a key he'd been given as a boy. And I doubt that he beheaded the man in his uncle's shop."

"All valid points. Go on," Ransome invited.

"Michael Pearson might be able to pick a lock and has a grandmother who's wearing mourning weeds, but why go through the trouble of staging such an elaborate display? He's about to leave for America with the girl he loves. Why kill his father now, especially when he doesn't stand to gain anything outright?"

"Revenge for the way he'd been treated all his life," Daniel said.

"Yes, but he could have simply hit Philip Hobart over the head and left him to die in the gutter. Why bother with the charade unless he had hoped to draw attention to someone else?"

"Such as?" Ransome asked.

"Either Charles Dafoe or his brother. But then why leave the remains in the Ferryman's cellar?" Jason replied.

"What would be Bram Hobart's motive for murdering his father?" Daniel asked. "And why would he behead the man and deliver the remains to Charles Dafoe? The two men had no disagreement that we know of."

"And why bother leaving the head at Newgate?" Ransome asked.

"Bram Hobart is certainly strong enough to have executed this plan, but I just can't conceive of a theory that would encompass all the evidence we have to date."

"I keep coming back to Charles Dafoe," Ransome said, his expression thoughtful. "And the evidence points directly to him." He folded down one finger. "Dafoe owed Philip Hobart money." The second finger went down. "The body was in his cellar, which only he and his wife had access to." Ransome folded down a third finger. "There's the grainy white powder from the oyster shells in the cellar and on the victim's clothes, nose, and gums." Fourth finger. "Mrs. Dafoe is in mourning and could have been the woman the vendor saw near Newgate on Tuesday morning." Ransome folded the final finger. "Charles Dafoe never expected the investigation to lead us to him, but when he realized he's a suspect, he reported the discovery of the body in order to deflect suspicion from himself. Then pointed us in the direction of Michael Pearson and made sure to tell Haze that the boy is handy with a lockpick and bears a grudge against his father."

"I agree with you, sir," Daniel said. "The evidence points to Charles Dafoe."

Ransome nodded decisively. "Bring him in, Haze. He's definitely our man."

"Yes, sir." Daniel pushed to his feet. He strode from Ransome's office and, after dispatching Constables Putney and Collins to pick up Charles Dafoe, walked out of the building without a backward glance.

Chapter 33

"Daniel, is something wrong?" Jason asked when he caught up with Daniel in the street.

"Were you even going to tell me?" Daniel growled, rounding on him. Jason had never seen him so angry, at least not with him.

"Tell you what?"

"Tell me about the offer Ransome made you. Is that why you are treating his wife, to get into his good graces? Was that the plan all along?"

Jason stared at Daniel, shocked to see the incandescent fury in his friend's eyes. "Is that what you really think?"

"I don't know, Jason. What else am I supposed to think?" Daniel retorted, but some of the heat had drained from his voice, possibly because Constable Ramsey had just stepped outside and was watching them, his brows furrowed in confusion.

"Daniel, I will forgive you this outburst because I know you're upset, but I would advise you to take a moment to consider what you're going to say next very carefully," Jason warned. Now he was angry as well and felt an overwhelming need to vindicate himself. "I operated on Laura Ransome because her life was in danger. Not now or at any time have I sought a position at Scotland Yard, nor have I ever done anything to undermine either your authority or your chance at advancement. I had not seriously considered taking the position Ransome offered me," Jason snapped. "But now I just might." He hadn't meant that last part, but it had just slipped out in anger, and the shock on Daniel's face made Jason feel ashamed. "How do you even know about the offer?"

Daniel lowered his gaze, his shoulders slumping with embarrassment. "Yates told me. It seems that Constable Collins overheard the conversation." Daniel looked truly miserable. "I had no right to speak to you that way. I was just taken unawares is all."

"I realize that, but instead of listening to gossip, you should have just come to me."

Daniel raised his gaze to meet Jason's. "I have my pride to get in the way of our friendship, and I'm deeply sorry to have offended you, Jason. I hope you can forgive me."

Jason sighed heavily. His gut feeling was to walk away and leave Daniel to come to terms with his feelings of resentment and inadequacy on his own, but if he walked away now, their friendship would never recover, and he wasn't ready for that to happen.

"Let's get a drink, Daniel," Jason said. "We can interview Charles Dafoe together once he's in custody."

Daniel nodded and smiled ruefully. "A drink would be nice," he said, and they set off for the nearest public house.

Jason suspected that Daniel wanted to discuss Ransome's offer in more depth but preempted him by returning to the case. If Jason were honest, he was still angry, and some part of him didn't want to let Daniel off the hook yet. And if he examined his self-awareness even further, he'd also have to admit that he didn't care to revisit Ransome's offer, not because it was unreasonable but because some part of him was excited by the prospect of accepting the job, and Jason couldn't bear to admit that to Daniel or have him guess.

"I'm not convinced that Charles Dafoe is the killer," Jason said once they were settled in a corner with their drinks before them. Jason had already had two glasses of wine, but given the way he was feeling, he allowed himself a half pint of cider, while Daniel had ordered a pint of bitter.

Daniel's eyebrows lifted in surprise. "But all the evidence points to Charles Dafoe. You heard Ransome, and he made a compelling argument."

"He did, but it's all just too neat, don't you think?"

"How do you mean?" Daniel asked.

"The remains could have been left in the cellar while the door was unlocked and the Dafoes were busy in the taproom. No one would think anything of someone delivering a barrel to a tavern. If that were the case, then Charles Dafoe told the truth, and the residue from the oyster shells never came in contact with the body. Likewise, his wife's mourning attire is not proof of anything, as Mrs. Barkley, Mrs. Hobart, and Mrs. Pearson are all in mourning."

"If you're correct, then that puts Bram Hobart, Clyde Barkley, and Michael Pearson back in the frame for murder," Daniel said. "Perhaps Clyde Barkley knew more of the victim's life than he was willing to admit, and Michael Pearson has lived nearby his whole life. He'd be intimately familiar with the goings on at the Ferryman, especially since his own home is a tavern."

"I don't think it's Clyde Barkley," Jason replied. "Or Michael Pearson."

"But what reason would Bram Hobart have to murder his father and stage such a bit of theater?"

"Aside from the inheritance, you mean?" Jason asked. "I'd say there might be another, much more personal reason."

Daniel stared at him, and Jason watched as Daniel tried to work out what he was referring to. "Come on," Jason said, and drained his glass. "I think we have a sculptor's studio to visit."

Chapter 34

If Bram Hobart was surprised to see them, he didn't show it. Instead, he offered a bland smile of welcome.

"Inspector Haze, to what do I owe the pleasure?" he asked.

"Mr. Hobart, this is my associate, Dr. Redmond. He performed the postmortem on your father's remains."

"Good afternoon, Mr. Hobart. I'm sorry for your loss," Jason said.

"Thank you, Dr. Redmond."

Bram didn't ask any questions about the postmortem or inquire why the man who'd autopsied his father was now in his studio. Given his lack of curiosity, Daniel saw no reason to enlighten him, not when any carelessly shared bit of information could tip Bram off to the true purpose of their visit.

"You never mentioned you had another brother," Daniel said as Bram turned his attention back to his current commission.

"You mean Michael?" Bram tossed over his shoulder.

"Yes, Michael Pearson."

Bram lowered the hand holding the chisel and sighed. "I saw no reason to bring Michael into it. He'd suffered enough at my father's hands."

"So you believe he is your father's son," Daniel said.

"Without a doubt. He resembles my father more in both character and appearance than I ever did."

"And you believe Michael is innocent of your father's murder?" Jason asked conversationally.

"Absolutely. Michael had nothing to gain by our father's death."

"But he did," Jason replied. "If you are the devoted brother you pretend to be, then surely you would include Michael in the distribution of your father's assets."

Bram shrugged, as if the thought had never occurred to him. "Of course Michael will receive his portion, but I have yet to learn just how much we're dealing with. I thought it best to wait until after the funeral to discuss the contents of my father's will."

"Is there a will?" Jason asked.

"Yes." Bram shot him a quizzical look. "Why wouldn't there be?"

"And is the will recent?" Daniel asked.

"I really don't know. What are you getting at, Inspector?"

"Nothing at all, Mr. Hobart. I was just wondering if your father had updated his will recently."

"Why would he?" Bram asked.

"Did you know he was ill at the time of his death?" Jason asked.

"No. He never mentioned he was unwell."

"And Mrs. Hobart? She never shared her concerns with you?"

"She would hardly confide in me in my father's presence," Bram replied. He seemed confused by Jason's question but didn't probe his reasons for asking.

"Did you never see Lucy privately?" Daniel queried.

Bram followed the direction of Daniel's gaze, which was squarely fixed on the delicate face of the angel he was sculpting. Daniel now knew exactly who the angel reminded him of.

Bram smiled coyly. "Lucy posed for me a few times. I was in need of a female model but couldn't afford to hire one. The reputable ones don't come cheap."

"It's an admirable likeness. Has she seen it?"

"No. My stepmother hasn't been to the studio since before Samuel died."

"There's nothing more difficult to bear than the loss of a child," Daniel said.

He hadn't meant to give so much of himself away, but his voice cracked, and he felt the familiar ache in his chest. Felix was never far away from his thoughts, even if he chose to pretend otherwise.

"No, there isn't. Lucy really hasn't been herself since Sam's death," Bram replied carefully.

"Mr. Hobart, may we look around your studio?" Daniel asked.

"What are you looking for?" Bram asked. His tone was light and inquisitive, and most people would have taken his reaction at face value, but Daniel was no longer a novice. He could tell that Bram's indifference was affected.

"We'll let you know when we find it," Daniel replied, matching his tone to Bram's. "Don't let us keep you from your work."

Bram Hobart shrugged. "Very well. Do let yourselves out when you're finished, gentlemen." He turned back to the angel that seemed to rise from the stone as if it were casting aside its earthly bonds. Part of the blade was visible now, and the sword trapped in stone reminded Daniel of an old Arthurian legend. The reference seemed strangely appropriate now that Daniel knew what Jason had inferred from the postmortem.

Leaving Bram Hobart to his work, Jason headed toward the back, while Daniel started by the door and strolled slowly between the rows of urns and statues, his gaze sweeping the floor and every visible surface. As before, a layer of fine dust covered the flagstones, but Daniel saw nothing suspicious until his gaze alighted on a life-size statue wrapped in sacking and lying on the handcart he'd seen on his first visit. The statue could easily pass for a body, just as a body could pass for a statue.

"Kindly help me lift the statue, Mr. Hobart," Daniel called out to the sculptor.

"That's a finished order ready to be collected by the client," Bram Hobart replied irritably.

"I'm not interested in the order, just the cart."

Bram nodded curtly and walked over to where Daniel waited for him. Together they lifted the wrapped statue and set it on the floor, leaving the cart for Daniel to examine. The mattress Bram used to cushion the bed of the cart still held the indentation of the statue's curves, but there were no obvious stains or anything that might be organic matter. The mattress was constructed of stuffed burlap and was about six feet long and three feet wide, big enough to hold a life-size statue or a fully grown person.

Daniel flipped the mattress and studied the underside, then ran his finger over a brown smudge near the top. If he was to lie on his back, his head would be in just about the same spot and would correspond to the location of the wound on the back of Philip Hobart's head. Daniel turned to Bram, but the sculptor was calm, amusement crinkling the corners of his eyes.

"Whose blood is that?" Daniel asked.

"Mine." Bram held out his hand to show Daniel a scabbed-over cut on the back of his hand. "I stained the padding when I was setting down the statue."

"But the blood is on the underside," Daniel pointed out.

"I didn't want the client to see it, so I turned the mattress over," Bram replied with exaggerated patience.

Much as Daniel wanted to make more of the stain, Bram had given him a plausible explanation. When dealing with tools and sharp bits of stone, he probably nicked himself quite often. Daniel nodded, and the two men replaced the wrapped statue on the cart.

"Why do you think I killed my father, Inspector Haze?" Bram asked as he returned to his angel and picked up the chisel he'd been using to sculpt the sword from the marble.

Daniel was just about to reply when Jason called out to him from the storeroom. "Can you come in here, Daniel?"

"What did you find?" Daniel asked when he entered the storeroom, a visibly annoyed Bram Hobart close on his heels.

It was a rectangular room that ran the length of the studio. A worktable was set against the far wall, and there was a shelving unit that took up the longest wall. It contained tools, pots of paint, small chunks of marble that were perhaps used to carve small items such as stars or spheres, carelessly arranged blueprints, and a leatherbound ledger.

"Please don't touch anything, Dr. Redmond," Bram said irritably.

Jason ignored him. "I found several things," he said.

Daniel was surprised to find a sword in Jason's hand, his elegant fingers gripping the hilt with practiced ease. For some odd reason, Daniel found it perfectly natural when Jason used the blade to point toward an elongated crate, looking for all the world like the Archangel Michael about to skewer Satan.

Bram Hobart stared at Jason as if he were a madman. "Why are you even here, Dr. Redmond?" Bram demanded. "What's your role in this?"

"I examined your father's remains, Mr. Hobart," Jason replied coolly as he laid the sword on the worktable. "And I know that you killed him."

Bram paled but didn't budge from his spot by the door. "And what makes you think I murdered my father?"

"You brought your father's body back to the studio after you hit him over the head. I expect you used the sacking you normally use to wrap your statues and placed his body on the cart. You then unwrapped him, laid his body atop this crate, and used the sword to behead him. I assume you use this sword as the subject for the blades you carve out of marble, but this weapon is surprisingly sharp and looks to have been sharpened and cleaned recently."

Bram smirked. "And what have you got to support this outlandish theory, Doctor?"

Jason used his foot to push the crate back a few inches. A brown substance had seeped into the spaces between the square flagstones of the floor. Jason bent down and picked up several black hairs that had been stuck to the dried blood.

"I'm fairly certain this hair matches the hair on your father's head," Jason said. "The strands were split when you lopped off his head. And the marble dust that covers every inch of this space got up his nostrils and into his mouth when the head fell to the floor and rolled over. Some also got on his trousers, since the crate is not long enough to support the entire body and the knees rested against the floor."

Jason cocked his head to the side and smiled at Bram in a way that chilled Daniel's blood. "There wasn't too much blood when you severed the head, since the victim was already dead, but some stained the collar of the victim's shirt and soaked in between the flagstones. You tried to clean it but weren't able to get it all out, so you covered the spot with the crate."

Bram Hobart shrugged. "That is pure supposition," he said calmly.

Jason turned to the shelf of supplies behind him and picked up a round tin with a familiar cover. He held it up. "Bixby's Pomade for Gentlemen," Jason announced. He opened the tin and showed the contents to Daniel and Bram Hobart. More than half the pomade had been used, and finger tracks were clearly visible in the waxy mass.

"You don't use pomade, Mr. Hobart," Jason said, eyeing Bram Hobart's shaggy, overgrown hair. "But your father did, and you thought it would work nicely to disguise the wound on his head, the actual cause of death. I expect you got this from your father's house, since you didn't want to be seen buying pomade from a local shop."

Bram Hobart stared at Jason balefully but didn't say anything, so Jason set the tin back and continued.

"Once you prepared the head, you laid it in a basket and gave it to your accomplice to deliver to Newgate on her way home. The next day, you procured a barrel and stuffed the body inside while you were still able to bend his limbs."

Jason's gaze never left Bram Hobart's face as he continued. "I assume you used the handcart and your father's key to get into the Dafoes' cellar, then cleverly fed Inspector Haze the story of the unpaid debt, thereby giving Charles Dafoe a motive and setting him up for your father's murder."

Daniel took up a position close to the door in case Bram tried to flee, but Bram stood perfectly still, his eyes blazing with anger.

"So why don't you tell us why I killed him, Dr. Redmond," Bram taunted. "Since you seem to have figured out everything else. Erroneously, I might add. What's my motive?"

"That's the most obvious part," Jason replied. "You were having an affair with your stepmother, and Samuel was most likely yours. Did your father finally catch on to what was going on right under his nose?"

Bram Hobart's response was lightning swift. He lunged for the sword, his fingers wrapping around the hilt with murderous intent. At that moment, Daniel saw a man who had nothing left to lose. Bram's gaze was wild, his teeth bared, and his fury directed toward the person who'd dared to stoke it. Bram charged, and the blade glinted dully as he thrust the sword at Jason, both hands now gripping the hilt for maximum impact. Neither Daniel nor Jason was armed, and even if they had been, there wouldn't have been enough time to draw and point the weapon. Daniel's only chance of saving Jason was to unbalance his attacker, since Jason had nowhere to go, boxed in as he was by the worktable and the shelves.

Daniel threw himself at Bram Hobart, his only thought to alter the blade's trajectory before it reached his friend. Seeing his chance, Jason twisted out of the way as much as the narrow space would allow. Bram howled with rage as he was knocked sideways, the blade missing Jason by mere inches and glancing off a hunk of marble with a bloodcurdling screech. Despite losing his balance, Bram didn't let go of the sword. He righted himself effortlessly and charged again, this time at Daniel, who stood between Bram and the door, his only chance at escape.

Daniel froze, unable to move as the blade sliced through the air, aimed at his chest. His limbs felt leaden, and his thoughts were as thick as treacle, all fusing into one incoherent mass, but his brain offered him one last gift. Daniel saw Sarah holding Charlotte, her eyes shining with love. Charlotte's little hand was splayed across Sarah's breast, her silky dark curls framing her cherubic face, her dark gaze fixed on her mother. Daniel smiled at the memory and wondered woozily if this was the last thing he'd ever see, but then both the thought and the image were knocked from his head as he hit the floor hard, his temple colliding with the corner of the crate that had been used to behead Philip Hobart.

Bram Hobart's body landed on top of him, forcing the air from Daniel's chest and slamming his head against the flagstone floor.

Daniel's head tolled like a bell and his vision dimmed at the edges as he fought to remain conscious. Operating on pure instinct, his body tensed, bracing for the excruciating pain of the blade piercing his organs and nailing him to the floor. But the pain didn't come, so Daniel permitted himself to shut his eyes and lie still for a moment. He heard thudding sounds and cries of pain, but even when he finally managed to open his eyes, he couldn't comprehend what was happening. His vision was blurred, and his thoughts seemed to form a tiny vortex, swirling like tea when he stirred in the sugar with one of those little spoons Sarah had liked so much.

Bram's weight was removed, and only then was Daniel finally able to draw breath. The fog began to clear from his mind, and he raised his head off the floor, surprised to find Bram Hobart slumped against the wall, his face white with agony. He was trembling violently, and his right arm appeared to hang at an odd angle.

Jason once again set the sword aside and spoke matter-of-factly. "Your shoulder is dislocated, Mr. Hobart. I will set it for you before we take you into custody."

Daniel stared at the two men, then shakily got to his feet. He could only assume that Jason had grabbed Hobart's wrist and wrenched his arm behind him with such force that he had dislocated the man's shoulder. Had the sword not fallen to the floor when Jason twisted the man's arm, Hobart might have sliced Jason's face or chest open.

Daniel breathed a sigh of relief when he ascertained that Jason wasn't hurt, but he did note that his friend looked shaken. Jason had balled his hands into fists, probably to stop them shaking, and took several deep breaths. After a few moments, his normal color returned and he relaxed his hands, ready to deal with the aftermath of Bram Hobart's attack.

Hobart remained immobile, his forehead glistening with perspiration, his lips white with suffering. Daniel could smell the rank odor of his sweat and had just enough time to turn away before he vomited all over the floor in the corner.

"Sit down, Daniel," Jason growled. "You're probably concussed."

Daniel wanted to protest, but he felt weak and dizzy, so he sat down on the crate and leaned against the wall, closing his eyes once again to stop the room from spinning. He needed a moment.

"Daniel, are you all right? Are you going to be sick again?" Jason asked.

"I'm fine. Just let me sit here for a minute."

"Keep your eyes open," Jason instructed.

Daniel forced his eyes open, even though all he really wanted was to go to sleep. It would have been so nice to lie in his bed, pull the coverlet up to his chin, and drift away. Perhaps he would even see Sarah again, but he had to follow Jason's instructions if he hoped to remain alert and walk out of Bram Hobart's studio on his own two feet. It was easier said than done though. His eyes seemed to close of their own accord, and he slumped further down the wall.

"Daniel," Jason barked. "Look at me."

"Stop yelling," Daniel muttered. "I can hear you."

"Dr. Redmond, please," Bram Hobart moaned.

Jason shot him a look that said he'd deal with him when he was good and ready, but the doctor in him prevailed. He couldn't bear to leave anyone in pain. A blood-curdling scream tore from Bram Hobart when Jason wrenched his shoulder back into its socket. Bram's breathing was ragged, and Daniel thought the man might be crying, but Daniel had closed his eyes again and didn't open them until Jason pulled up his lids and stared into his eyes, as if he could see inside Daniel's brain.

"You'll be all right," Jason said. "You hit your head hard, but I don't think there's any serious damage."

"How do you know?" Daniel asked weakly.

"I don't. I'm just being optimistic."

"Oh," was all Daniel could manage.

"I don't think it will be necessary to cuff Hobart," Jason said. "He's as weak as a newborn kitten."

Daniel nodded. He didn't feel much stronger than a kitten himself, but the nausea had passed, and his thoughts were once again arranging themselves into a logical pattern.

"We need to get him to the Yard," Daniel said.

Jason nodded and hauled Bram to his feet. "One wrong move, and I'll dislocate your shoulder again," Jason promised, and Daniel was in no doubt that he meant it.

"You are like no doctor I ever met," Bram grumbled.

"And you're like no son I've ever encountered," Jason replied. "Why'd you kill your father? Surely there were other ways to resolve your differences."

"I killed him because he didn't deserve to live," Bram replied. He sounded a little stronger, and Daniel saw anger flare in his eyes. Daniel hoped Bram would explain his answer, but he didn't elaborate.

"Let's go," Bram said instead. "I'm ready. And I'm not going to fight."

Daniel found a length of sacking and wrapped the sword, then followed Jason and Bram Hobart outside.

Once they got Hobart to Scotland Yard, Daniel handed him over to Sergeant Meadows and turned to Jason, who watched warily as the man was led down to the cells.

"I think we should speak to Lucy Hobart before we interview Bram," Jason said.

Daniel nodded. "I agree. When presented with the evidence, she will either confess or lie to protect her lover. Either way, we'll have a clearer idea of what happened to bring about Philip Hobart's death. Should we speak to her at home, do you think?"

"I think it would be best to interview her in a more formal setting. She might be more willing to tell us the truth when faced with the possibility of an arrest."

"I have Charles Dafoe down in the cells," Sergeant Meadows said when he returned to the foyer. "I think he's itching to have a go at Bram Hobart."

"Let him go." Daniel turned to Constable Collins, who'd just appeared at the end of the corridor. "Constable, I need you to bring in Mrs. Hobart."

"Right, guv. On my way."

"I'll accompany him, in case Mrs. Hobart feels unwell," Jason volunteered. Daniel turned toward the door, but Jason forestalled him. "I want you to have a cup of strong, sweet tea and lie down in the cells until I return. Don't go to sleep. Just rest for a while. Sergeant Meadows, please have someone keep an eye on Inspector Haze. He took a hard knock on the head."

"Yes, sir," Sergeant Meadows replied, and grinned in a way that suggested Daniel wasn't going to get a moment's peace.

Daniel knew better than to argue, so he nodded his assent and took himself off.

Chapter 35

Daniel felt considerably better by the time Jason returned. He'd spent a peaceful hour down in the cells, and the tea and sausage roll Constable Putney had brought him went a long way toward restoring him. Daniel had thought that Bram Hobart might try to reason with him, but Bram remained silent, which was just as well, since there was nothing he could say that would help him evade a charge of murder.

When Daniel joined Jason and Lucy Hobart in the interview room, he was shocked by how pale and drawn Lucy looked in the sullen light of the late afternoon, her gaze radiating anxiety.

"Inspector Haze, why am I here?" she cried as soon as Daniel assumed his seat. "Dr. Redmond wouldn't tell me anything."

Lucy Hobart wasn't cuffed, even though she had to be Bram Hobart's accomplice and the woman Mrs. Hobson had seen outside the prison on Tuesday morning. There was little possibility of her running when both Jason and Daniel were in the room and Constable Collins just outside.

"Mrs. Hobart, I apologize for the lack of an explanation," Daniel said solicitously. "But we have some questions to put to you."

"What sort of questions?"

"We arrested your stepson for the murder of your husband," he said, his gaze never leaving Lucy Hobart's face.

She went even paler, her eyes widening in shock. "You arrested Bram? Why?"

"Because we found traces of blood in his studio, as well as the sword he'd used to behead his father. There was also the pomade he had used to cover up the head wound that killed him."

"The blood can be anyone's, and Bram uses the sword as a prop," Lucy Hobart said, striving to keep calm. "And anyone could have hit Philip over the head."

"But it wasn't anyone. It was Bram Hobart, and he will hang for murder," Daniel replied. "And I think the reason he murdered his father was you."

Lucy looked like she was going to be ill, but Daniel didn't acknowledge her distress. Instead, he waited, curious to see what explanation she would come up with to exonerate her lover.

"Bram didn't kill his father," Lucy choked out at last.

"No? Then who did?" Jason asked, his tone inquisitive rather than accusing.

"It was an accident," Lucy cried.

"Why would anyone go to such lengths to cover up an accident?"

"Bram did it to protect me. He was afraid I'd be charged with murder."

"You would not be charged with murder if you hadn't committed one, Mrs. Hobart," Daniel said. "How did your husband die?"

"Philip had not been well these past few months. He suffered from a lack of appetite and was always very tired toward the evening. He frequently felt dizzy and nauseated."

Daniel nodded. This corresponded with what Jason had said about Philip Hobart's condition. "Go on."

Lucy Hobart drew a steadying breath. "On the night he died, he stood up too quickly, lost his balance, and fell. His head hit the edge of the mantel."

"So why did you think you'd be charged with murder, Mrs. Hobart?" Daniel asked. "If that's what really happened, his death would be easily explained."

"Because that isn't what happened," Jason said. He bent down and extracted a heavy silver candlestick from a sack at his feet. The candlestick had a scrolled square base with pointed corners. "I retrieved this from your drawing room after Constable Collins escorted you outside, Mrs. Hobart. You had cleaned it well, but some blood remained trapped inside the scrollwork. I imagine a good polish would have taken care of that, but you didn't want to ask Hattie to polish the candlesticks immediately after your husband's death and it would have looked odd if you decided to polish them yourself. Hattie would have become suspicious, and given that she's disgruntled already, she might have used that information against you."

Lucy Hobart stared at him, as if realizing for the first time that he was on to her and this wasn't a voluntary interview that would end with her returning home.

"You hit your husband over the head with this candlestick," Jason said as he weighed the candlestick experimentally in his hand. "It's heavy enough to crack someone's skull, and I imagine you applied considerable force because you were angry."

"Why would I be angry?" Lucy whispered.

"I imagine Mr. Hobart found out about your affair with his son. Perhaps he threatened you, or maybe even hit you in his anger, which would explain your careful gait. You're in pain," Daniel said, and Lucy's eyes brimmed with tears. "You were frightened, so you grabbed the first thing you had to hand and bashed him over the head," Daniel continued, but out of the corner of his eye, he could see Jason shaking his head.

"You hit him from behind," Jason said, "which leads me to believe that your husband never saw it coming. It was either premeditated or you attacked him after an argument had already finished. Did he hurt you, Mrs. Hobart?"

Lucy Hobart cried softly, tears sliding down her pale cheeks and dripping onto the black crape of her gown.

"I didn't know what I was doing until it was too late," she whimpered. "I was so overcome with grief and rage that I acted on impulse."

"What did your husband do to incite such a reaction?" Jason asked softly.

"He murdered Sammy," Lucy wailed. "He held a pillow over his face until he suffocated."

"And why did he do that? Was it because he discovered that the child wasn't his?" Daniel asked.

Lucy nodded. "As I said, Philip had not been well for months. I begged him to see a physician, and he finally agreed. Had I known how that visit would change our lives, I never would have suggested it."

"And what did the physician tell him, Mrs. Hobart?" Jason asked.

"Philip was always in robust health," Lucy said. "He was hardly ever ill, and he never saw a doctor when he was a young man." She drew a shuddering breath. "The doctor examined him. That was when he found the tumor in his…" She couldn't bring herself to name the part of her husband's anatomy that had been affected. "He told Philip that it's unlikely that he'd fathered Samuel." Lucy was sobbing now, her narrow shoulders quaking as she wrapped her arms about her middle.

"Did your husband suspect that you were carrying on with Bram before his visit to the doctor?" Daniel asked. Lucy shook her head.

"Did he confront you about the affair after?" Jason asked.

"Not directly, but I caught him watching me and Bram. And he seemed colder to Samuel."

"Did Samuel bear a resemblance to his natural father?"

Lucy nodded. "He looked more like Bram every day."

"So what happened on Monday night?" Daniel asked. "Samuel has been gone for some weeks now. Did you always suspect that your husband might have had a hand in his death?"

"Not for a moment. I told Philip at dinner that I was going to go to Bram's studio the following day, to sit for him. I had modeled for Bram in the past. Philip knew that. He'd never lost his temper with me before, but that enraged him. I'd never seen him so angry. He said that if he was to go to his grave knowing he'd been so thoroughly betrayed by his wife and his son, then there was something I should know. He took Sammy from us because he was the one thing we both loved so dearly. He had suffocated him with a pillow."

"But you didn't hit him then," Jason said. "Your husband went out after supper."

Lucy nodded. "He went to the Queen's Arms. That's where he normally went when he wanted a drink. I thought he might go to the Ferryman, but I don't suppose he wanted Charles Dafoe to know the truth of his life. And Charles would have realized something was wrong. He'd known Philip since he was a boy."

"What happened then?" Daniel asked.

"I had a word with Hattie. I needed to make certain she hadn't overheard what was said, and I didn't think she had. She was tired and wanted only to finish in the kitchen and retire to her room. I retired as well, but I couldn't go to bed. Knowing what Philip had done had broken something in me. What he'd done was monstrous," Lucy cried. "Evil. He was no better than his father."

"So, what did you do?" Jason asked.

"I went downstairs and had a drink. Then another. I needed something to dull the pain, but nothing could erase the agony of knowing that Sammy's death was my fault. I couldn't spend another day married to Philip, nor did I think he deserved to live, not even one more day. I had betrayed him, yes, but he had murdered an innocent child. So I waited for Philip to come back. I grabbed the candlestick and stood behind the drawing room door when I heard him come in. I knew he'd come into the drawing room to turn off the lamps. When he entered, I hit him over the head. He staggered, then turned and lunged for me. He slammed me into the doorjamb, then pushed me to the floor and kicked me in the stomach. I thought he was going to kill me."

"And then?" Daniel inquired. He could picture it all in his mind and feel the churning fury, fear, and grief Lucy Hobart must have felt that night.

"He collapsed, and I knew he was dead. Once I realized what I had done, I was terrified. I had committed murder. I cleaned up the blood, wiped the candlestick, and put it back on the mantel. Then I laid Philip on the settee, making it look as if he'd fallen asleep, in case Hattie came down and saw him in the drawing room. I even had the presence of mind to cover the pillow so that the blood from the wound wouldn't leave a stain," Lucy said. She seemed to wonder at her own ingenuity before she continued. "I ran all the way to Bram's studio. He always worked late, so I knew he'd be there. I told him what had happened. He was horrified and shocked, but he didn't fault me for what I had done. He brought the cart he uses for his orders and some sacking and took Philip's body away. I went back to the studio with him. I couldn't bear to remain in that house."

"You were the one to leave the basket on the steps of Newgate," Jason said. "You were seen."

Lucy nodded. "We didn't know how to explain Philip's sudden absence, so Bram came up with a plan. He said that if we left the head at Newgate, the police would assume the murder had something to do with a past case and never look at us too closely. And it was his idea to cover up the head wound. He asked me to bring Philip's jar of pomade."

"Were you there when Bram beheaded the body?" Daniel asked, curious if this fragile-looking woman had stood by and watched her lover desecrate her husband's corpse.

"No. I stepped outside. I couldn't bear to look. Bram handed me a covered basket and told me what to do. I have no recollection of getting to the prison or coming home afterward," Lucy confessed.

"You were in shock," Jason said.

"Yes, I suppose I must have been. I woke up in my own bed the next morning, dressed, and went downstairs. Pretending everything was normal was the hardest thing I've ever had to do."

"Thank you, Mrs. Hobart," Daniel said. "I think we've heard enough." He stood and walked to the door. "Take Mrs. Hobart down to the cells, Constable," he instructed Constable Collins. "And bring Mr. Hobart to the interview room."

"Yes, sir."

"I can't help but feel pity for her," Jason said as soon as Lucy Hobart was out of earshot. "Philip Hobart's death is a form of justice. To kill that child was an act of unfathomable cruelty."

"We can't go taking justice into our own hands."

"She could easily have gotten away with it had Bram Hobart not interfered," Jason mused.

"You reckon?"

"It would be difficult to prove that the blow to the head was not the result of an accident, especially if Mrs. Hobart had the presence of mind to dispose of the candlesticks or have Hattie polish them. Had the police not been summoned, she could have buried her husband, and no one would have been the wiser. In his desire to protect his love, Bram Hobart has sentenced her to death."

"Do you think he realizes that?" Daniel asked.

“I’m sure the thought has crossed his mind.”

Their conversation was cut short by the arrival of the man himself.

Chapter 36

When Bram Hobart was ushered into the interview room, he looked as if he'd just seen a ghost, which in essence he had. Given her confession, Lucy Hobart wasn't long for this world, since no judge, no matter how compassionate, would absolve her of murder. Bram took a seat and nailed Daniel with a gaze that crackled with defiance.

"Lucy. Is. Innocent," he announced. He enunciated each word, as if that made them true.

"Mrs. Hobart has confessed to murder," Daniel replied calmly.

"She's trying to protect me," Bram said with equal calm. "I killed my father."

"How did you kill him?"

"I hit him over the head with a candlestick."

Jason shook his head. "You didn't."

"And how can you possibly know that?" Bram demanded. "It was me. I struck him after he confronted me about my relationship with Lucy."

"You are taller than Philip Hobart by at least three inches," Jason said. "Therefore, the angle and the position of the wound would have been quite different had you been the one to strike him. The blow was administered by someone who's much shorter than you."

"That's absolute bollocks," Bram retorted furiously.

"The postmortem results say different. They support Lucy's version of what happened."

"The results of the postmortem are nothing more than an educated guess. I can demand a second postmortem, and if the surgeon challenges your conclusions, you'll have nothing."

"We have a murder, a weapon, and a very compelling motive," Daniel replied. "And if we ask Mrs. Hobart to pick up the candlestick and swing it at someone of a similar height to your father's, the head wound would be in approximately the same spot. Lucy murdered your father when she discovered that he'd smothered Samuel."

"There's no proof Samuel was murdered. My father was taunting Lucy because he wanted to punish her for loving me instead of him. They argued, but I was the one to kill him," Bram insisted. "I wanted to set her free."

"Mr. Hobart, I can obtain an exhumation order for your son," Daniel said.

Bram Hobart seemed to shrink into himself at the mention of an exhumation. "And how would you be able to prove that he was murdered?"

"Every act of violence leaves discernable scars," Jason said.

"Please, don't disturb my son's grave," Bram said hoarsely.

"We will if we have to," Daniel replied.

Jason thought Daniel was being unnecessarily cruel. They had their confession and a continuous, plausible chain of events. There was no need to torture these bereaved parents. Bram Hobart obviously thought the same because all the fight seemed to go out of him.

"It would finish Lucy if she thought Sammy was exhumed and carved up. I will tell you whatever you want to know."

Daniel sighed, and Jason knew he was relieved not to have to carry out his threat. Only a man who'd lost a child could understand the pain of having their child's remains disturbed. "Tell us everything, from the beginning," Daniel said.

Bram nodded. "I never thought my father would remarry. It's not that he had been so devoted to my mother; it's just that he had little use for women, or for anyone, really. There was an aloofness about him, a detachment no one could quite penetrate. I thought it was the natural effect of his work, but I don't believe he ever cared much about the people whose lives he took, not enough to be affected by their deaths, at any rate.

Bram drew a ragged breath, as if recalling those times when he had been alone with a man who never quite noticed him. "My father was a solitary man, and the only person he seemed to genuinely want to spend time with was Charles Dafoe. Maybe it was that he felt a debt of gratitude to the Dafoes for taking him in when he had no one in the world, or that he'd forged a bond with Charles before he shut himself off to anyone or anything that might touch his soul."

Bram went silent for a moment, his gaze fixed on his cuffed wrists. "Everything changed when he met Lucy. For us both. Father was smitten. I don't know if it was her youth or beauty, but he was determined to have her, and have her he did. Incidentally, Lucy is the daughter of Graham Cornett," Bram announced, and watched Daniel and Jason eagerly as he waited for a reaction.

"Graham Cornett?" Daniel repeated, as if needing to reassure himself that he'd heard correctly. "*The* Graham Cornett?"

Jason turned to Daniel, hoping for an explanation. He'd never heard of Graham Cornett, but Daniel obviously had, and the name meant something to him.

"Graham Cornett was hanged five years ago," Daniel said. "He was convicted of murdering his wife and three daughters. Slit their throats while they slept."

"What was his motive?" Jason asked, horrified by the scene Daniel had just painted.

"He never gave a reason for his actions. He simply came home one day, waited until his womenfolk were asleep, and murdered them in their beds."

"But not Lucy?"

"Lucy was seventeen at the time," Bram said. "And she was the one to discover the bodies."

"Why did he spare her?" Jason asked.

"Presumably because he needed someone to keep house for him," Bram said bitterly.

"So your father met Lucy after the execution?" Daniel asked.

"Before. Lucy came to see him."

"What did she want? A quick death for the man who'd slaughtered her mother and sisters?" Jason asked angrily.

"No. She wanted him to suffer. She was willing to give my father everything she had that was of any value if he would prolong Cornett's suffering. She also asked that he untie his hands. She wanted to see him fight for breath, claw at the rope, and jerk like a marionette. She wanted vengeance."

"Did your father oblige?" Daniel asked.

"He didn't want the few coins Lucy could scrape together or the silver ring that had belonged to her mother. He wanted Lucy herself. So he tied Cornett's hands loosely enough that the man was able to free them. Public hangings had yet to be outlawed, so the crowd got quite a show that day."

"And Lucy agreed to marry your father in exchange?" Jason asked. He was appalled by this bartering of lives, but he was in no position to comprehend Lucy's frame of mind at the time.

Bram shot Jason an angry look, no doubt furious that Jason was judging the woman he loved. "Lucy had nowhere to go and nothing to fall back on. She had nothing to recommend her for a respectable position, and no one would allow a convicted murderer's daughter into their home. My father offered her a life of safety and comfort. And aching loneliness," Bram added. "She was an ornament. My father's property, just like the candlestick she used to bash him over the head. He hardly ever spoke to her. For him, the joy lay in possession."

"Was the marriage ever consummated?" Jason asked, wondering if Philip Hobart's ability to perform had been impaired by his condition and if he had suspected right away that Samuel wasn't his.

"Yes, it was, but my father couldn't—" Bram's voice trailed off. "He blamed it on Lucy. Said she was useless as a wife, and it was her lack of affection that contributed to his bouts of impotence. Lucy was distraught. She was trapped in a loveless marriage, with nothing to call her own, and no way out. And after a few years, she came to realize that the child she longed for would never come to be, not if she remained married to my father."

"And that's where you came in?" Daniel asked.

"It was never my intention to begin an affair with my stepmother. Initially, I knew nothing of their marriage, only that Lucy was obviously lonely. I think I was the only person Lucy saw outside of my father and Hattie. My father had no friends or known associates, and he had never introduced her to the Dafoes. It suited his purposes to isolate Lucy."

"So how did it start?" Jason asked.

"I invited Lucy to visit my studio and made a joke about her posing for me because she had the face of an angel. She loved the idea. She said it would get her out of the house and make her immortal. And the rest came naturally," Bram said.

"Did your father realize that the child wasn't his when Lucy told him she was pregnant?" Daniel asked.

Bram shook his head. "My father was too shortsighted to see that Lucy might have her own needs. He simply assumed that one of their few successful couplings had led to a pregnancy. He was happy about the child. He thought it would give Lucy something to do, and it soothed his wounded pride. No man wants to admit that he can't get a child on his beautiful young wife. Lucy was happy too," Bram said softly. "She just wanted someone to love, someone that was truly hers. I think we could all have gone on like that for years, if not for the visit to the doctor. That's when he began to suspect that Lucy had been unfaithful."

"Would your father really murder his own grandson?" Jason asked. "Is it not possible that Samuel died of natural causes?"

Bram let out a mirthless bark of laughter. "Whatever compassion my father once had was beaten out of him by his own father and then by the life he'd chosen for himself. He was incapable of any depth of feeling, for anyone, but he was capable of rage, and vengeance. And vengeance he got," Bram said as his eyes filled with tears. "Sammy was light and joy and hope, all the things that had never lived in that house." He looked at Daniel, imploring him to help.

"Why did you do it, Mr. Hobart?" Jason asked. "Why did you behead your father? Surely there were other, less gruesome ways to cover up the murder. You could have thrown his body off a bridge. If it was discovered, the head wound could be explained by his head colliding with the stonework or hitting a rock."

Bram Hobart's shoulders sagged. "My first thought was to make it look like revenge, but the prevailing reason was to avoid a postmortem. I thought that if the cause of death was obvious, no one would bother with getting to the truth. How could I have known that you would be the one to perform the postmortem?" he said bitterly. "Few other surgeons would bother to look for a head wound or to swab the nose and mouth for marble dust."

"You tried to frame an innocent man," Daniel said.

"Once I realized what I had done, I panicked. So I used my father's key to let myself into the Ferryman's cellar and left the barrel there. Not for a moment did I imagine that Charles Dafoe would alert the police."

"What did you think he would do?" Jason asked.

"I thought he'd dispose of the barrel as soon as he realized that his failure to repay the loan made for a powerful motive."

"And would you have allowed Charles Dafoe to die for a crime you had committed?" Jason asked, not bothering to hide his disgust.

Bram didn't reply. Instead, he fixed his gaze on Daniel, and there was something in the set of his jaw and the squaring of his shoulders that spoke to a decision.

"Inspector Haze, allow me to take the blame. I will sign a confession. I will speak to the press if that's what it takes. I will shout from the rooftops that I killed my father in a jealous rage. Please, let Lucy go. She deserves another chance at life after the losses and cruelty she's been forced to endure."

"I'm sorry, Mr. Hobart, but I cannot bend the law to my will every time I find myself sympathetic to the killer," Daniel replied coolly. "Mrs. Hobart was the one to strike the fatal blow. She will be charged with the murder of her husband." Daniel didn't add that Lucy would hang. That was self-evident.

Bram angrily wiped away his tears, the iron cuffs on his wrists jangling. "And what about me?" he demanded. "Will I hang as well?"

"It's up to the judge presiding over your case to determine the sentence. The snatching and desecration of a body is not considered a felony, so it's not punishable by death, but you might receive a prison sentence or be ordered to pay a fine."

"So I will live," Bram said miserably.

"You will live."

"That's cold comfort." Bram sighed heavily and looked Daniel squarely in the eye. "May I have a moment with Lucy?"

Daniel started to shake his head, then seemingly changed his mind. "All right. I will allow it."

"Thank you, Inspector. I would also beg you for a moment of privacy."

"Mr. Hobart," Daniel exclaimed. "Surely you don't intend to—"

"I mean nothing improper, Inspector Haze. I only want a moment of solitude with the woman I love. Surely there is no way for us to escape from Scotland Yard."

"Very well." Daniel pushed to his feet. He opened the door to allow Constable Collins inside. "Take him down, Constable, and give him a few minutes alone with Mrs. Hobart. Be sure to lock them in."

"Yes, sir," Constable Collins replied, and took Bram Hobart by the arm. "Let's go, then, lover boy," he said nastily.

"I can't tell you how glad I am this case is now closed," Daniel said once Constable Collins had escorted Bram Hobart from the interview room. "I think this one will stay with me for a while. That poor child."

"I recommend a pleasant distraction," Jason said, thinking that he could use something to lift his spirits as well. This case had disturbed him, and there was still no word on the *Arcadia*.

"I will go to Birch Hill tomorrow and spend the day with Charlotte. I miss her desperately."

"A day with Charlotte will do you good," Jason agreed. "When do you mean to bring her home?"

"I need to find a new nursemaid. Perhaps I will place an advertisement in the paper when I return. Harriet would love to raise Charlotte, but I mean to keep my daughter with me."

"I'm sure Mrs. Elderman wouldn't mind coming to London for a few weeks," Jason suggested.

Daniel smiled at him ruefully. "You don't think I can be trusted to hire a competent replacement for Rebecca?" he said, completely misinterpreting Jason's suggestion.

"I'm sure you can, but it's good to have a second opinion. If you don't care to consult your mother-in-law, perhaps Katherine can help you vet potential candidates. She's an excellent judge of character."

Daniel nodded. "I just might have to take you up on that. I'm not ready to invite Harriet to stay. She might never leave. She's lonely on her own and wants nothing more than to be a part of Charlotte's life. But if I invite her to live with us, I will never be able to move on from Sarah's death. Harriet will keep Sarah's memory alive without even trying, and I couldn't bear that, Jason. I need to distance myself if I hope to have any sort of future in which I don't end up a miserable old man."

"You won't hear an argument from me," Jason said. He was ready to go home and hoped Lily would still be awake so he could spend a few minutes with her.

Jason replaced the candlestick in the sack he'd wrapped it in and handed it to Daniel to store in the evidence cupboard until the trial, while Daniel closed his notebook and pushed it into his pocket. They had just left the interview room when a flustered Constable Collins came flying down the corridor.

"He's killed her. Oh, God, he's killed her!"

The three of them sprinted toward the staircase that led to the cells, but Jason knew they were too late as soon as he saw Lucy Hobart's lifeless gaze. She lay cradled in her lover's arms, her head resting against his chest. From the appearance of her neck, it wasn't hard to figure out how Bram Hobart had murdered her, just as it wasn't difficult to understand why. He'd spared her a trial and an execution, and in turn had condemned himself to death, an outcome he clearly desired.

Bram met Jason's gaze squarely. His eyes shimmered with tears and his bottom lip trembled, but Jason saw no remorse in his gaze. Perhaps the two had agreed on this course of action if it ever came to it, or maybe it had been a spontaneous reaction to an inevitable conclusion. Either way, Bram Hobart was a dead man, and Michael Pearson was a rich one, since he'd now inherit the lot.

"Call in the undertaker, Constable," Daniel said softly, as if speaking too loudly would disturb Lucy's rest. "And then arrange Mr. Hobart's transport to Newgate Prison. I think he'll get a warm welcome there."

Turning on his heel, Daniel walked away.

Chapter 37

"Allow me to offer you a ride home," John Ransome said when Jason stepped outside a few minutes after Daniel had gone. "I'm on my way to see Laura."

"I'll draw up the discharge papers tomorrow," Jason promised once they'd settled in the carriage. "I think Mrs. Ransome will be more comfortable recuperating at home."

"Thank you." Ransome gave Jason a searching look. "We all make choices, Jason," he said as the brougham pulled away from the curb and merged with the early evening traffic. "The Hobarts made choices they couldn't walk away from."

Jason didn't want to think about the Hobarts anymore. He didn't believe in the inevitability of fate or generational curses, but if this family's history was anything to go on, these people were truly damaged. From Philip Hobart's parents to Lucy's tragic family to the death of an innocent child, perhaps this line was best expunged before more innocent lives were lost or taken. There was still Michael Pearson, but he seemed to have been brought up by people who cared for him and had his Saskia to love. Now that he would inherit Philip Hobart's estate, he'd have a much better chance at a blameless life.

Jason was relieved when the carriage stopped before his house in Kensington, and he alighted after wishing John Ransome a good night and sending his regards to Laura. He was grateful to the superintendent for not taking the opportunity to press him about the position of chief inspector. From a policing perspective, it had been a fine day's work, but Jason couldn't shake the dread that had seeped into his soul and hoped that the Hobarts would rest in peace. All of them. He briefly wondered what would happen to the angel that wielded a sword and bore Lucy Hobart's face. Perhaps it would guard the final resting place of the woman who had inspired it.

The house was quiet when Jason let himself in, only Fanny appearing as if by magic to welcome him home and take his things. It was just past five, so too early for Lily to go to sleep, but perhaps she and Katherine were in the nursery.

"Where's her ladyship?" Jason asked.

"They're in the back garden, sir."

"Thank you, Fanny."

Jason walked through the house and toward the door that led to the walled garden behind the house. Katherine sat on a wrought-iron bench while Lily toddled down the stone path, stopping to look at the birds perched in a nearby tree. She looked pretty as a picture in her sky-blue coat and matching bonnet.

"Papa," Lily cried when she saw Jason, and he lifted her into his arms and planted a kiss on her nose. Lily laughed and Jason laughed with her, suddenly feeling a little lighter after the awful happenings of the day.

"You've made an arrest," Katherine said, watching him from her perch on the bench.

Jason nodded. "We have."

"Who was it?"

"Lucy Hobart murdered her husband, and Bram Hobart helped her to cover it up."

"Why did she do it?" Katherine asked.

"Hobart smothered their child when he discovered Lucy had been unfaithful to him with his own son."

"It's like something out of a Greek tragedy," Katherine said. "Heartbreaking and almost too theatrical to be real."

"Oh, it's real." Jason settled on the bench next to his wife, Lily in his lap. "Bram Hobart murdered Lucy after she confessed, and now he will hang."

"Goodness me," Katherine exclaimed.

"He thought he was doing her a kindness," Jason explained.

"And was he?"

"Perhaps. Neither one of them could ever walk away from what happened. They were doomed the moment they gave in to their feelings for each other."

"How sad," Katherine said. "Well, I trust Daniel is pleased to have the case closed."

"He's relieved the case is closed, but pleased is not a term I would use to describe him just now."

"Oh?"

"John Ransome offered me the position of chief inspector," Jason said.

Katherine stared at him, her mouth opening slightly in surprise. "Chief inspector? But why you?"

Jason shrugged. He suddenly felt too tired to analyze Ransome's motives.

"He knows you'll make him look good," Katherine said, smiling knowingly.

"There are other competent detectives at Scotland Yard."

"But none of them are of the nobility. Having someone like you to lead the other detectives will raise the profile of the police service and maybe attract more promising young men to join when they see your photograph in the paper and feel inspired by the difference you make to their ilk."

Jason chuckled. "Their ilk?"

Katherine smiled sadly. "My dear, no one cares about the plight of the poor, or the endless bodies pulled from the river or found in dark alleys. The police service was formed to protect the rich and powerful, and there's nothing better than one of their own to represent the service."

"Am I one of their own?" Jason asked, surprised by Katherine's description.

"You are to them, and they will trust in you and hope that the position of chief inspector is just the start. Once Commissioner Hawkins retires, John Ransome will take his place and a new superintendent will take charge of Scotland Yard. I think Ransome wants that man to be you."

"I hadn't considered that," Jason said.

"No, but I'm sure he has. Have you spoken to Daniel about this?"

"Not in detail, but he's aware of Ransome's offer."

"I can't imagine he's happy about it."

"He isn't."

"What will you do?" Katherine asked.

Jason let a squirming Lily down and leaned against the back of the bench, watching his daughter head straight for the dolly she had dropped. "If I'm completely honest, there's a part of me that's intrigued. I could really make a difference, if only by introducing new avenues of training for the detectives and teaching them how to spot certain physical evidence that they might otherwise miss, not being medically trained. But there's another part of me that thinks the whole idea is absurd. I am a surgeon. I make a difference already, even if most days I don't feel like it. Perhaps I'd be reaching too high."

Katherine smiled warmly and placed her hand over Jason's. "Jason, if you truly wanted this, the conversation we're having would be very different. You want me to talk you out of this because deep down you're not ready for the responsibility."

Jason laughed. "You know me so well, Katie. And you're right. Exciting as it might be, I'm not ready to take on Scotland Yard."

"That doesn't mean that there won't come a time when you might feel differently."

"But the opportunity would have passed," Jason replied.

"I don't believe so. As long as John Ransome is on the police service, you will always have a way in if you want it."

Jason smiled at Katherine. "You're right, and I thank you for your advice." He reached out, took her hand, and brought her fingers to his lips.

"You need never thank me. But you are welcome to show me your appreciation later," she said playfully. "Now, it's time for Lily's supper."

Katherine stood and scooped up the child, ready to head inside. "Oh, I forgot. Two letters came for you this afternoon. I left them on the desk in the library."

"Thank you, Katie," Jason said, and followed Katherine inside.

She headed upstairs to the nursery, where she would feed Lily, and Jason decided to stop by the library to read his correspondence before he headed upstairs himself to say goodnight to Lily and change for dinner. Jason felt a pang of unease when he examined the two pieces of mail. The first was a note from the steamship company, and the second a letter from Mr. Hartley. The latter looked dog-eared and stained, and Jason wondered if it had got lost, then been found, and then finally delivered to the correct address. The note from the steamship company was crisp and bright, likely posted only that morning.

Jason settled in his favorite studded leather wingchair. The library was cold despite the pleasant warmth outside, and he wished a fire had been lit but saw no reason to bother since he'd be heading upstairs once he finished his brandy. He considered the two missives and decided to open the letter from Mr. Hartley first. It was brief and to the point, much like the man himself. It was dated nearly a month ago.

March 8, 1869

New York

Dear sir,

Per your request, I have undertaken a journey to Boston to ascertain the whereabouts of Mary O'Connell nee Donovan, and her children. It didn't take long to discover that Mary's husband, Sean O'Connell, had counted himself part of a gang of Irish thugs whose main avenues of income were from running prostitutes, enforcers, and hitmen for hire. Sean O'Connell was at one time a trusted lieutenant but lost the trust of the leaders and was treated accordingly.

O'Connell's body was left on the doorstep for his wife to find with a demand that she reimburse the funds O'Connell had appropriated or she would be next. Mary fled to New York, where she boarded a ship bound for London. I trust that by the time you receive this letter, Mary will be with you and will have explained the situation in person.

The invoice for time spent and expenses incurred on your behalf is enclosed. Please do not hesitate to contact me should you require assistance stateside.

Your servant,

M. Hartley

Hartley Investigations

Jason glanced at the invoice, then refolded the letter and stuffed it into his pocket, lest anyone come upon it by accident. He'd have to find a way to tell Katherine and Micah about the murder of Mary's husband. But not before he knew what had happened to Mary.

Bracing himself for more bad news, Jason tore open the note from the steamship line. It was from Mr. Cleese, and Jason's heart sank when he saw the stark words on the white card bearing the company's logo.

Dear sir,

It is with a heavy heart that I inform you of the sinking of the *Arcadia*. All souls were lost.

With respect,

H. Cleese

Grinnell, Minturn & Co.

The note fluttered to the floor as Jason stared into the unlit hearth. What he saw was not the brick and mortar of the fire box but a sunbaked clearing, the grass browned by merciless heat, the sky so bright it hurt the eyes. Suddenly, he thought he smelled the heavy perfume of overripe peaches and felt the hot breath of the Georgia afternoon on his sunburned face, the broken stones of the crumbling wall of the encampment digging into his shoulders. Torn canvas fluttered in the stifling breeze, and a swarm of horseflies hovered above the bloated corpses that had been left to rot while the guards sat in the shade of a leafy tree, dicing and drinking. Jason could almost feel the emaciated body of the little boy as he held him in his arms, whispering words of comfort as Micah wept for his father and brother who were among the dead.

It was then that Jason had promised Micah that he would look after him forever, even if forever meant only a few more days or weeks as they slowly starved to death, their fate of no interest to anyone. Jason hadn't expected either of them to survive, but they had, and here he was, about to break the poor boy's heart again. How much grief could one child take without being left forever damaged by the tragedies he'd endured? Were the Donovans cursed as well? And would Jason's love and support be enough to shore up Micah in the days to come?

Jason didn't much care what had happened to Sean O'Connell. He'd obviously been a petty criminal who hadn't had the brains God had given him to protect either himself or his family from the consequences of his greed. But Jason did care about Mary and Liam and the setback Micah would suffer once he found out that his only family was lying at the bottom of the sea, their remains picked over by fish and broken apart by the mighty currents of the Atlantic. Micah didn't have a single grave to visit should he crave the comfort of spending a few minutes remembering his family at their final resting places. Even his mother's grave in Maryland had been desecrated, destroyed by marauding soldiers who had been only too happy to take their anger and frustration out on a Catholic cemetery where most of the names etched into the stones were Irish.

Jason bowed his head and said a prayer for them all, hoping that their souls were at peace and that Micah would eventually recover from his immeasurable loss. Then he picked up the card from Mr. Cleese, locked it in a drawer, and headed upstairs to change for dinner.

Epilogue

March 27, 1869

Jason paced the drawing room like a caged tiger, unable to sit still, not when the clock was ticking down to a task he'd do anything to avoid. Any minute now, Joe would be back with Micah, and Jason would have to impart the terrible news. Katherine watched Jason's anguish, her eyes warm with sympathy, but didn't bother with empty platitudes. After all, what could she say that would make any difference? All they could do was support Micah in his grief, and Katherine already wore her most somber gray gown, while Jason wore a black armband to show respect for the dead. They would not adopt full mourning, since Mary and her children were not blood relatives, but if Micah wished to observe a year of mourning, Jason would ensure he had what he needed.

Jason had lived through some awful holidays, both during the war and after, when he had struggled to recuperate both physically and mentally, not only from the abuse he had suffered but the loss of all those he had loved. This Easter would come a close second to those dark days. Jason nearly jumped out of his skin when the sound of the brass knocker reverberated through the house, the hour of reckoning having finally arrived. He met Katherine's worried gaze and paused on his way to the drawing room door. Joe would not be knocking, so it had to be a visitor.

"Constable Collins for you, my lord," Dodson said as he entered the room. "It seems your presence is required at a crime scene."

Jason sighed and went to greet the constable. This was remarkably bad timing, but also a welcome distraction.

"Good afternoon, Constable. What happened?" he asked the young man who stood awkwardly by the door, his helmet under his arm.

"Two young children, sir," Constable Collins said. "Discovered in a trunk in the village of Fox Hollow."

"Fox Hollow?"

"It's in Essex, sir."

"Why did they not report it to the Brentwood Constabulary?" Jason asked.

"It seems you were requested by name, sir."

"Who by?"

"Lady Foxley. Will you come?"

It took Jason a moment to place the name, then he nodded. "Of course."

"Will you be needing your medical bag, sir?" Fanny whispered, her eyes huge with horror as she appeared behind Jason.

"I very much doubt it, Fanny, but I'll take it all the same."

"I'll just wait outside, sir," Constable Collins said as Fanny went to fetch Jason's things.

Jason felt terrible leaving just before Micah got home, but some part of him was glad of the reprieve. He simply couldn't bear to face the boy, and even a few more hours might give him the courage to tell Micah the truth of what had happened. Jason shrugged on his coat, set his top hat on his head, and yanked open the door—only to come face to face with Mary, who was clutching a sleeping Liam to her chest.

"Hello, Captain. I've come home, if you'll have me," Mary said shyly, and walked into Jason's arms, which was just as well since he was mute with shock.

Jason had no idea what manner of miracle had brought Mary to his door, but it was obvious she had never boarded the

Arcadia. His heart went out to the victims and their families, but as he held Mary and a sleepy Liam against him, all he cared about was that his unorthodox little family had not been irrevocably fractured.

It was there that Micah found them a few minutes later, Jason holding tightly to the newly resurrected. It was going to be a happy Easter after all.

The End

Please stay a few minutes longer to read an excerpt from

Murder of Innocents, A Redmond and Haze Mystery Book 14

But first, I would like to tell you about my new Victorian murder mystery series, **Tate and Bell Mysteries**.

The first book, **The Highgate Cemetery Murder,** will be released on February 29, 2024. Please turn the page for a brief excerpt.

An Excerpt from The Highgate Cemetery Murder

Prologue

All Saints' Day

The silence was unnerving, the forbidding vaults and ancient monuments glistening with moisture after last night's rain. The trees, their brilliant autumn colors muted against the pewter smudge of the morning sky, looked for all the world like they were weeping for the dead. The cemetery was deserted, the paths muddy and unkempt.

Victor Tate bent his head into the gathering wind and planted his hand on his bowler to keep it from blowing off his head. He was both determined and reluctant to see to the morning's errand. It was only right that he should come today and lay flowers on Julia's grave, it being her birthday, but the memory of his clever, beautiful wife broke his heart all over again when weighed against the painful reminder of her untimely death nearly three years ago.

Julia would have been twenty-five today, a woman in her prime, possibly a mother, had the consumption not done its ugly work and devoured her from the inside, leaving behind nothing but a pitiful bag of bones too exhausted to keep fighting the ravaging illness. They'd had such a short time together, less than two years, but Victor had not remarried as everyone said he should. Perhaps he never would, not unless someone captured his heart the way Julia had. He didn't think it was likely to happen, but life was full of surprises, both good and bad, and he made every effort to keep an open mind and treat every day as if it were a blank page in the book that was life.

Victor's step slowed as he approached the lane where Julia was buried. He'd thought it'd get easier with time, but the lichen-covered gravestone aroused the usual feelings of guilt and shame. He knew he should come more often, clear away the wilted flowers and pull up the weeds that threatened to choke the monument, but he always found an excuse, unable to face the lonely spot without ruminating on the brevity and unfairness of life.

Victor looked around, his myopic vision turning the scene into a melancholy watercolor. Something in his surroundings didn't seem quite right. It looked like an angel on one of the gravestones was moving, its stone robe and marble tresses rippling in the wind. Victor fumbled for his spectacles, pulled them out of his pocket and put them on without taking his eyes off the terrifying seraph. The image crystallized, and Victor let out a strangled cry, dropping the poppies he'd brought to lay on Julia's grave and stepping on them in his distress.

A young woman hung on a marble cross like a Christian martyr, her wrists bound to the crossbar, her head tilted to the side. She wore nothing but a flowing chemise, the fabric whipping around her bare legs and hanging off her arms like broken wings. What appeared to be a human heart, held in place by a thin chain or a string, was suspended from the woman's neck, still oozing blood. The woman's eyes were partially open, as was her mouth, and Victor thought he heard a cry for help carried on the wind.

"I'm coming," he cried as he took off at a run. "Hold on."

Alerted by the sound of his voice, a figure materialized behind the cross. The man was about Victor's own age, late twenties. His bowler was pulled low over his eyes, and his caped greatcoat gave him the appearance of a bat about to take flight. For a moment, their eyes met, and both froze, immobilized by indecision and surprise. And then the man was moving, weaving between the stones before disappearing from Victor's view altogether, his dark shape swallowed by the unkempt greenery beyond the last row of graves. It was either follow the man or rescue the poor creature who had been so cruelly treated. The choice was obvious.

It took Victor several long moments to reach the cross, but he needn't have hurried. The blue gaze that looked down on him was not only fixed in death but tinged with red, as if the woman's eyes were glowing. The mouth he'd imagined to be frozen in a scream was slack, the lips bluish. The woman's flesh was as cold and white as the marble beneath her feet. She was dead, and probably had been for some time, but silent tears slid down her pale cheeks and dripped onto her feet. Victor stared up, paralyzed with terror. He'd heard it said that statues of the Virgin were sometimes seen to shed real tears, but he'd always dismissed the stories as fantastical tales of popish fervor. Above him, rainwater slid unnoticed down the amber leaves of an overhanging branch and dripped onto the young woman's immobile face, turning her from a grotesque corpse into a weeping angel.

Victor turned away and hastened toward the exit, desperate to get away from the terrifying spectacle.

An Excerpt from Murder of Innocents

Prologue

The house was silent and dark, the gallery, hung with portraits of long-dead baronets and their pasty-faced ladies, lost in shadow. The wooden staircase creaked as Amy warily trudged up the stairs, the flame of her candle wavering in the drafty emptiness. She hated her first chore of the day, partly because the task was disgusting and demeaning and partly because the gloomy, empty corridors frightened her. There was something malevolent about the ancient house, its low ceilings and narrow passageways making her feel trapped, and the snooty ancestors' painted eyes following her every move with their painted eyes.

Eager to get the unpleasant task over with, Amy crept into the baronet's bedroom and slid the chamber pot from beneath the bed. She needn't have bothered to be quiet. He was out cold, his breath reeking of spirits and the chamber redolent with the odors of a man with healthy appetites, both for food and self-pleasure. Amy stepped outside, emptied the nightsoil into her bucket, then returned the chamber pot to the room and shut the door.

Her lady's bedroom was next, followed by the rooms of the upstairs servants whose nightsoil fell under the upstairs maid's remit. Amy was passing one of the unused bedchambers when she became aware of a strange odor. Putting her apron over her nose to keep out the noxious smell, she pushed the door open and peered inside.

The sun was just coming up and pale pink light streamed through the leaded windows, dispelling the murky darkness within. The room was empty, the massive tester bed hulking above her like some ancient ship, its curtain sails limp in the stagnant stillness. Amy lowered her apron and sniffed. The malodorous smell appeared to be coming from the carved sea chest at the foot of the bed. Inching forward, she gingerly lifted the lid. The smell assaulted her senses, but she forgot about her own discomfort as her hand flew to her mouth and tears spilled down her cheeks.

A sob tearing from her chest, Amy dropped the heavy lid and hurried from the room, her shoes making a terrible clatter on the stairs as she ran for help. She prayed there was still something to be done, but deep inside she knew. Death had come to Fox Hollow.

Chapter 1

Saturday, March 27, 1869

Even with the windows closed, Jason noticed the change in the air. It smelled of loamy earth, new grass, and pungent manure. The sky was clear, the ever-present coal soot that hovered over London replaced by puffy white clouds. It had rained earlier, but now the sky was a brilliant blue, the blossoming blackthorn and cherry plum buoyant against the backdrop of cobalt. On any other day, Jason would have enjoyed an outing to the country, but not today. For one, the brougham was trundling toward Fox Hollow, where two young children had died in suspicious circumstances. For another, he desperately wanted to be at home with his family.

Jason longed to see Micah, who had just arrived in London to spend Easter with the Redmonds, and talk with Mary. Mary Donovan, now O'Connell, and her son Liam had unexpectedly appeared on his doorstep that very morning, nothing short of an Easter miracle since the ship they'd reportedly sailed on from America had gone down off the coast of Ireland, all souls aboard lost. Mary had boarded another ship, narrowly avoiding certain death, but Jason would have liked to welcome her properly and hear more about the troubles that had forced Mary to flee Boston. Still, he could hardly complain. His family was safe and under the same roof once again and would spend Easter together as they had done before Mary decamped to America.

As he and Daniel neared their destination, Jason's thoughts turned to the grief-stricken parents who'd just lost both their children. Nothing would bring back the deceased, and Jason wasn't at all sure it would be a comfort to the family to learn how the boys had died. Regardless of whether they had been murdered or had died accidentally and might have been saved had they been discovered in time, they were gone. The knowledge would only give the parents reason to blame themselves and question their every decision leading up to the tragedy, wondering again and again if they might have done something differently that would have prevented the deaths of their babies. But if the children had been murdered, the killer could hardly be allowed to evade capture, so Jason supposed it was a moot point. His job was to determine the cause of death, while Daniel's job was to bring the culprit to justice.

Given Daniel's daughter Charlotte's recent abduction, Jason wished someone else had been tasked with investigating the deaths of the children. Daniel still felt the aftershocks of those few days and was particularly sensitive to anything involving small children. He would have gladly declined the assignment, but it seemed that Daniel and Jason had been requested by name, a state of affairs Superintendent Ransome both welcomed and resented. The summons had come from a noble personage, which always guaranteed a high-profile case, but the baronet's country seat happened to fall outside the jurisdiction of Scotland Yard, and the investigation would infringe on the territory of the Essex Constabulary and take up resources that would otherwise be allocated to inquiries that took place in London. Jason was paid a nominal fee for his involvement, which he donated to a charity for fallen women, but Daniel, being one of Ransome's most trusted detectives, was more difficult to spare when the Yard was snowed under with cases of varying importance.

Jason glanced at Daniel, who sat staring out the window, his gaze fixed on the fields and forests of his native Essex, his shoulders squared, his jaw tight with tension. Daniel turned to face Jason, his expression one of dismay since it seemed that his thoughts were running along the same line as Jason's.

"I just don't understand why Lady Foxley requested us by name," he grumbled. "That woman always did treat everyone as if they were her flunkeys and should jump to attention when she so much as graced them with her presence."

Daniel had good reason to resent Lucinda Foxley and didn't think any interaction with her would go any better than their previous encounters in Birch Hill. Just because Lucinda was now married didn't mean she had changed or had come to see the error of her ways. Lucinda Foxley's understanding of right and wrong was fluid at best, and her privileged upbringing and autocratic father had damaged her beyond repair, a happenstance that wasn't her fault but still made her extremely difficult to deal with. The Lucinda they had known was impulsive, callous, and utterly devoid of compassion, even toward those close to her.

Jason had no wish to belittle Daniel's feelings, since his irritation was perfectly justified, but thought he could defuse whatever residual anger Daniel felt at being ripped away from London to do Lucinda's bidding by focusing on the positive aspects of the summons.

"Presumably we were asked for by name because Lucinda Foxley trusts us to conduct a thorough investigation," he said.

"But why is she even involved?" Daniel countered. "The children can't be hers, since she married quite recently."

"No, but perhaps she's worried about her reputation and standing in the village."

Daniel hmphed. "As well she should be. Wherever Lucinda Foxley goes, death follows."

Lucinda Chadwick, as she was then, had been a suspect in two previous investigations. She had managed to avoid the repercussions and a stain on her name, but that didn't mean she was wholly innocent or even remotely sorry. Daniel had written her off as a bad seed, but Jason was prepared to give Lucinda the benefit of the doubt since she had been very young at the time of the investigations. He hoped marriage had had a positive effect and she was now content with her lot, but Daniel doubted that a wild and unrepentant nature like Lucinda's could ever be fully tamed. Perhaps Sir Lawrence had found a way to calm his tempestuous bride, or perhaps he'd given her leave to do as she would, and the result had proved tragic.

"Daniel, our duty is to two little boys. We will either rule the deaths accidental or open an investigation. Either way, we're here to do a job and should leave our personal feelings about Lucinda Foxley at the door."

Looking chastised, Daniel nodded. "You're right, and I will do my best to forget the beating I received at the hands of that woman or the role she played in the death of the poor young man who only wanted to discover the truth about his family. You have my word that I will try to remain neutral and objective."

"You always are," Jason reassured him, even though that wasn't strictly true.

It was difficult to remain objective when one's feelings and family were involved, but Jason trusted Daniel to do the right thing and knew that whatever the outcome, Daniel would remain courteous and professional.

Chapter 2

When it finally came into view, the house wasn't at all what Jason had expected. With a name like Fox Hollow, he had thought it might be quaint, but the sprawling Tudor manor that sat solid and proud amid the greening lawns put him in mind of the Dark Ages. When this house had been built, England had been a place of unfathomable ignorance, ruthless political maneuvering, and merciless religious persecution. It was also a time when America, the country of his birth, had been nothing but rivers and forests, the people that inhabited the land living without fear of extinction. A time no one cared to remember.

The house boasted four timber-framed sections, each one with its own steeply pitched roof and a jettied upper floor. Two massive brick chimneys were positioned on either side, and the mullioned windows were divided into ten panes, the diamond-shaped segments of glass reflecting the afternoon sun. Jason couldn't see the grounds beyond, but he was sure there was a kitchen garden, an herb garden, and probably a walled rose garden, where the ladies sat in the shade of the arbors on warm days or took the air when the weather turned cold. There was a well-tended herbaceous border that must be stunning in the summer, potted plants, and flowers that had yet to bloom planted beneath the ground floor windows. There was probably a number of outbuildings discreetly tucked away behind the hulking structure, each with its own purpose and designated staff. The house appeared untouched by time, a haunting relic of centuries gone by and lives lived in isolated splendor.

The carriage rolled through the open gates and continued down the drive until it came to a stop before the black-painted door studded with iron nails. The door promptly opened to reveal a woman in her forties, presumably the housekeeper. She was dressed in black bombazine, and an intricate silver chatelaine, the sort Jason had never seen up close, hung from her waist, five household appendages affixed to stylized chains glinting in the early afternoon light. There was a thimble, sewing scissors in an engraved sheath, a tiny notebook, what appeared to be a pen, and a heart-shaped container the size of a walnut that probably contained smelling salts. The woman's dark hair was covered by a black lace cap, and her pale blue eyes seemed to radiate relief when Daniel stepped from the brougham and tipped his bowler.

"Are you the gentlemen from Scotland Yard?" the housekeeper asked, her gaze sweeping over Jason and Daniel. "Inspector Haze and Dr. Redmond?"

The form of address wasn't lost on Jason, and he didn't correct her. He and Daniel often downplayed Jason's rank for the sake of an investigation since it made Jason seem more approachable, particularly to working people.

"I'm Inspector Haze," Daniel said, and held up his warrant card for the woman's inspection. "And you are?"

"Mrs. Buckley, the housekeeper. Do come inside. My lord," she added deferentially, and inclined her head to Jason as a sign of respect.

The foyer smelled of musty wood and beeswax and was dominated by a wide dark-wood staircase that was handsomely carved and soared majestically toward the upper floor. The overhanging gallery overshadowed the outer parts of the foyer, and the light filtering through the windows was so distorted by the panes as to seem almost otherworldly. No gas lamps were in evidence, and the tall candles in iron holders were not lit so early in the day. The interior was so outmoded as to make one feel as if they'd time-traveled into the distant past.

"Is Lady Foxley expecting us?" Daniel asked as he took in his surroundings, his nose twitching with distaste. Not from a noble family himself, Daniel had little appreciation for country seats and dusty relics, particularly when they were achieved through marriage rather than birth.

"I'm afraid my lady felt unwell and needed to rest. I'll tell Sir Lawrence you're here," Mrs. Buckley replied.

She instructed a young parlormaid to take their coats and hats and invited them to wait in the parlor, which was dominated by an arched stone fireplace that was big enough for Jason and Daniel to stand in side by side. The fire had not been lit and the room was chilly, damp, and unpleasantly gloomy, the light seemingly leached by the coffered ceiling made of dark wooden squares, each adorned with a five-petaled flower. Several faded tapestries hung on the walls, and a framed document, written in Old English and dated October 2, 1563, was on display, the missive written in flowing script and embellished with the wax seal of Elizabeth I, the wax yellowed with age. It appeared to be a pardon bestowed on some long-dead Foxley who had probably come dangerously close to losing his head.

Jason and Daniel settled into the hardback chairs that resembled thrones and were extremely uncomfortable since the cushions were so threadbare, they barely padded the seats. The same parlormaid that had taken their things brought two cups of mulled wine, the spiced drink filling the room with the pleasant aromas of honey and cloves. After taking a sip, Jason set the cup aside. He liked the idea of mulled wine a lot more than he enjoyed the taste. Daniel drained his cup, glad of a hot drink after the long drive.

Creaking came from somewhere above, and then the unmistakable sound of a heavy tread as the master of the house descended the stairs and approached the parlor. Jason had not seen Lawrence Foxley in nearly two years. Outwardly, Sir Lawrence had not changed. He was still in fine physical form, his bearing erect and his clothes fashionable and expensive. The cabochon ring on his pinky reflected the afternoon light, his watch chain gleamed, and his buttons shone with polish. The fair hair that he'd worn artfully tousled while courting Lucinda Chadwick was now longer, the sideburns edged sharply just beneath Sir Lawrence's fleshy cheekbones, the points angled toward a sensual mouth. There were no obvious signs of ill health, but Jason got the impression that Sir Lawrence overindulged in spirits and had grown slightly thicker around the middle.

The baronet smiled, and Jason saw genuine grief in his blue eyes. "Lord Redmond, Inspector Haze, I thank you for coming. Would you care for some tea? Or perhaps something a little stronger?"

"Thank you, no," Daniel said. "We quite enjoyed the mulled wine. Sir Lawrence, if you would be so kind as to tell us why we were sent for?"

Sir Lawrence nodded and sank onto the plush red settee that showed considerable signs of wear, particularly in the center. "I was going to send word to the Brentwood Constabulary, but Lucinda begged me to send a message to Scotland Yard. She's quite distraught."

"Can you tell us what happened?" Jason asked.

Sir Lawrence's mouth dipped, and he sighed heavily, his shoulders dropping. "Our cook, Mrs. Powers, has—had," he amended, his expression pained, "two boys. John was six, and Bertie was four. The boys had the run of the estate and spent hours playing outside in all weather. When they didn't come home for supper last night, Mrs. Powers became worried, so we organized a search party. We looked for hours but found no sign of the children. The boys' father and I even followed the path along the river, in case the children had fallen in and been pulled along by the current."

Sir Lawrence sighed again, even more audibly this time. "This morning, the upstairs maid, Amy, smelled something foul coming from one of the unused chambers. The odor was coming from an old sea chest. When she opened the chest, she found the children. They were dead and had probably been for hours."

"Might it have been an accident?" Daniel asked. "Could the children have become trapped in the chest and suffocated?"

Sir Lawrence shook his tawny head. "I don't believe so, Inspector Haze. The trunk was not locked when Amy entered the room, so the children could have climbed out at any time if they were playing a game. And someone would have heard them if they had called for help. There's always someone about. It would seem that the boys became ill and passed before they could call out. Mrs. Powers is convinced that her children were murdered."

"Who would want to murder two little boys?" Jason asked.

"I don't know," Sir Lawrence said, his voice quavering and his eyes misting with tears. Jason hadn't taken Sir Lawrence for an emotional man, especially when it came to those who served him, but he appeared sincere in his grief.

"Has anything been moved since the maidservant discovered the children?" Jason asked.

Sir Lawrence shook his head. "Mrs. Powers wanted to take the children home and lay them out, but I explained how important it is for the police to see the deceased as they were found. I locked the room, so no one has been inside since the boys' parents saw them this morning."

"Then you had better show us," Daniel said.

He looked grim, and Jason shared his apprehension. Accustomed as he was to handling the dead, he found it difficult to remain emotionally detached when the deceased were children.

"I hope you will forgive my presumption," Sir Lawrence said before taking them upstairs, "but I thought it best not to mention your noble title to anyone except Mrs. Buckley, my lord. It would prevent the servants from speaking frankly in your presence, and I need to know who did this."

"There's no need to apologize," Jason said. "You made the right decision. And now I need to see the deceased."

Made in the USA
Middletown, DE
25 March 2025